THE CONFOUNDING CASE OF THE CARISBROOK EMERALDS

THE CASEBOOK OF BARNABY ADAIR: VOLUME 6

STEPHANIE LAURENS

THE CONFOUNDING CASE OF THE CARISBROOK EMERALDS

THE CASEBOOK OF BARNABY ADAIR: VOLUME 6

#1 New York Times *bestselling author Stephanie Laurens brings you a tale of emerging and also established loves and the many facets of family, interwoven with mystery and murder.*

A young lady accused of theft and the gentleman who elects himself her champion enlist the aid of Stokes, Barnaby, Penelope, and friends in pursuing justice, only to find themselves tangled in a web of inter-family tensions and secrets.

When Miss Cara Di Abaccio is accused of stealing the Carisbrook emeralds by the infamously arrogant Lady Carisbrook and marched out of her guardian's house by Scotland Yard's finest, Hugo Adair, Barnaby Adair's cousin, takes umbrage and descends on Scotland Yard, breathing fire in Cara's defense.

Hugo discovers Inspector Stokes has been assigned to the case, and after surveying the evidence thus far, Stokes calls in his big guns when it comes to dealing with investigations in the ton—namely, the Honorable Barnaby Adair and his wife, Penelope.

Soon convinced of Cara's innocence and—given Hugo's apparent tendre for Cara—the need to clear her name, Penelope and Barnaby join Stokes and his team in pursuing the emeralds and, most importantly, who stole them.

But the deeper our intrepid investigators delve into the Carisbrook household, the more certain they become that all is not as it seems. Lady Carisbrook is a harpy, Franklin Carisbrook is secretive, Julia Carisbrook is overly timid, and Lord Carisbrook, otherwise a genial and honorable gentleman, holds himself distant from his family. More, his lordship attempts to shut down the investigation. And Stokes, Barnaby, and Penelope are convinced the Carisbrooks' staff are not sharing all they know.

Meanwhile, having been appointed Cara's watchdog until the mystery is resolved, Hugo, fascinated by Cara as he's been with no other young lady, seeks to entertain and amuse her…and, increasingly intently, to discover the way to her heart. Consequently, Penelope finds herself juggling the attractions of the investigation against the demands of the Adair family for her to actively encourage the budding romance.

What would her mentors advise? On that, Penelope is crystal clear.

Regardless, aided by Griselda, Violet, and Montague and calling on contacts in business, the underworld, and ton society, Penelope, Barnaby, and Stokes battle to peel back each layer of subterfuge and, step by step, eliminate the innocent and follow the emeralds' trail…

Yet instead of becoming clearer, the veils and shadows shrouding the Carisbrooks only grow murkier…until, abruptly, our investigators find themselves facing an inexplicable death, with a potential murderer whose conviction would shake society to its back teeth.

A historical novel of 78,000 words interweaving mystery, romance, and social intrigue.

PRAISE FOR THE WORKS OF STEPHANIE LAURENS

"Stephanie Laurens' heroines are marvelous tributes to Georgette Heyer: feisty and strong." *Cathy Kelly*

"Stephanie Laurens never fails to entertain and charm her readers with vibrant plots, snappy dialogue, and unforgettable characters." *Historical Romance Reviews*

"Stephanie Laurens plays into readers' fantasies like a master and claims their hearts time and again." *Romantic Times Magazine*

Praise for The Confounding Case of the Carisbrook Emeralds

"(An) alluring mystery brimming with red herrings, lots of intrigue, and that perfect touch of romance for which Laurens is rightly revered." *Angela M., Copy Editor, Red Adept Editing*

"Laurens crafts a story as elegant as the gentlemen and women who populate it." *Kim H., Proofreader, Red Adept Editing*

"I really enjoyed this well-written historical mystery novel! The characters unravel exciting plot twists and turns as they investigate the disappearance of a famous set of emeralds." *Kristina B., Proofreader, Red Adept Editing*

OTHER TITLES BY STEPHANIE LAURENS

Cynster Novels

Devil's Bride

A Rake's Vow

Scandal's Bride

A Rogue's Proposal

A Secret Love

All About Love

All About Passion

On A Wild Night

On A Wicked Dawn

The Perfect Lover

The Ideal Bride

The Truth About Love

What Price Love?

The Taste of Innocence

Temptation and Surrender

Cynster Sisters Trilogy

Viscount Breckenridge to the Rescue

In Pursuit of Eliza Cynster

The Capture of the Earl of Glencrae

Cynster Sisters Duo

And Then She Fell

The Taming of Ryder Cavanaugh

Cynster Specials

The Promise in a Kiss

By Winter's Light

Cynster Next Generation Novels

The Tempting of Thomas Carrick

A Match for Marcus Cynster

The Lady By His Side

An Irresistible Alliance

The Greatest Challenge of Them All

Lady Osbaldestone's Christmas Chronicles

Lady Osbaldestone's Christmas Goose

Lady Osbaldestone and the Missing Christmas Carols (October 18, 2018)

The Casebook of Barnaby Adair Novels

Where the Heart Leads

The Peculiar Case of Lord Finsbury's Diamonds

The Masterful Mr. Montague

The Curious Case of Lady Latimer's Shoes

Loving Rose: The Redemption of Malcolm Sinclair

The Confounding Case of the Carisbrook Emeralds

The Murder at Mandeville Hall (August 16, 2018)

Bastion Club Novels

Captain Jack's Woman (Prequel)

The Lady Chosen

A Gentleman's Honor

A Lady of His Own

A Fine Passion

To Distraction

Beyond Seduction

The Edge of Desire

Mastered by Love

Black Cobra Quartet

The Untamed Bride

The Elusive Bride

The Brazen Bride

The Reckless Bride

The Adventurers Quartet

The Lady's Command

A Buccaneer at Heart

The Daredevil Snared

Lord of the Privateers

The Cavanaughs

The Designs of Lord Randolph Cavanaugh (April 24, 2018)

Other Novels

The Lady Risks All

The Legend of Nimway Hall – 1750: Jacqueline

Medieval (As M.S.Laurens)

Desire's Prize

Novellas

Melting Ice – from the anthologies *Rough Around the Edges* and *Scandalous Brides*

Rose in Bloom – from the anthology *Scottish Brides*

Scandalous Lord Dere – from the anthology *Secrets of a Perfect Night*

Lost and Found – from the anthology *Hero, Come Back*

The Fall of Rogue Gerrard – from the anthology *It Happened One Night*

The Seduction of Sebastian Trantor – from the anthology *It Happened One Season*

Short Stories

The Wedding Planner – from the anthology *Royal Weddings*

A Return Engagement – from the anthology *Royal Bridesmaids*

UK-Style Regency Romances

Tangled Reins

Four in Hand

Impetuous Innocent

Fair Juno

The Reasons for Marriage

A Lady of Expectations An Unwilling Conquest

A Comfortable Wife

THE CONFOUNDING CASE OF THE CARISBROOK EMERALDS

This is a work of fiction. Names, characters, places, and incidents are either products of the writer's imagination or are used fictitiously and are not to be construed as real. Any resemblance to actual events, locales, organizations, or persons, living or dead, is entirely coincidental.

THE CONFOUNDING CASE OF THE CARISBROOK EMERALDS

ISBN: 978-1-9922789-11-8

Cover design by Savdek Management Pty. Ltd.

Savdek Management Proprietary Limited, Melbourne, Australia.

www.stephanielaurens.com

Email: admin@stephanielaurens.com

❀ Created with Vellum

CHAPTER 1

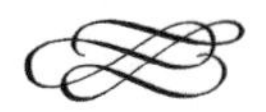

APRIL 7, 1839. LONDON

"*Where is she?"*

The feminine bellow echoed through the front hall and into the breakfast parlor, where Cara Di Abaccio was seated at the table with her cousins, Franklin and Julia Carisbrook. Startled, all three raised their heads; together with the butler, Jarvis, and the footman, Jeremy, they stared at the doorway.

A heartbeat passed, then in a rush of heavy footsteps and angrily swishing skirts, Cara's aunt, Livia, Lady Carisbrook, stormed into the room. She was a tall, full-figured woman with dark hair, perennially pinched features, and jet-black eyes. Currently garbed in a frilly and much-beribboned dressing gown, her hair restrained beneath a silk night-cap, Lady Carisbrook halted just inside the door. Her face contorting in fury, she raised one arm and pointed at Cara. "There you are, you conniving little thief!"

Her eyes growing even rounder, Cara stared in utter incomprehension. "Aunt…?"

"Don't you 'aunt' me! I always knew you were a sly little trollop—I warned Humphrey how it would be. But would he listen? No—of course not! He had to give house room to his scandalous sister's get, and worse, he insisted you be treated as part of the family, living alongside Franklin and Julia. *Pshaw!*" Her cheeks mottled with rage, Lady Carisbrook advanced on the table. "And now, miss, we see the result. My emeralds—the Carisbrook emeralds—are gone!"

Lady Carisbrook flung her hands in the air. "Vanished!" She returned her gaze, black eyes flashing, to Cara. "You've been here four weeks, just long enough to learn what's what, and now, you've stolen the emeralds."

Feeling as if she was having a bad dream, Cara set down her knife and fork and slowly shook her head. "No, aunt. I haven't—"

"*Don't* bother denying it. The emeralds—necklace, earrings, case, and all—are gone, and we all know who took them!" Lady Carisbrook cast Cara a look brimming with loathing and contempt; her lip all but curled. "You're the only foreigner in the house."

With that unarguable pronouncement, Lady Carisbrook turned her adamantine gaze on Franklin and Julia, seated opposite Cara and as stunned as she. "Make sure the thieving minx remains in this room until the police arrive."

All the blood drained from Cara's face, from her head. Giddy, she stared at Lady Carisbrook while Franklin and Julia, equally white-faced and flabbergasted, did the same. Until then standing frozen behind the pair, Jarvis shot a wide-eyed look over their heads at Jeremy.

Commandingly, Lady Carisbrook swung toward the butler. "Jarvis—send for Scotland Yard. Inform them we have a thief they need to come and take away."

Without another glance at any of them, Lady Carisbrook stalked from the room.

Leaving behind a stunned silence and a cloud of foreboding.

Sergeant Wilkes stepped over the threshold of Lord Carisbrook's John Street town house in a state of nervous trepidation.

A veteran of the force, Wilkes did not like the looks of this assignment; handling crimes in Mayfair was very definitely not his beat. His bad luck that it was Sunday morning, and he'd been the senior man on duty when the Carisbrook footman had come in to report the theft of a set of priceless emeralds. Still, according to the footman, the household had already apprehended the thief and merely required the villain to be clapped in shackles and hauled to the station to be charged. Such action was well within Wilkes's scope, and he'd brought Constable Fitch to assist if necessary.

With Fitch at his heels, Wilkes had followed the footman down the area steps and through the staff door. Wilkes looked ahead as the shadows of a long, unadorned passageway closed around them, and he spied a tall, lean, middle-aged butler waiting at the corridor's end.

Wilkes removed his helmet, tucked it under his arm, and told himself he could manage this. He walked up to the butler and halted. "Sergeant Wilkes of Scotland Yard." He flicked a hand over his shoulder. "And this is Constable Fitch. We understand you've had a spot of bother."

The butler's features remained rigid. "Indeed." With a fractional inclination of his head, he turned. "If you will come this way."

Wilkes wanted to ask about the emeralds and the thief, but he assumed he'd have his answers soon enough, so he held his tongue and, in his heavy boots, clomped behind the butler up a narrow staircase and into the front hall.

Before Wilkes realized what the man was about, the butler strode to a door, opened it, walked inside, and announced, "Two officers from Scotland Yard, ma'am. As you requested. A Sergeant Wilkes and a Constable Fitch."

From within the room came a cold female voice. "Excellent. Show them in, Jarvis."

Despite his rush of nervousness, Wilkes's feet carried him on. He only just had time to register the oddity in the butler's words—*As you requested? Why had the man phrased it like that?*—before he found himself entering a drawing room.

A gorgon sat on a sofa set perpendicular to the fireplace in which a cheery fire blazed. Through beady black eyes, she watched Wilkes advance. Her lips were thin and tightly pursed, and her expression stated more loudly than words that she was unimpressed by what she saw.

Wilkes halted on the fringed edge of a thick rug that looked expensive. Feeling Fitch halt just behind him, Wilkes essayed an awkward bow. Straightening, he adopted his blandest expression and assumed he was facing the lady of the house. "Lady Carisbrook. We understand your staff have apprehended a thief."

"Exactly."

The lady's voice—tone and diction—reminded Wilkes of steel being sharpened.

Lady Carisbrook continued, "My husband's foreign-born niece has stolen the Carisbrook emeralds. You need to take her away, find out what she did with my jewels, and return them to me." Lady Carisbrook stared at Wilkes for three seconds, then waved her hand in arrogant dismissal. "You may go."

Wilkes blinked. Behind him, Fitch shifted his weight. Wilkes cleared his throat. "If I could ask, my lady, if the girl—your husband's niece—stole the emeralds, where are they now?"

Lady Carisbrook frowned. "It's your job to find out, Sergeant."

Wilkes clamped down on the desire to retreat. "When was the last time the jewels were seen, ma'am?"

"I wore them last night. When I returned to the house, I put them in their case and left the case on my dressing table. This morning, after the Italian girl delivered my breakfast, I saw the case was gone."

Wilkes frowned. "But you didn't see her take the case?"

"No. But I was hardly watching her every move."

"Has the girl left the house since the jewels went missing?" Wilkes flicked a glance at the butler—Jarvis—who had moved to stand to one side, maintaining a clear line of sight to the gorgon.

At Wilkes's question, Jarvis's expression grew even more rigid.

In contrast, Lady Carisbrook bent an uncomprehending look on Wilkes. "I'm sure I don't know."

Wilkes exchanged a sidelong glance with Fitch, then drew breath and stated, "In that case, my lady, we'll need to speak with the rest of the household and search the premises."

"Good God, no!" Lady Carisbrook looked utterly appalled. "I won't have police tramping through my house—the very idea! Especially as there's no reason whatever to put us all out. The matter is simple—the Italian girl stole my emeralds. Search her and her room by all means and then take her away. I refuse to harbor a foreign criminal under my roof for an instant longer!"

Wilkes's heart was steadily sinking; so much for his hopes of a straightforward case. In his experience, when one of the upper ten thousand suggested a case was a "simple matter," invariably, said case proved anything but.

Lady Carisbrook continued, "No one else could possibly be the thief—our staff have all been with us for years. It's perfectly obvious that Cara Di Abaccio is the culprit." Lady Carisbrook pointed at the door—this time accompanying the gesture with an arrogantly commanding look. "Do your job, Sergeant, and remove her from this house!"

Wilkes was out of his depth. He bowed to her ladyship, turned, and with Fitch beside him, made for the door.

Jarvis moved to hold the door for them, then followed them from the room. After closing the door with a soft click, the butler paused, looking at Wilkes. Jarvis hesitated, but then, strengthening what appeared to be a rigid control over his features and especially his tongue, offered, "Miss Di Abaccio is in the breakfast parlor with her cousins—Mr. Franklin Carisbrook and Miss Julia Carisbrook. If you'll come this way."

Wilkes cocked an eyebrow at Fitch, who dutifully pulled out his notebook and started scribbling as they walked.

Jarvis led them to a room on the other side of the house.

Wilkes followed Jarvis inside. A highly polished round table with six straight-backed chairs arranged around it stood at the center of the room, and a sideboard sporting numerous covered dishes sat against one wall. Large windows looked out on a small square of garden and admitted the weak sunlight of the April morning, illuminating the three people seated about the table.

A gentleman in his mid- to late twenties with dark-brown hair and a young lady of perhaps twenty-one years sat facing the door; they looked up as Wilkes and Fitch entered. Their features were tense. Both looked helpless; their gazes locked on Wilkes as if hoping he would rescue them. From what, he had no idea.

The third person at the table was another young lady. Glossy black hair hung in heavy ringlets from an artfully fashioned knot at the back of her head; when she swung to look at Wilkes, he saw that the black mane was drawn severely back the better to reveal a countenance of quite startling loveliness. Wide, black-lashed, emerald eyes fixed on his face. The young lady had a finely drawn and straight, if longish, nose—a Roman nose without a doubt—and her lips were deep rose and lushly curved above a softly rounded but determined chin.

From the honeyed tint of her complexion, Wilkes took her to be the Italian girl—Miss Cara Di Abaccio, their supposed thief.

Wilkes halted a few paces into the room and managed to suppress a disbelieving snort. He'd collared more thieves than he could count, but, he reminded himself, this was the ton, and he knew better than to allow appearances to sway him. Still…

He favored the three with a short bow. "I'm Sergeant Wilkes, and this is Constable Fitch. We've been sent by Scotland Yard in response to Lady Carisbrook's summons."

Wilkes studied the three faces turned his way; all remained pale and expectantly tense, as if waiting for some axe to fall. He wouldn't have said he was a sensitive sort, yet even he felt certain that there was more going on than simply a misplaced accusation of theft.

He returned his attention to Miss Di Abaccio.

She met his gaze steadily, but, he sensed, with bated breath.

"Miss Di Abaccio. As I assume you are aware, Lady Carisbrook has accused you of stealing her emeralds."

"I didn't take them." Cara Di Abaccio's voice was low and husky. She shook her head. "I would never do such a thing."

She spoke calmly, evenly—with transparent honesty. But underneath, Wilkes sensed she was afraid.

Afraid of what?

Given he couldn't be sure, Wilkes merely inclined his head in acknowledgment of her statements; he could hear the *scritch* of Fitch's pencil as he jotted down her words. "Be that as it may, miss, we need you to come with us."

For an instant, he wondered if she would resist, but then, slowly, she pushed to her feet. She drew in a deep breath and tipped up her chin. "Very well, Sergeant." Then her façade wavered, and her fear shone through. "May I fetch my coat and bonnet?"

Her uncertainty—the underlying vulnerability—tugged at Wilkes, and he hurried to assure her, "This will probably just be temporary, miss. Just until we can figure out what happened. And—" He paused, then, looking into her wide eyes, went on. "As it happens, we'll need to search your room, miss, so you'll have time to collect whatever you want to take with you."

Her expression eased enough to be noticeable.

Wilkes darted a glance around the room. His words had lowered the tension in all those watching—not just in her two cousins but in Jarvis and the silent footman, too.

Wilkes shot a glance at Fitch and saw his own dawning understanding reflected in the constable's eyes. No one in that room believed Cara Di Abaccio was the thief—that she'd been the one to take the Carisbrook emeralds.

Everyone thought Lady Carisbrook had chosen her as a scapegoat.

Wilkes swallowed a groan. Ton cases—they were *never* straight-forward.

"Thank you, Sergeant." Miss Di Abaccio nodded in patent gratitude. She glanced once—fleetingly—at her cousins, then looked at Jarvis. "Perhaps, then, we should go to my room."

Jarvis signaled to the footman. "Henry will show you up."

Wilkes softly humphed, but didn't argue. Obviously, Cara Di Abaccio knew the way to her own room, but Wilkes wasn't averse to a non-Yard witness able to testify to anything found—or not found—during the upcoming search.

Without another word, Cara Di Abaccio swept out of the room and into the front hall. She paused to allow Henry to lead the way up the main staircase, then followed. Wilkes trooped behind her, with Fitch bringing up the rear.

Miss Di Abaccio's bedchamber was a smallish room on the first floor, toward the end of one wing of the house and facing the street. A medium-sized two-door armoire stood against one side wall, with a modest dressing table next to it. A washstand and a chest of drawers lined the opposite wall, flanking a small fireplace with a neat fire still smoldering in the grate. Opposite the door stood a tester bed with a pretty chintz coverlet that matched the curtains hanging at the windows to either side. A flat-topped traveling chest draped with a colorful shawl sat at the bed's foot.

The windows were shut against the noise rising from the street. It was only early April; there was unlikely to have been any reason the windows would have been opened for months—not unless Cara Di Abaccio had wanted to toss a jewel case to an accomplice waiting in the street.

Wilkes crossed to one window. A quick survey of the lock showed it hadn't been unsnibbed recently—indeed, not for some time.

Fitch had moved to check the other window. He looked at Wilkes and infinitesimally shook his head, then turned to survey the room.

After noting that the footman had taken up a stance against the wall just inside the door and Cara Di Abaccio was holding herself rigidly upright in a similar position on the other side of the door, Wilkes scanned the space with an experienced eye.

Searching the sparsely furnished room wasn't going to take long.

Cara clasped her hands, her fingers twining and gripping tight, and watched as the burly policemen searched through her belongings. They wouldn't find anything…

At least, nothing put there by her.

Her always-active imagination threw up the horrifying specter of her aunt hating her enough to have hidden—or had her horrible dresser hide—the jewel case containing the Carisbrook emeralds somewhere among Cara's things.

Chilled, Cara examined the mental vision, then drew in a breath through lungs painfully constricted and, by an effort of will, banished the image.

If her aunt hated her that much…there was nothing she could do.

From the moment she'd arrived in John Street, she'd known Lady Carisbrook disapproved—mightily—of her; her uncle Humphrey's sincerely warm welcome hadn't lessened the impact of her ladyship's cold glare and her grudgingly uttered and stilted words. From the instant of setting eyes on her, her aunt had wanted her gone.

Cara had no idea why and had worked to ensure she did nothing to incite her aunt's active malevolence.

Apparently, she'd failed.

Moving about the small room in their heavy uniforms and coats, the policemen were surprisingly quick and efficient. To Cara's relief, they didn't tumble her few possessions about but lifted, looked, and set things back.

Finally, the pair exchanged a glance, then the older man—the sergeant, Wilkes—turned to her. "Perhaps, miss, you would like to pack a small bag. Just the essentials to tide you over for a few days."

She drew in a deeper—freer—breath and nodded. "Thank you. I will." It seemed her aunt hadn't tried to…what was the English term? Pin the crime on her? Regardless, the jewel case wasn't in her room. Did that mean it was truly missing?

As she pulled her empty traveling valise from beneath her bed—unexpectedly grateful that she hadn't sent it upstairs to the attic—Wilkes said to his helper, "Check with the staff." Cara felt the sergeant's gaze briefly touch her face but, setting her bag on the bed, didn't meet it. Wilkes looked back at his man. "Ask around and learn what they can tell us about Miss Di Abaccio's movements late last night and this morning."

The other man snapped off a salute, shut the notebook in which he'd been jotting, and made for the door.

Cara set about systematically packing as much as she could into the valise.

Ignoring the footman, Henry, who watched her with sympathetic resignation, Wilkes studied her as she moved about the room. After a time, he grunted. "You didn't take the jewels, did you?"

Pressing a folded gown into the case, Cara looked up and, across the bed, met Wilkes's eyes—kindly brown eyes, their expression steady. "No." After a moment, she straightened and went on, "I can't imagine why anyone would think I would." She spread her hands. "What would I do with them?"

Wilkes frowned. "Wear them?"

She made the scoffing sound her aunt and her cousin Julia had told her ladies in England never made and moved to the dresser and pulled open the top drawer. "The Carisbrook emeralds are famous for their age and quality. But the design is very old and...heavy." She turned back with her underthings in her hands. Without looking at either Wilkes or Henry, she prosaically laid them in the case. "They would look"—she frowned—"outré." She searched for the English words. "Awkward and clumsy—silly—on me. I am far too small, too"—straightening, she gestured, indicating a massive bosom—"not-large to carry off such a piece."

Henry made a strangled noise, and Wilkes's face turned decidedly pink. He cleared his throat. "I see. Then I assume your aunt imagines you would sell them."

About to close her case on her meager wardrobe—all the clothes she'd brought with her to England—Cara paused and met Wilkes's gaze. "As I am what the English call a 'poor relation,' perhaps that is what my aunt thinks in making her accusation." Cara shrugged. "Who can tell what is in her mind? But I only arrived in England a month ago. I have never been here before, so I know no one, and through the past four weeks, the only people I have spoken to outside my aunt's or my cousins' presences have been the staff of this house. And my uncle, of course."

"Your uncle—Lord Carisbrook." Wilkes frowned. "Her ladyship said you were his niece."

Cara nodded. "My mother was his younger sister. She eloped with an Italian painter. But both my parents died of an illness last year, and Lord Carisbrook—who was made my guardian in my parents' wills—insisted I come here to London and live with his family." Cara thought back to that moment when she'd received his lordship's summons; in the straits she'd been in, the directive had appeared a godsend. She looked down at her valise. "It was a very kind offer."

She moved back to the dresser and reached for the bottom drawer.

"So where is your uncle at the moment? It's Sunday—most gents of his ilk would be at home."

"He left for his estate in Surrey on Friday." Cara studied the contents of the bottom drawer. "He isn't expected back until later today." She honestly wasn't sure if, in the circumstances, her uncle would defend her against his wife's accusation. He'd been kind, but even when he was in

London, he held himself aloof from the household, from Cara, and Franklin and Julia, too, as well as his wife.

Cara bit her lip. She couldn't allow herself to think of what might come. She needed to preserve what hope she still had and wait to see where this latest bend in her life's road would take her. Her recent experiences had taught her that clinging to hope and being open to whatever possibilities Fate deigned to offer was the surest route to survival.

Refocusing on the pencils, crayons, and sketchbooks stored in the drawer, she debated her options. She couldn't take her wooden art case in which she normally transported her supplies; it was too big and bulky. Along with her easel—also far too big to carry—the art case, still holding her paints, was pushed to the back of her armoire. But she could probably take all her drawing supplies if she crammed things in and didn't worry about crushing her clothes.

Wilkes had said "essential" things, and to her, her drawing implements were as essential as air—far more important than clothes. She stacked the pencils, crayons, and books, lifted them from the drawer, and turned to the bed and the valise.

Wilkes continued to watch, but as if he wasn't truly seeing her press and push and rearrange her things until she could shut the case. He seemed to shake himself back to the present as she buckled the straps.

When she straightened and reached for the bag's handle, Henry stepped forward. "Allow me, Miss Cara."

She gladly surrendered the case; even though she'd been among them for only four weeks, she'd come to know and like the staff. "Thank you, Henry."

She looked at Wilkes. He walked to the door, opened it, and led the way out. Cara drew in a breath, raised her head, and followed him into the corridor.

Henry shut the door, then quickly caught up to her. He glanced at the back of Wilkes's head, then murmured, "Don't you worry, Miss Cara—we'll make sure the master knows what's happened the instant he steps through the door."

She smiled, although it was a weak effort. "Thank you, Henry. And please thank the others, too." She paused, then, as they neared the stairs, added, "And please assure everyone that no matter what her ladyship thinks, I did not touch her jewels."

"No, miss. Of course not."

Henry sounded vaguely offended that she'd imagined the staff would think such a thing.

Wilkes heard the exchange and inwardly grimaced. Staff in a house like this always knew what was what; the more he heard, the more he was convinced that Lady Carisbrook's accusation was all a hum.

He started down the stairs, unsurprised to hear Miss Di Abaccio's footsteps lightly but determinedly descending behind him. She was a sensible young lady with a decent spine, and he liked her the more for it. Lots of young ladies would have had the vapors. Just the thought made him shudder, a reaction he endeavored to suppress.

Jarvis was waiting in the front hall, along with Fitch. Wilkes could tell from Fitch's demeanor that he'd learned something pertinent from the staff, but rather than asking for a report then and there and prolonging what—judging by Jarvis's and Henry's torn expressions—was already a fraught moment, Wilkes met Jarvis's gaze. "Please inform Lord Carisbrook that we have detained Miss Di Abaccio for the moment. We'll be taking her to Scotland Yard."

Jarvis inclined his head in acknowledgment, his expression signaling that he was glad to have been given such a definite order.

As if to confirm that, Jarvis's gaze cut across the hall.

Wilkes followed the butler's glance and saw Lady Carisbrook standing in the drawing room doorway with her arms folded beneath her impressive bosom, vindictive triumph all over her face.

Wilkes glanced at his "prisoner." Miss Di Abaccio was standing with her back ramrod straight and her head held high. Her gaze remained steady, fixed on Wilkes; she didn't spare a glance for her aunt.

Wilkes looked again at Lady Carisbrook and saw an ugly sneer further distort the lady's countenance. Then she uncrossed her arms, stepped back, and shut the drawing room door.

The words "good riddance" hadn't been uttered but had been most effectively conveyed.

Another glance at Miss Di Abaccio confirmed that her composure remained intact.

Feeling ever more convinced of her innocence, Wilkes gestured to the door. Jarvis opened it, and Wilkes solicitously ushered Miss Di Abaccio out and down the steps.

Fitch moved past and went to open the door of the plain black police carriage they'd arrived in.

Wilkes guided Miss Di Abaccio to the carriage. Henry, who had followed, stowed her valise in the boot, then saluted her before turning away.

"Thank you," she softly called before allowing Wilkes to help her into the carriage.

Wilkes clambered in after her and settled on the seat beside her.

Fitch joined them and, after shutting the door, fell onto the facing seat.

The instant the carriage rattled off, Wilkes met Fitch's sharp eyes. "What did you learn?"

Fitch's gaze shifted to Miss Di Abaccio, and he politely inclined his head. "The staff said her ladyship came home in the small hours from some ball, and Miss Di Abaccio, as well as the son and daughter, were with her. Seems they all went upstairs—it was close on two o'clock—and her ladyship was wearing the jewels then. Miss Di Abaccio and the others all went to their own rooms. The next thing the staff knew, at about half past eight this morning, her ladyship came raging downstairs and accused Miss Di Abaccio of stealing the emeralds."

Wilkes grunted and shook his head. "Who knows what's going on in the lady's mind? The instant we get to the station, collar a runner and send him off to Greenbury Street. This is definitely one for Senior Inspector Stokes and his friends."

Hugo Adair slipped through the throng of worshippers who, at the end of the morning service, had spilled onto the porch of St. George's Church at the corner of Hanover Square. Tall enough to see over most heads, Hugo scanned the crowd, searching for a glimpse of glossy black curls framing a face of Madonna-like sweetness whose features, instead of exuding serenity, glowed with vibrant liveliness.

Cara Di Abaccio's face held so much life—radiated so much engaging vivacity—that Hugo could literally stare at her for hours and had whenever he could get away with such unwavering absorption.

He'd taken to assiduously escorting his mother to Sunday service precisely for that reason.

But today in the church, when he'd located Lady Carisbrook's hatted head among the devoted—not difficult given her ladyship had a fetish for extravagant headgear that put all others to shame—he hadn't seen Cara in her usual position, seated three places past her ladyship, with

Franklin and Julia, the Carisbrooks' children and Cara's cousins, between.

The thought that Cara must be ill and languishing at home alone prodded Hugo on as he quartered the shifting crowd, searching for the Carisbrook party.

He'd first encountered Cara Di Abaccio three weeks before, at an alfresco luncheon one of his sisters had dragged him to. He'd been instantly smitten; he was willing to admit that, no matter how silly it made him sound.

Smitten. It was the right word. Struck beyond recovery, he'd been drawn to Cara—to her laughing eyes and her fascinating smile and the warm glow that suffused her face when she looked at him.

Since their first meeting, he'd tracked her through the ton, attending the same events she did. Given his family's connections, that hadn't proved all that hard. His only concern was that, sooner or later, his mother and sisters would learn of his doings and insist on meeting Cara before he and she had progressed to the point family introductions.

Hugo paused at the edge of the crowd to sweep the gathering again. *There!* The gauzy creation with countless tiny ribbon bows in a hideous shade of puce could belong to no other than Lady Carisbrook. Of course, her ladyship was holding court right in the middle of the crowd. Muttering a curse, Hugo dived in again, smiling and nodding and resisting all attempts to waylay him.

Something was wrong—or at least, not right. His instincts were pricking as they hadn't in a long while—not in all the months since he'd sold out of the army and returned to civilian life.

He'd spent nearly a decade in the cavalry, serving in a regiment of Hussars. With the wars long over, he'd seen no battlefields—just as well given he'd discovered a year ago that dead bodies left him nauseated. Instead, his time had been consumed by parades and balls and looking the part as he rode with his troop in this or that procession or guard. Being tall and dark haired and possessing broad shoulders and a long lean frame, he had excelled at the activity of looking the part. For the rest of his time, along with a circle of like-minded friends, he'd engaged in the usual hedonistic pursuits at which gentlemen of his class also excelled, wine, women, and song being the least of them. Gambling hard, riding to hounds, consorting with opera dancers, and even more reckless adventures had filled uncounted days and nights.

Then, abruptly, his interest in such activities had died. Whether it was age or something else, he didn't know, but one day, he'd simply had enough. Restless and dissatisfied, he'd sold out.

A month later, during the Season last year, his mother had hauled him off to a ball in the vain hope he would stumble on some sweet young miss who would fix his peripatetic interest and get him off his mother's hands, or at least that was how she'd phrased it. Instead, he'd gone out to smoke a cheroot and stumbled over a dead body—a lady with her head bashed in.

After that experience, he'd lost his taste for cheroots.

But through what had followed, he'd seen more of his cousin Barnaby Adair and his wife, Penelope. Both were, each in their own way, decidedly eccentric, yet they'd found purpose in their lives, and through being in their company, Hugo had realized that that—purpose—was what he lacked and what he needed to find.

He'd left town and retreated to his family's estate in Wiltshire. Enfolded in the peace of the country, he'd set his mind to the task of defining what he wanted to do—to achieve with his life.

Long walks and talks with his father had helped, and he'd realized that his answer lay in the one thing he was especially good at and that he truly enjoyed.

Breeding hounds.

His father had always bred hounds, and during his earlier years, Hugo had helped and had nudged their dogs into a higher category of quality. His father had continued the work while Hugo had been in the army, and the breeding kennels had advanced to a point where their name was well known, and gentlemen and hunt masters came to buy dogs for their packs.

Hugo had spoken for hours with his father, discussing the prospects, the ins and outs, and had ultimately won his sire's agreement that he could take over the fledgling enterprise. He was eager to do so, but his father had made one non-negotiable stipulation—that Hugo allow his mother to have one last try at finding him a suitable bride.

That stipulation was the only reason Hugo was in town—the only reason he'd been there to fall under Cara Di Abaccio's spell.

He knew he was handsome, dashing, and all the rest. He was well born, well-connected, and despite being a second son, would be no pauper. Yet even over the few short weeks she'd been in town, from watching Cara discourage other would-be suitors, Hugo already knew such considerations were of no importance to her.

She was a rebel like him—a free spirit who, while acknowledging the tenets of society, allowed them no real purchase.

He'd discovered she was an artist—that she had an artist's soul—and she loved animals, all animals, as he did.

He didn't yet know if she felt for him in the same way he was already willing to admit—at least to himself—that he felt for her. He hadn't yet reached the point of speaking—of seeking the consent of her uncle and asking her to marry him—but day by day, he was edging closer to that precipice.

He was almost at the point of looking forward to falling over it.

To falling irrevocably in love.

That had worked for Barnaby; Hugo couldn't see why it wouldn't work for him.

Indeed, just as his inherently reckless nature had made him perfect for dealing with the potential risks faced by any cavalryman, those same traits paved the way for him to take the biggest risk of all and venture his heart on love.

That was one life gamble that, hour by hour, he was drawing closer to taking.

Finally, his patience well-nigh exhausted, he slid between two older matrons into a gap behind Lady Carisbrook. He concentrated on her, and as the surrounding chatter faded, her voice reached him clearly. She was declaiming to an audience of her cronies; usually, Hugo judged that most of her ladyship's toadies were secretly bored by her diatribes, but today, all gave the appearance of hanging on her ladyship's every word.

"Of course," she stated, "I always knew she wasn't to be trusted, but not even *I* would have *dreamed* that the wretched girl would steal my emeralds!"

Her ladyship paused, allowing the expected oohs, aahs, and sycophantic murmurings to run their course before continuing, "Naturally, I had no alternative but to summon Scotland Yard, and they came and took the wretched ingrate away."

Hugo's instincts flared, not just prodding but screaming. His blood ran cold. She couldn't mean Cara?

He listened to the responses from the other ladies, but comments such as "after all you'd done for her," "after taking her in," and "a viper under your own roof" could have applied to a favored maid as much as to Cara.

Suddenly desperate, Hugo turned and searched the crowd again. Franklin and Julia were usually found within feet of their mother, but not today. "Where are they?" he muttered.

Then he spotted the pair. They were clinging to the edge of the crowd, and neither looked the least bit happy.

Hugo all but barged his way to them.

He planted himself directly before the pair, making their eyes go wide. "Cara," he rapped out, using his captain's voice. "Where is she?"

Julia looked stricken and wrung her hands, but volunteered nothing.

Hugo shifted his gaze to Franklin, who apparently understood the threat in his eyes.

Franklin swallowed and said, "This morning, Mama accused Cara of stealing the Carisbrook emeralds. Mama had them last night, and this morning, they were gone, and she said Cara had taken them."

His jaw clenching, Hugo ground out, "I heard your mother mention Scotland Yard."

Julia nodded frantically. "It was horrible. Two policemen came and took Cara away."

For one instant, Hugo told himself he'd misheard. In the next, that part of him that had made his commanders beg him to remain in the army surfaced, pushing through the accumulated layers of sophisticated-gentleman-about-town camouflage.

"Right." Hugo didn't know what his face looked like, but both Franklin and Julia straightened and lost some of their irritating vagueness.

Franklin looked at him with blatant hope, while Julia put a hand on his sleeve and ventured, "Please, can you think of any way to get her out of there—wherever they've taken her?"

He would do that or die trying. But…he searched Franklin's and Julia's faces. "You don't believe Cara's guilty."

"Of course not," Franklin muttered, his features growing grim. He stared at Hugo. "Do you?"

Hugo blinked, then spoke what he realized was the truth. "It didn't even occur to me."

With that, he swung around and scanned the carriages drawn up by the curbs on both sides of the street. He spotted his mother's and quit the church porch and strode for it.

He found his mother's footman, Jenks, waiting in the carriage's shade. "Find my mother and tell her I've been called away. I'll see her at home later."

Jenks tipped him a salute.

Hugo spun on his heel and stalked off toward Scotland Yard.

CHAPTER 2

Senior Inspector Basil Stokes climbed the steps of Scotland Yard with heavy boots. He was not in a good mood. Why the ton couldn't observe the Sabbath quietly without screeching about some crime, thus allowing him to enjoy his day off, was beyond his ability to understand.

At that very moment, he should have been sitting down to a Sunday dinner of roast capon in the smiling company of his wife and his young daughter. And every Sunday, he looked forward to the hours of the early afternoon, when he took Megan to the park to play. It was the only time during the week that he got to spend solely with her, and she with him.

Scowling blackly, he reached the entrance, pushed open the swinging door, and marched inside. Spotting Wilkes, who had summoned him, leaning on the counter at the end of the hall, Stokes growled, "Why can't the nobs take Sunday off like normal people?"

Wilkes grimaced and straightened, but held his ground. "Nothing for it, I'm afraid, sir. This one's got your moniker all over it."

Stokes halted before the desk—just as the doors behind him were flung open with such force that the handles hit the walls.

Shock colored the face of the sergeant behind the desk, and Wilkes stiffened. Stokes whirled to confront the threat.

A gentleman Stokes recognized but couldn't immediately place came stalking down the hall. The man's features were grim, his dark hair sweeping across a lowered, decidedly pugnacious, and—yes—threatening brow.

In one comprehensive glance, Stokes took in the man's large fists—clenched—and that, after one swift raking glance about the hall, the man's dark-blue eyes had fixed on him.

It was the eyes that jolted Stokes's memory into dredging up the connection.

Stokes relaxed, the tension that had invested his muscles draining. He nodded to the gentleman as he halted—still openly belligerent—before him. "Adair. What can we do for you?"

Wilkes blinked. "There's more of them?"

Both Adair and Stokes shot Wilkes a glance—Adair's glowering with incipient menace, Stokes's amused—then Adair returned his gaze to Stokes. "I understand two of your men attended the Carisbrook residence this morning and, at Lady Carisbrook's direction, removed Miss Cara Di Abaccio." Hugo paused, then demanded, "Where is she?"

Stokes managed not to blink; his previous interactions with Barnaby Adair's cousin had left him viewing Hugo as not precisely weak but perhaps not as strong and forceful a character as others of Barnaby's family.

Rapidly realigning his thoughts with the reality standing, all but vibrating with the potential for violent action, before him, Stokes looked at Wilkes, who now appeared both interested and concerned. When Stokes arched a brow, Wilkes, his gaze shifting to Hugo, nodded.

Calmly, Stokes met Hugo's eyes. "I've only just walked in, having been summoned to deal with what I suspect is the case in which you apparently hold an interest." Just what interest that was, Stokes was keen to learn. When investigating in the ton, having someone on the inside made life much easier; if, in this case, Hugo was already in such a position, Stokes would be happy to enlist him.

And if Hugo's interest was what Stokes suspected it might be, enlisting Hugo wouldn't be difficult.

Wilkes, who had assisted Stokes on several ton cases, read the signs and volunteered, "I put the young lady in your office, sir."

Stokes noted that the news that he was taking control of the case had lessened the dangerous tension gripping Hugo. Stokes tipped his head toward the stairs. "Why don't you come with me, and we can see if we can straighten this out?"

Hugo inclined his head, still stiff, yet clearly accepting Stokes's olive branch. "Thank you."

Stokes gestured to the stairs, and Hugo fell in beside him. As they climbed, Stokes said, "I've yet to be briefed, so I'm coming into this blind. What have you heard of the case?"

Hugo was looking down, placing his large feet on the treads. "I escorted my mother to church at St. George's. Lady Carisbrook, her son and daughter, and Miss Di Abaccio normally attend, but today, I didn't see Miss Di Abaccio. After the service, while the congregation was mingling, I heard Lady Carisbrook exclaiming to her friends that a 'wretched girl,' an 'ingrate,' had stolen her emeralds. Lady Carisbrook didn't name the girl in my hearing, but I found Franklin and Julia—her ladyship's children —on the edge of the crowd, and they told me her ladyship had accused Cara of stealing the emeralds and summoned policemen from here, and two men came and took Cara away." Hugo glanced back at Wilkes, who was following them up the stairs. "You haven't charged her, have you?"

The words were calm and quiet, leaving the menace underlying them all the more evident.

"'Course not." Wilkes sounded faintly offended.

A fact that, to Stokes, spoke volumes.

On reaching the top of the stairs, Stokes gestured Hugo and Wilkes into a small alcove off the corridor. "Right, then. Before I meet Miss Di Abaccio, perhaps you'd better tell me what's happened so far." He nodded at Wilkes. "You first."

Wilkes straightened to attention and gave a succinct account of his unexpected foray into Mayfair. "We were told the household had apprehended a thief." Wilkes dutifully detailed Lady Carisbrook's allegations regarding Miss Di Abaccio stealing the Carisbrook emeralds and her ladyship's insistence that he and Fitch remove the young lady from the house. "When we spoke with her, Miss Di Abaccio denied doing the deed. We searched her room and found no evidence to say she had." Wilkes shifted his gaze to Hugo. "And Fitch and I got the distinct impression no one else in the house—staff or her cousins—thought Miss Di Abaccio guilty."

Hugo snorted. "Of course she's not guilty. Lady Carisbrook's just seized on her emeralds being misplaced to throw Cara out of the house." He paused, then frowned. "Was Lord Carisbrook at home?"

Wilkes tipped his head, acknowledging the point. "No, he wasn't."

Stokes studied Wilkes's face, then Hugo's. "Are you saying that if his lordship had been there, this wouldn't have happened? Or, at least, that Miss Di Abaccio wouldn't have been accused?"

Hugo nodded decisively. "Miss Di Abaccio is his lordship's niece and also now his ward. He's a reasonable man—an honorable older gent. In contrast, Lady Carisbrook is a pompous tartar. I don't know that she cares for anyone or anything other than preserving what she sees as her position —her station in life."

Stokes pulled a face. "I see. One of those." As a scion of the gentry rather than the aristocracy, Stokes was well aware of the arrogant stances taken by some of the latter species. Stokes thought for a moment, then demanded of Hugo, "Tell me what you know of the Carisbrook emeralds."

Hugo grimaced. "I've only seen them a few times—the stones are squarish and set in a heavily ornate gold necklace with matching earrings. Given the design, the parure probably hails from Elizabethan times—very showy, heavy, and large."

"As they're referred to as the Carisbrook emeralds, I take it they're famous?" Stokes asked.

Hugo shrugged. "As such things go. Not as famous as the Cynster emeralds, but nearly as old."

Stokes grunted and turned to Wilkes. "Clearly, the Carisbrook emeralds aren't going to be easy to hide. So where did you search?"

Defensiveness crept into Wilkes's expression. "We searched the girl's —Miss Di Abaccio's—room. Lady Carisbrook said the jewels were in a case and it was the whole case that was taken, but neither it nor any jewels were in Miss Di Abaccio's room. And she couldn't have been hiding them on her person, either."

"Where else did you search?" Stokes asked.

Wilkes actually blushed. "We wanted to search the house, but her ladyship wouldn't have it. She'd fixed it in her head that Miss Di Abaccio, who as you might expect from the name is a foreigner, had taken the jewels, and that was that. She—her ladyship—seemed to think it was just a matter of us taking Miss Di Abaccio away and browbeating the location of the emeralds out of her, then we'd get the jewels and return them to her ladyship. She wouldn't even allow us to speak to the staff."

Hugo gave vent to a low, angry growl.

Stokes knew exactly how Hugo felt. Stokes stared at Wilkes, but the sergeant didn't quail, and to give him his due, the situation wasn't his fault; dealing with the likes of Lady Carisbrook required bigger guns. "Right, then." Stokes glanced at the large clock at the end of the corridor. "It's now past midday, and the theft occurred sometime before…"

He looked at Wilkes, and the sergeant supplied, "Eight-thirty in the morning. That was when Lady Carisbrook noticed the case was gone." Without waiting to be asked, Wilkes added, "She last saw the jewels when she took them off after coming in last night—about two in the morning, that was."

"So our thief has had at least six hours, if not eight, to dispose of the emeralds." Stokes exhaled in frustration. He looked down for a moment and gathered his thoughts. "It might be shutting the door after the horse has bolted"—he glanced at Wilkes—"but given that most thefts like these are carried out by someone in the household, living in the house, I want a cordon of men placed around the Carisbrook residence, front and back. If any member of the household leaves, they're to be followed. If anyone calls and then leaves, once they're on their way, intercept them and ask for their name and their business in the house." He paused, then added, "And tell Gilbert downstairs that I want four men, yourself included, to accompany me to the house once I finish speaking with Miss Di Abaccio."

"Yes, sir." Wilkes saluted and, at Stokes's nod, left to clatter back down the stairs.

Stokes glanced at Hugo. "I take it you would like to see Miss Di Abaccio."

Hugo straightened; he was an inch or so taller than Stokes. "I intend to stand beside her through this ordeal."

Stokes considered what he could read in Hugo's face, then inclined his head. "Very well. Let's see what she can tell me."

He led the way down the corridor to his office.

The door stood ajar. Stokes paused on the threshold to see Constable Fitch, who Stokes had thought a hardened case, encouraging a black-haired young lady who was balancing a cup and saucer in one hand to make her selection from a plate of biscuits… Stokes recognized his own shortbread biscuits, made by his wife, Griselda.

Caught in the act, Fitch met Stokes's eyes and colored, but didn't straighten or remove the plate. "We thought to make Miss Di Abaccio comfortable, sir."

Stokes snorted softly and waved the words aside. He focused on his supposed thief, sitting primly on a straight-backed chair to the side of his desk, and instantly understood Wilkes's, Fitch's, and most especially Hugo's reactions. Miss Cara Di Abaccio was the sort of female guaranteed to provoke the protective instincts of any male who gazed upon her. It wasn't the perfection of her features—indeed, her mouth was a trifle large for the current standard of beauty—but the innocence conveyed in those large green eyes that would compel any red-blooded male to instantly leap to her defense.

As a married man with a two-year-old daughter, Stokes considered himself largely immune from such compulsions, yet even he felt the weight of Cara Di Abaccio's spell. The thing of it was, gazing at her widening eyes and sensing the trepidation pouring from her, Stokes seriously doubted Miss Di Abaccio had any notion of her innate power—which only made him more certain that her apparent innocence was no façade.

He stepped into the room, and Miss Di Abaccio turned and put the saucer on the desk and, in something of a fluster, grasped her small reticule, until then lying in her lap, looked up at Stokes, and made to rise—

Stokes waved her back and found himself nodding politely to her. "Miss Di Abaccio."

Uncertain, with her wide eyes fixed on his face, she subsided onto the chair.

Fitch threw Stokes what was almost a warning look and retreated with the biscuits.

Then Hugo stepped into the room; until that moment, he'd been concealed by the corridor's gloom.

Stokes looked at Miss Di Abaccio in time to take in the fact that her eyes could, indeed, grow bigger yet. She stared at Hugo, and her lips formed a silent "Oh."

For his part, Hugo had eyes only for her. He moved past Fitch, bent to take Miss Di Abaccio's hand—which she wordlessly surrendered—and bowed gracefully over it. "My dear Cara, please be assured that neither I nor Inspector Stokes here"—with his other hand, Hugo indicated Stokes—"nor the police nor anyone with half a brain place any credence whatever in your aunt's assertions." Straightening, Hugo spied another chair; without releasing Miss Di Abaccio's hand, he reached out, dragged the chair over, set it beside hers, and sat.

He clasped both his hands around the one of hers he'd appropriated, looked into her eyes, and in a tone that brooked neither dissent nor disbelief, stated, "We'll soon get to the bottom of this."

With that, calm and assured, Hugo raised his gaze and fixed it on Stokes.

Stokes looked down at the pair. He was receiving the distinct impression that, having possessed himself of Miss Di Abaccio's hand, Hugo had no intention of letting it go—literally or figuratively.

Muting a humph, Stokes rounded his desk and sat in his comfortable office chair.

Between them, Fitch and Hugo resited his and Miss Di Abaccio's chairs so that they were sitting side by side to Stokes's right, facing the desk and able to meet his gaze.

"First things first." Stokes glanced at Fitch, who dutifully drew out his notebook and pencil, then Stokes transferred his gaze to Miss Di Abaccio. "I understand you are Lord Carisbrook's niece and his ward. Were you born in England?"

"No. In Italy." Miss Di Abaccio's voice was low in tone, faintly husky, and her accent converted ordinary words into something vaguely exotic. "My father was Italian, and my parents lived there. My mother was Lord Carisbrook's younger sister. When my parents died of a fever last year, Lord Carisbrook became my guardian and was kind enough to insist I come to England and live with his family here. He and the household have made me very welcome, and I will always be grateful for that."

Fitch scribbled diligently, and Stokes nodded. "I see." He mentally kicked himself for not asking Hugo earlier, but he needed to know. "Forgive my bluntness, Miss Di Abaccio, but did you inherit substantial assets?"

Hugo's face darkened, and he shook his head, but Miss Di Abaccio's countenance showed no hint of discomposure.

"No, no—I have no money. I am…" She glanced at Hugo. "A poor relation." She looked at Stokes. "Lady Carisbrook has told me that is my state."

Stokes found his opinion of Lady Carisbrook sinking minute to minute, but it seemed her accusation at least had the merit of understandable motive, if nothing else. "When did you join the Carisbrook household?"

"I arrived in London in the second week of March, so it is now four weeks that I have been here."

Fitch cleared his throat.

When Stokes looked inquiringly his way, the constable—an experienced man—said, "Begging yours and Miss Di Abaccio's pardon, sir, but her ladyship did say as Miss Di Abaccio was the only foreigner in the house—set great store by that point, her ladyship did—and also that all the staff have been with the household for years."

Stokes digested that news, then looked at Cara Di Abaccio. "Miss Di Abaccio, did your aunt welcome you into her home?"

Miss Di Abaccio looked down at her hands, still entangled with Hugo's. "I… She…" Then she drew breath and said, "I cannot properly answer that, sir."

The glare Hugo was directing at him convinced Stokes to leave that point, at least for the moment.

Stokes humphed and tugged at his lower lip. Prejudices—it seemed more than one—had prompted Lady Carisbrook to determinedly and with intent point her finger at her niece-by-marriage. Prejudice wasn't proof, yet setting her ladyship's accusation aside, the fact remained that the Carisbrook emeralds, unquestionably highly valuable, had gone missing, presumed stolen.

That was the crux of this case.

And as such, it fell to Scotland Yard—and therefore to Stokes and his team—to solve the crime, apprehend the culprit, and if possible, retrieve the emeralds.

Stokes refocused on Cara and Hugo. Cara was still sitting primly with her eyes downcast, her gaze apparently on Hugo's hand, still surrounding one of hers in her lap, while Hugo had his head bent, murmuring reassurances that Stokes could be trusted to see everything put right.

Stokes swallowed a snort. He was touched by Hugo's confidence, but Stokes knew his limits. To deal with this case, he would need those bigger guns he'd thought of earlier.

As for Cara Di Abaccio's innocence, in his experienced view, the strongest evidence to date on that subject was Hugo's belief in it. Hugo was an Adair, and Stokes had a high regard for the instinctive intelligence of the members of that family.

Conscious that time was passing and that there was nothing he needed to ask Cara Di Abaccio that couldn't be asked, and possibly better asked, later, Stokes looked at Fitch. "I'll speak with the duty magistrate and clear a search of the Carisbrook residence. Meanwhile, tell Wilkes to go to Albemarle Street and request the assistance of Mr. Barnaby Adair."

"Yes, sir!" Fitch put up his notebook, eager to get on. "Should Wilkes ask Mr. Adair to join us here?"

"No." Stokes rose to his feet. "Tell him"—his lips quirked; it was

Sunday after all, and Penelope, Barnaby's wife, was sure to be at home as well—"and anyone who might think to accompany him to meet us outside the Carisbrook house."

Fitch snapped off a salute and headed for the door.

Stokes looked at Hugo and saw the determination and hope in his face, then nodded to him and Miss Di Abaccio. "Wait here. My meeting with the magistrate won't take long."

Stokes, Miss Di Abaccio, Hugo, and Wilkes were waiting—not particularly patiently—in a supposedly anonymous large black coach drawn up to the curb opposite Number 12 John Street when Barnaby Adair, with his wife, Penelope, on his arm, strolled up and rapped on the carriage's side.

Stokes humphed, leaned forward, and swung open the door.

Standing on the pavement, the handsome couple looked into the carriage with undisguised curiosity.

Over the years, the pair had assisted Stokes with a significant number of cases in which the wrongdoers had proved to be members of society's upper echelons. As the third son of an earl, Barnaby had the entrée into circles beyond Stokes's reach. More, having been born into such circles, Barnaby and Penelope possessed a wealth of contacts, as well as understanding how the nobs thought and why they acted as they did; such insights had proved invaluable in solving the aforementioned cases. In addition, Barnaby's father, the Earl of Cothelstone, was one of the directors of the Metropolitan Police. Given that and their history of success, the commissioner now took it as a given that when a case involving the ton arose, Stokes would handle it and would consult with Barnaby and Penelope Adair.

Stokes's gaze ranged over his friends; he hadn't seen them for a few weeks. Many a villain had looked at Barnaby, seen a typical gentleman of his class, and underestimated his intelligence and his devotion to seeing justice done—more fool them. As tall as Stokes, but leaner and more elegantly dressed, Barnaby exuded the aura of a gentleman about town. His pale skin, aristocratic features, halo of guinea-gold curls, and bright-blue eyes were a visual foil to Stokes's darker, more saturnine features, his close-cropped black hair, and eyes of steely gray. Despite their differences—in looks, background, and social standing—they'd grown to be successful associates in solving crimes and, along the way, had become close friends.

That friendship had solidified further when their wives—Barnaby's Penelope and Stokes's Griselda—had become firm friends, too. Then last year, courtesy of another case, their small circle had expanded to include Heathcote Montague, renowned man of business to the ton, and his wife, Violet, who these days divided her time between organizing Montague and organizing Penelope.

Framed by the carriage doorway, Penelope met Stokes's eyes and smiled delightedly. Petite, dark-haired, supremely well connected among the ton, a darling of the grandes dames and with the ear of all the most important hostesses, Penelope was a force to be reckoned with. Her primary interests beyond her and Barnaby's son, Oliver, lay in translating old and generally obscure tomes for various learned institutions while simultaneously, along with her three sisters, overseeing the activities of the Foundling House in Bloomsbury—which in part explained why she needed Violet to organize her days.

Yet it was Penelope's intellect that was her most striking attribute; it manifested in a vibrant interest in all about her that shone in her dark eyes, magnified by the spectacles she habitually wore. She was now a matron of twenty-six years, yet her enthusiasm for life—and for justice—remained undimmed.

Together with Penelope having taken astute survey of the occupants of the carriage, Barnaby smiled and arched his brows. "I gather our assistance is required."

Behind the lenses of her spectacles, Penelope's eyes gleamed. Her gaze had fixed on Hugo and the lady sitting beside him, and Penelope's expression turned openly intrigued.

Stokes waved the pair inside; the coach was cavernous, built to carry at least six large men. He waited until Barnaby helped Penelope up and followed her in, shut the door behind him, and sat beside her on the seat opposite Stokes, Hugo, and Cara Di Abaccio before stating, "The Carisbrook emeralds have been stolen."

Penelope heard the call to arms, but in that moment, she was far more interested in the young woman seated beside Hugo. From the lady's coloring, she instantly deduced her identity. "Miss Di Abaccio, isn't it?" Smiling brightly, Penelope held out her hand. She bit back the words: *Hugo's mother has mentioned you.*

Briefly, Miss Di Abaccio met Hugo's eyes, then leaned forward and lightly clasped Penelope's fingers. "Yes, that is I. I am afraid you have the advantage of me, ma'am."

Penelope grinned. "I'm Penelope Adair." She waved at Barnaby. "And this is my husband, Barnaby Adair." She shifted her gaze to Hugo's face. "Hugo's cousin. We occasionally assist Inspector Stokes when his cases involve members of the ton."

Having exchanged a nod with Hugo and Wilkes, Barnaby reached across Penelope and shook Miss Di Abaccio's hand. "A pleasure, Miss Di Abaccio, although I could have hoped that we would meet under less fraught circumstances." Barnaby transferred his gaze to Stokes. "So... when did the emeralds go missing, and what has their disappearance to do with Miss Di Abaccio?"

Stokes gestured to Wilkes, who obliged by giving a concise report of what he'd learned on attending the Carisbrook house in response to Lady Carisbrook's summons, then Stokes filled in what his questioning of Miss Di Abaccio had added to the picture.

When he fell silent and looked invitingly at her and Barnaby, Penelope couldn't hold her tongue. "Good Lord!" Despite her years observing the ton, she was genuinely shocked. She looked at Cara Di Abaccio. "Lady Carisbrook's behavior toward you falls well beyond the line of what can be excused. Even had she been overset by nerves—and from my albeit distant knowledge of her, that's something I find difficult to believe—to treat you in such a manner without proof and then deny the police the opportunity to search the house and interview the staff is a monstrous injustice!" She paused, then went on, her tone hardening, "As for insisting you deliver her breakfast tray every morning..." Lips setting, she shook her head. "Words fail me."

Barnaby, too, was distinctly unimpressed. "To accuse you of stealing as she did and insist on your removal from beneath your guardian's roof... Such actions require strong justification, which, from all we've heard, is notably lacking." After a second's pause, he asked, "Tell us about the others in the family. We"—he glanced at Penelope—"are acquainted with Lord and Lady Carisbrook, at least by name. Who else of the family is currently residing in the house?"

Penelope noticed that Hugo had taken one of Miss Di Abaccio's hands and now surreptitiously squeezed it in support.

Miss Di Abaccio—Cara; it was a great deal easier to think of her by her first name—raised her head and replied, "There are only two of the Carisbrook children who yet live at home—the second son, Franklin, and the third and last daughter, Julia. The older three children are married and live elsewhere."

Penelope nodded. "Franklin Carisbrook is about my age, so I know next to nothing about him, and even less about Julia, who is younger."

"She's twenty-three," Cara said. "Two months older than me."

Penelope—along with Barnaby—fixed Hugo with an interrogatory look.

Hugo grimaced. "I don't know either well." He glanced at Cara. "I've only recently spent time in the circles they frequent."

Only since Cara joined the family was Penelope's guess. "Nevertheless," she persisted, "what are your thoughts on the pair?" She pushed her glasses up on the bridge of her nose and fixed her gaze on Hugo's face. "If you think, you'll discover you've observed more than you realize."

Hugo straightened on the seat. He frowned faintly, obediently casting his mind over all he'd heard and seen. Eventually, he offered, "I can't tell you much of Julia Carisbrook, other than..." He glanced apologetically at Cara, then went on, "Well, she's twenty-three, well-looking enough, but...too reserved—no, too self-effacing. As if she's unsure she truly wants to attract any gentleman's attention."

Penelope nodded decisively. "She lacks confidence—hardly surprising with a mother like Lady Carisbrook." To Stokes, she explained, "I understand Lady Carisbrook is a firm believer in managing her children's lives to the smallest detail."

"Oh yes," Cara murmured. "You are right—it is just like that."

Encouraged, Hugo went on, "Franklin is...very unhappy with his mother's constant meddling with his life—with her hands on his reins, if you like. But I get the impression he's intent on something—as if he's glimpsed a way out and is determined to seize it."

"Julia and I," Cara said, glancing up and meeting Hugo's eyes, "think that Franklin has found a sweetheart, but we don't know who or where." Cara looked at Penelope. "Franklin is often from the house—visiting friends, he says, but..." She shrugged. "A sweetheart can be a friend, yes?"

"Indeed." Penelope nodded. "And to add my knowledge to our pool, third-hand though it is, it's widely known that Lady Carisbrook is a shrewishly arrogant harpy. She adheres to the school of thought that holds that the only way to secure one's own station in life is to make all those on social rungs below yours constantly aware of their place." Penelope dipped her head to Cara. "Her insistence on you delivering her breakfast tray is an example of that. But her ladyship treats all and sundry in the same way—if one is not of higher standing than she, one is not worthy of her consideration."

Beside Penelope, Barnaby shifted. "In contrast to his wife, Lord Carisbrook has the reputation of being a true gentleman, one of the old school, perhaps, but all the more gracious for that."

Cara averred, "My uncle has been nothing but kind."

Barnaby inclined his head. "Miss Di Abaccio—Cara, if we may?" When she nodded, he went on, "It would greatly help us all if you would answer my next questions with the utmost frankness." He trapped her gaze. "I take it you and your uncle are on good terms?"

Readily, she nodded. "I am beholden to him, and he has been so very kind. I hold him in the highest esteem, and I fear I will never be able to repay him, so I have vowed I will always do my best to make him content with me."

Barnaby smiled at her phrasing and smoothly asked, "And Franklin?"

"We are friends, I would think." She glanced at Hugo. "Franklin, too, has been…welcoming, you would say." She shrugged. "He is my cousin, and I would help him if he asked for aid, but outside the house, I know little of his life—only what we see when he attends with us at balls and parties."

"I see. And your cousin Julia?"

"She and I are friends. Close friends, as we are of an age and neither of us have wed."

"So you and she get along well?" Penelope asked.

Cara nodded. "Yes, very well." She paused, then glanced at Hugo and said, "Sometimes, I think Julia is very happy I am now there, with her at the balls and parties, so that when the young gentlemen come to speak with us, I can…what is the phrase? Keep them amused? Then she can watch and speak to those she wishes to." She pursed her lips, then added, "I am not as…quiet as she."

"You're not self-effacing and are significantly more confident," Hugo stated.

Cara flashed him a smile, one that had Penelope mentally blinking. Truly, Cara Di Abaccio was a lovely girl who, apparently, had no idea of the power of her smiles.

"That," Barnaby said, "brings us to the critical question." He caught Cara's eyes. "How would you say you got on with Lady Carisbrook?"

Cara wrinkled her nose, then said, "I cannot like her, and I know she is not at all happy to have me in her house—under her roof, as she puts it—but I do not argue with her, if that is what you mean. She is my uncle's wife, and I will honor him in all things, even if that means holding my tongue and…what is the word…tolering? No—tolerating. Even if I must tolerate Lady Carisbrook's slights, I will do it for my uncle." She held Barnaby's gaze and shook her head. "I would not cause strife in his household, not when he has welcomed me into it so warmly and generously."

Penelope nodded decisively. For a second, she studied Hugo's expression—his close to adoring expression—and found it hard to fault him; Cara Di Abaccio's stance did her credit. Turning her mind to the issue of the missing emeralds and how what they'd learned might impact on that, she asked, "What of the staff? Did you have any trouble with any of them?" When Cara met her gaze, Penelope added, "Sometimes, being a foreigner can be difficult."

"Oh no." Cara shook her head. "All the staff—well, all except for Simpkins, Lady Carisbrook's dresser—have been friendly and helpful. And as for Simpkins"—Cara shrugged—"she casts me dark looks when she thinks no one else can see, but other than that, she keeps her distance, and our paths rarely cross."

Familiar with the duties of a lady's maid of the level to be termed "a dresser," Penelope accepted that Cara and Simpkins wouldn't often have reason to even exchange words. "Very well. It's useful that you've made friends with the staff—perhaps you can shed light on one possible scenario regarding the disappearance of these emeralds. Given Lady Carisbrook's reputation, which suggests she would be unbearably arrogant and overbearing to her staff, is there any chance that one of them might have taken the emeralds—perhaps as a means of striking back at her ladyship for some especially hurtful action?"

But Cara was already emphatically shaking her head. "No—I cannot believe that would happen."

"Why not?" Stokes asked.

"Because all the staff are deeply, deeply loyal to my uncle, and the emeralds are his." Cara looked at all their faces, willing them to understand. "It is to his lordship the staff owe their allegiance—like me, they revere him because he is always kind, and so they, too, tolerate her ladyship for his sake. None of the staff would have stolen the emeralds."

Barnaby pulled a face and shifted, stretching his long legs. "Barring some pressure both unforeseeable and immense, I suspect your assessment of the staff will prove correct." When Penelope turned to him, he met her gaze. "I can't imagine any of the staff at Cothelstone stealing from the family, either."

Reluctantly, she nodded and looked at Stokes. "I can't think of anything more we might learn while inside this coach."

"Indeed." Stokes reached for the door handle, but the sound of a carriage rattling up and slowing made him pause.

They all turned their heads and peered out at an old traveling coach that rolled to a stop before the Carisbrook house.

Cara swiveled on the seat to look more directly out of the window. "That's Uncle Humphrey's carriage. He's back!" Relief rang in her voice.

Penelope exchanged a swift glance with Stokes, then reached across and tugged Cara's sleeve; capturing the younger woman's gaze, she drew her away from the window. "If it is your uncle, you can't go and speak with him—not yet. Not until we ascertain what the situation is regarding the emeralds and Lady Carisbrook's accusation against you."

"I'm sorry to say"—Stokes leaned forward to meet Cara's eyes—"that until such time as Lady Carisbrook withdraws her charge against you, you will officially need to remain in police custody."

"That doesn't mean that anyone is imagining putting you in a cell." Barnaby caught Hugo's eye before his cousin could voice any protest. "There's also the consideration that until we solve the mystery of the emeralds, no matter your supporters inside the Carisbrook house, you might not be safe within its walls."

That pulled both Cara and Hugo up short. After a moment of staring at Barnaby, Cara glanced at Hugo, just as he glanced at her. Hugo squeezed her hand. "We need to do as Barnaby, Stokes, and Penelope recommend. They're used to sorting out situations like this."

Cara looked cast down, but then she drew in a breath, raised her head, firmed her lips, and nodded. "Yes. You are no doubt right." She glanced from Barnaby to Penelope, then looked at Stokes. "So what now?"

"I'd say that's his lordship, right enough." Wilkes's observation had them all looking across the street in time to glimpse an elderly gent in an old-fashioned coat climb the steps, traverse the porch, and be admitted into the house.

Stokes reached again for the door handle. "I believe that's our cue to cross the street and evaluate the scene of the crime."

"And," Penelope said, as she stood and followed Stokes from the carriage, "meet the other major players in this family drama."

They left Cara with Hugo in the carriage, watched over by the police driver.

Penelope took Barnaby's arm, and alongside Stokes, they crossed the cobbles and halted on the pavement at the foot of the three steps leading up to the narrow porch before the black-painted door of the Carisbrook town house.

Stokes was signaling to various men, calling them to him. They came running up and collectively reported that no one had left the house since they'd been sent to keep watch. Stokes grunted. "It's possible we shut the door too late. However, given the apparent unlikelihood of any of the staff being involved, then our principal suspects must be the family, and after coming home so late—or rather early in the morning—and then going to church, it's unlikely they've ventured out again." He smiled grimly. "At least not yet, and not without the staff or other members of the family being aware of their absence."

"Indeed." Penelope regarded the door with determination. "Shall we?"

Of course, she led the way up the steps, but she paused on the porch to allow Stokes to do the honors and thump on the door.

"There is a bellpull, you know." She pointed to the chain hanging on the wall to the right of the door.

Stokes eyed it with disfavor. "Everyone expects the police to bang on their doors—they'd be disappointed if we didn't."

A few smothered guffaws came from the men behind them.

Stokes cast his eye over his assembled force. He'd brought enough men to mount a speedy yet effective search of the premises. As well as Wilkes, Fitch, and four of the six junior constables he'd drawn to keep watch on the house, Morgan and Philpot, the constables assigned to his regular team, had somehow heard that something was up and had reported for duty, day off or not. Stokes was happy to have them; they knew his ways, and he could rely on them to act as he would wish.

Barnaby and Penelope were both standing with their heads dipped, faint frowns on their faces. Stokes turned back to the still-closed door. His summons should have been answered by now.

Barnaby caught his eye. "There's some sort of argument going on in the hall. Knock again."

Stokes already had his fist raised. This time, he hammered on the door, then paused and called loudly, "Police!"

Penelope swallowed a giggle and sent him a droll look. Shouting

"Police!" in this neighborhood was a surefire way of ensuring staff scurried to open the door.

A bare second later, a tall, thin individual, garbed in butler black and with a face blank with shock, swung the door wide.

Stokes had hoped to overhear something useful—possibly even incriminating—but all the voices in the front hall had abruptly fallen silent.

Regardless, he didn't waste the moment. Holding up his warrant card, he declared, "Inspector Stokes of Scotland Yard. I have reason and authority to search these premises."

With that, he marched through the door—causing the butler to take a stumbling step back.

Stokes sensed Barnaby and Penelope close behind him, and his men filed in after them. He halted three paces on and rapidly scanned the tableau before them.

The frozen tableau. It was as if they'd barged onto the stage of a theater right in the middle of a scene of high drama, and all the players had halted in shock and turned to stare at them.

CHAPTER 3

In one comprehensive glance, Stokes took note of the five people in the front hall.

The butler stood, stunned and stupefied, by the still-open door, staring in transparent horror at the men massing at Stokes's back. Lord Carisbrook—it had to be he—stood in the middle of the space, leaning on a cane and half facing a younger gentleman Stokes took to be Franklin Carisbrook. The latter appeared to have been expostulating, conveying fraught news to his father; Franklin's face had been filled with incredulity and concern even before Stokes had stormed in. In Franklin's shadow, a young lady, presumably his sister Julia, hovered, all but wringing her hands. Farther down the hall, a handsome footman stood stony faced with his back to the wall; before his gaze had switched to Stokes and company, the footman had been frowning expectantly at his master.

Then, as if a switch was flicked, life returned to the paralyzed cast.

The butler leapt to close the front door, plunging the front half of the hall into gloom.

Blinking in patent astonishment, Lord Carisbrook swung to face Stokes, and Franklin stepped to his father's shoulder.

Before his lordship could speak, Stokes said, "Lord Carisbrook." Stokes half bowed to the older man. "I understand you've just arrived home, my lord. I daresay your son"—Stokes glanced at Franklin—"has been attempting to explain the recent events that have occurred in this house. To summarize, a report of the theft of a jewel case containing the

Carisbrook emeralds was made this morning, and a Miss Cara Di Abaccio, your ward and resident of this house, was accused by Lady Carisbrook of having stolen the jewels."

"So Franklin just said." An angry flush mottled Lord Carisbrook's cheeks. "But that's preposterous! *Preposterous!* As if dear Cara would do such a thing."

Franklin's and Julia's faces echoed that sentiment, the expressions in their eyes now tinged with dawning hope.

Lord Carisbrook huffed and turned. His gaze probed the farther reaches of the hall, then rose over the stairs to the gallery. "But where is Cara?"

"As to that, my lord," Stokes replied, "Lady Carisbrook insisted Miss Di Abaccio be removed from this house. She is currently in police custody."

Slowly, Lord Carisbrook turned to look at Stokes; his expression was the epitome of aghast incredulity. "What?"

Then his lordship's chest swelled ominously. Jaw setting pugnaciously, he struck the hall tiles with his cane and thundered, "Stuff and nonsense! There is no possibility—*none*, I tell you—that dear Cara is involved."

"Don't be ridiculous, Humphrey."

The words jerked everyone's attention to the stairs, to the lady of quite remarkably haughty mien who was slowly—with deliberately measured steps—descending.

"Lady Carisbrook," Penelope whispered from her position at Stokes's elbow.

To that point, Stokes had spoken in discreet tones and his voice was deep, while Penelope had barely murmured and the others of their party hadn't spoken at all. Stokes looked upward. The floor above overhung the front half of the hall, giving it a lower ceiling and shrouding the space before the door in deep shadow. From the top of the stairs—from where she had no doubt surveyed those in the hall below before commencing her descent—Lady Carisbrook apparently hadn't seen Stokes, much less the group behind him; she didn't know they were there.

Her gaze on the stairs, she continued to descend while her arrogantly strident tones rolled oppressively over them all. "Of course that thieving Italian minx is to blame. Don't say I didn't warn you how it would be when you insisted on taking her in. Treating her as if she was one of the family—really!"

Lord Carisbrook shifted uncomfortably. "Livia, please—this is most unseemly. You know very well that Cara is no thief."

"Indeed?" Her ladyship's tone took on an even uglier edge. "If not her, then whom, pray tell? Are you seriously suggesting that Simpkins or one of the maids, all of whom have been with us for years, suddenly upped and stole the emeralds? Why now? Why wait for years?" Lady Carisbrook halted on the last stair and narrowed her eyes on her husband. "I'll tell you why the emeralds disappeared last night. It was because that was the first time since that treacherous child came to this house that the jewels were within her reach."

Lord Carisbrook opened his mouth, but her ladyship raised a hand and scathingly declared, "There is absolutely no point in attempting to defend her. I told you no good would come of giving house room to your scandalous sister's whelp, much less embracing her as part of the family—and now look what's happened." Dramatically, Lady Carisbrook flung out her hands. "She's been here mere weeks, and my emeralds are gone!"

Silence—seething with more emotions than Stokes could immediately identify, anger and resentment among them—fell.

He seized the moment to calmly walk forward, finally impinging on Lady Carisbrook's awareness. She blinked, and her expression blanked; her hand tightened on the newel post.

Stokes halted beside Lord Carisbrook and half bowed to her ladyship. "Lady Carisbrook. I am Senior Inspector Stokes of Scotland Yard. In response to your report, I am here to investigate the disappearance of the Carisbrook emeralds. Your allegations are of interest to us"—with a flick of his hand, Stokes indicated the rest of their group—"and we are here to gather the proof required to substantiate them."

Her ladyship recovered her aplomb. "Excellent!" Her eyes—Stokes thought they were black—lit with malicious expectation.

He turned to Lord Carisbrook. "My lord, allow me to introduce the Honorable Mr. and Mrs. Barnaby Adair. As you might have heard, they act as occasional consultants to the Yard in resolving matters such as this."

Lord Carisbrook had noticed Barnaby and Penelope, but until that moment, he hadn't considered what their presence meant; his expression suggested he didn't know whether to be glad or sorry—reassured or mortified—to be meeting them in such circumstances.

A gentle smile on her lips, Penelope glided forward. "Lord Carisbrook—a pleasure, although would that it had been some less bothersome event that brought us here." She held out her hand, and prompted by ingrained good manners, Lord Carisbrook took it and bowed.

"Mrs. Adair." His lordship sounded faintly strangled.

While Barnaby followed Penelope in exchanging greetings with his lordship, Stokes watched Lady Carisbrook, to whom Barnaby and Penelope's presence had come as a rude shock. From her ladyship's stunned and horrified expression, Stokes surmised she hadn't looked further than accusing her niece-by-marriage and getting her out of the house; Lady Carisbrook hadn't considered what initiating a police investigation would entail.

Stokes had no doubt that in her eyes, he and his men were bad enough —minor inconveniences, yet people she could dismiss, whose opinions didn't matter to her—but the addition of Penelope and Barnaby to the investigation elevated the situation to a very different level.

Leaving Lady Carisbrook struggling to assimilate a reality she hadn't foreseen, Stokes spared a glance for Franklin and Julia Carisbrook. Both appeared uncertain as to what reaction they should have toward the unfolding events, yet there was a hint of hope on both their faces—hope for what, Stokes couldn't yet say.

"As you might know, sir," Barnaby replied in response to Lord Carisbrook's query as to Barnaby's and Penelope's purposes in being there, "my father, the earl, is one of the directors who assist the commissioner in overseeing the workings of the police force. Over the years, my wife and I have assisted Inspector Stokes with several cases involving members of the ton, and the commissioner and the directors have concluded that it is very much better for Stokes to have our insights available to him so that he can most appropriately respond to crimes within our level of society."

As Barnaby had hoped, Lord Carisbrook read between his lines and was somewhat mollified. "Ah—I see." His lordship clasped his hands over the head of his cane, hesitated, then raised troubled eyes to Barnaby's face. "As to what's most appropriate in this case...I wonder, Mr. Adair"—his lordship turned to include Penelope and Stokes with his gaze —"whether it's possible to, er, *cancel* the report my wife made. I'm sure the emeralds will turn up somewhere, and the accusation against my niece is really beyond absurd—"

"Oh no you don't!" Lady Carisbrook stepped off the stair and swept down on them, outrage radiating from every pore. Her eyes blazed as she glared at her husband. "My emeralds—the *Carisbrook* emeralds—are missing! They were stolen from my room—filched from under our own roof! It is beyond insupportable! Of course, the police must hunt for them—what are the police for?"

"Indeed, ma'am." Stokes leapt on the opening. "Given that a formal report of a crime has been made and the emeralds are, as you've confirmed, missing, then we at the Yard are duty bound to get to the bottom of it. My men and I—assisted by Mr. and Mrs. Adair—are here to do precisely that. With his lordship's and your permission, we propose to conduct a comprehensive search of the house." Stokes tipped his head toward Lord Carisbrook. "As his lordship says, the emeralds might well turn up."

Barnaby hid a smile as Stokes's tone grew chillier and he continued, "In addition, we will need to interview everyone in the household. I'm sure you understand that as a very serious accusation has been made against Miss Di Abaccio, proofs will need to be assembled to either confirm the accusation or show it to be without foundation."

Her face a picture of dismayed chagrin, Lady Carisbrook all but rocked back on her heels.

Didn't think of that, did you? Penelope thought rather viciously; she'd already taken against Lady Carisbrook, and she hadn't yet exchanged a word with the woman. Apparently, her ladyship had only just realized that making an accusation against her husband's ward that was subsequently proved to be false would reflect badly on her. Penelope could find little sympathy for her ladyship's predicament.

Stokes turned to Lord Carisbrook. "With your permission, my lord, I will instruct my men to search the house thoroughly to establish that the emeralds are no longer under this roof."

Lord Carisbrook closed his eyes—whether searching for inspiration, patience, or strength, Penelope couldn't tell—then he opened them and, lips tight, nodded. "As you say, Inspector, the wheels of justice must now turn." His lordship shot his wife an indecipherable look, then gestured widely, indicating the house. "You and your men may search wherever you wish."

Penelope caught Lord Carisbrook's eyes and smiled approvingly. No matter how reluctant, he'd made the right decision. His attempt to discourage the investigation—to rescind his wife's report—had come as no surprise; gentlemen of his lordship's ilk always did their utmost to avoid all hint of scandal.

Her ladyship, on the other hand, craved being the center of attention among her peers; Penelope suspected she'd grasped the chance to accuse

Cara, believing that would give her what she wanted, without due consideration of any adverse effects.

"I will be in my study, Inspector." Lord Carisbrook turned away, but paused with his gaze on Penelope and Barnaby. "If you would call on me there when this business is complete, Mr. and Mrs. Adair, I would appreciate a moment of your time."

Barnaby inclined his head. "Of course."

Penelope gave his lordship—and Franklin, who, after one hard glance at this mother, turned to walk beside his father—a reassuring smile.

From the corner of her eye, she watched Lady Carisbrook vacillate, then, elevating her chin to a dismissively haughty angle, her ladyship turned and swept to the open doorway of the drawing room.

Julia Carisbrook dithered. She looked longingly after her father and brother, but then reluctantly followed her mother. She went into the drawing room and shut the door.

Penelope looked at Stokes and arched her brows. "So—what's our plan?"

Stokes turned to the butler—whose name proved to be Jarvis—and instructed him and the footman, Jeremy, to gather all the staff in the servants' hall, to wait there until they could be questioned. Stokes sent Morgan to oversee the staff. Morgan grinned insouciantly and went. A baby-faced constable who appeared much younger and less experienced than he was, Morgan had the gift of the gab and could charm any maid or cook to divulge her most secret of secrets and was a dab hand at gaining the trust of most men, too.

With the staff out of the way, Stokes led the rest of his company, Barnaby and Penelope included, up the stairs. He sent the younger constables up to the top floor and the servants' quarters, while along with Barnaby, Wilkes, Fitch, Philpot, and Penelope, Stokes settled to search the rooms on the first floor—those the family occupied and also the empty guest bedchambers.

Penelope immediately wandered down the corridor, searching for Lady Carisbrook's room. She found it—along with a ferret-faced woman sitting in a chair by the window and busily stitching the seam of a gown sporting an overabundance of frills. Penelope narrowed her eyes on the woman's face. "Simpkins, I take it."

Like any experienced dresser, Simpkins cast her eyes over Penelope's stylish carriage dress in fine plum-colored wool with its matching velvet facings, immediately deduced her station, and rose and dipped into a passable curtsy. "Yes, ma'am."

"You're wanted in the servants' hall." Penelope held the door open and waited.

Simpkins reluctantly set aside her work. "Her ladyship didn't say—"

"His lordship has returned to the house and is aware of the directive." Penelope's tone brooked no challenge.

Simpkins's lips thinned, but she bowed her head and went.

Penelope remained in the corridor to make sure the dresser went downstairs, but instead, Simpkins paused and knocked on another door.

A young maid looked out.

Penelope swiftly walked down the corridor.

Seeing her approaching, the maid bobbed a curtsy. "Ma'am?"

"And you are?"

"Polly, ma'am. Miss Julia's maid."

"I see. As I've just told Simpkins, all the staff have been called to the servants' hall. You should go there straightaway."

"Yes, ma'am." Polly bobbed again, stepped out of the room, and shut the door. Then, looking past Penelope, she gasped and stared. "Oh—what are those men doing up here?"

Penelope turned to see Stokes and Philpot crossing from room to room closer to the main stairs. "They're policemen. They're searching for the emeralds."

She looked back in time to see that the news had come as a shock to both women. They had to have known of her ladyship's accusation against Cara, but plainly hadn't foreseen that the result might be this.

Polly turned wide eyes on Simpkins. "Police," she breathed. "We'd better get downstairs."

On the one hand, Simpkins didn't want to go, but on the other, she plainly felt a similar compulsion to retreat to the relative safety of the servants' hall. She stepped back. After nodding to Penelope, both women turned, walked to the end of the corridor, and descended via the narrow back stairs.

Penelope stood staring after them for a moment, then returned to her ladyship's room.

She was soon joined by some of the others; they searched diligently, opening every cupboard and drawer, lifting mattresses and piles of clothes, looking behind curtains, and peering into every space. They'd all searched houses before, often for items smaller than a jewel case; they knew the likely spots for concealment, but were thorough in looking absolutely everywhere.

The constables dispatched upstairs returned, reporting, to no one's surprise, that they'd found nothing in any of the staff's rooms. With the additional help, the search of the first-floor rooms was soon completed.

The company regathered at the top of the stairs.

"It occurs to me," Penelope said, "that a parure of jewels like the Carisbrook emeralds would normally be kept in a safe."

Barnaby nodded. "We'll need to ask how the emeralds were stored. Her ladyship intimated that they weren't usually accessible, at least not to Cara."

Stokes humphed and turned to his men. He delegated Wilkes to take the others and search all the rooms downstairs, barring only the study and the drawing room. "We'll do those last."

Wilkes snapped off a salute, and the men clattered down the stairs.

Stokes looked at Barnaby and Penelope. "Meanwhile, I suggest we join Morgan and see what the staff can tell us before we interview the family."

With an expectant smile, Barnaby waved Stokes down the stairs, then with Penelope by his side, followed.

They made their way to the servants' hall.

As usual, Morgan had calmed everyone with his easy banter. The staff had assembled around the long rectangular table that occupied the center of the servants' hall. They'd all taken their no doubt customary seats around the table and, as Stokes, Barnaby, and Penelope walked in, came to their feet.

Stokes halted at the head of the table and let his gaze pass over the company, noting each face.

Beside him, Jarvis cleared his throat. "Inspector. We stand ready to assist you and your colleagues in whatever way we can."

Stokes inclined his head. "Good. As you can imagine, we have a range of questions, but at present, our focus is on understanding the order of events prior to the emeralds being found to be missing." With a wave, he indicated that everyone should sit again.

Jarvis and Jeremy gathered three extra chairs that they set around the head of the table, causing everyone to shuffle along, but once Stokes sat, with Penelope to his right and Barnaby on his left, the scrapes ceased, and with Morgan observing from the foot of the table, everyone settled and gave their attention to Stokes.

"First," Stokes said, leaning his forearms on the table and clasping his hands, "I can tell you that we have searched all the bedrooms in the house, your rooms included, and have confirmed that the emeralds are no longer above stairs. A search of all the downstairs rooms is currently under way, but we don't expect to find the jewels in his lordship's study, or the pantry, or anywhere else." One of the maids giggled nervously, and the tension in the room lightened. Stokes smiled faintly and continued, "At this point, no suspicion is being directed at anyone at all. As I said, our next step is to learn what we can of the movement of the jewels prior to them disappearing."

Stokes cut a glance at Penelope. In a situation such as this, her knowledge of ton households made her the most appropriate person to take point.

She caught his gaze, glanced around the table, then focused on Jarvis and the housekeeper, seated next to him. "Perhaps we might start with the last time Lady Carisbrook wore the emeralds. We understand that was on Saturday, when her ladyship wore the emeralds to her evening events. Is that correct?"

"Yes." The confirmation came from Simpkins, who was seated opposite the housekeeper.

Everyone looked her way, but Simpkins folded her lips and said nothing else.

Penelope arched her brows and calmly returned her gaze to Jarvis. "Was her ladyship still wearing the jewels when she returned to the house?"

Jarvis nodded. "Yes, ma'am. I saw them when I took her cloak."

"Excellent." Penelope now turned her gaze on Jeremy, sitting on the other side of Simpkins. "Did you see the jewels, too?"

Jeremy nodded. "Yes, ma'am. I was in the front hall to take Miss Carisbrook's cloak and Mr. Carisbrook's coat and hat."

"All three returned to the house together?" Stokes asked. He was busily scribbling in his notebook.

"Yes," both Jarvis and Jeremy replied.

"Good." Penelope turned her gaze on Simpkins. "I take it that when her ladyship reached her room, she was still wearing the emeralds."

"Of course," Simpkins said. Without further prompting, she went on, "As usual, she took them off as soon as she'd walked in—she crossed straight to her dressing table and had me undo the clasp on the necklace while she took off the earrings, then she laid all three pieces into the case, shut it, and left it to one side of the dressing table."

"The case," Penelope said. "Describe it."

Simpkins shrugged. "A normal jewel case covered in black velvet." She held up her hands, indicating a shape about nine inches long and six inches wide. "The necklace fitted around the inside, and the earrings sat in the middle."

For all her dour attitude, Simpkins seemed willing enough to share what she knew.

"Very well," Penelope said. "So we have the emeralds in their case sitting on one end of her ladyship's dressing table. What time was that?"

Simpkins frowned, uncertain, and looked at Jarvis.

After a moment of thinking, the butler offered, "It must have been close to two o'clock. Between half past one and two."

Penelope looked at Simpkins. "Did anyone else come into the room while you were with her ladyship?"

Simpkins paused as if thinking back, then replied, "No."

"Was the jewel case still on the dressing table when you left?" Penelope asked. "Did you actually see it there close to the time that you left the room?"

"I didn't look at it again, not after her ladyship closed it and set it aside, but it must have been there. I know her ladyship didn't go back to her dressing table, not once she rose from it, and I certainly didn't." Simpkins compressed her lips and fell silent.

After a moment of studying Simpkins, Penelope nodded. "Very well." She looked around the table. "So you left Lady Carisbrook in her room. Did anyone else enter the room before morning?"

Looks were cast across and up and down the table, but no one spoke.

Eventually, all eyes returned to the head of the table, to Stokes, Barnaby, and Penelope.

Stokes inwardly sighed. He was certain the staff were holding back something, even if they hadn't lied. He took up the questioning. "Who was the first person into the room come morning?"

A nervous clearing of a throat came from farther down the table, then a young maid squeaked, "That was me. I went in to clear the grate and start the fire. Her ladyship's fire is always the first."

Stokes wasn't surprised to hear that. "And what time was that?"

"Sharp on six o'clock, sir." The maid looked at Jarvis. "Mr. Jarvis saw me go up."

"Indeed, Inspector," Jarvis confirmed. "Missy is always reliably prompt to her duties."

"I see." Stokes made a point of jotting something down, then without looking up, asked, "Missy, when you went into her ladyship's room, did you see the jewel case on her dressing table?"

"Oh no, sir!"

Stokes glanced down the table to see that Missy was all earnest eyes.

"I always keep my eyes down," she assured him. "Just crept in and made straight for the fireplace, did my business, then crept out again." She glanced at Jarvis. "I never look about."

Jarvis nodded approvingly, as did the housekeeper beside him. "Quite right, Missy. Exactly as you ought."

Stokes hid a grimace and looked down at his notes. "So who was next into the room?"

The staff traded glances, then Jarvis spoke. "That would have been Miss Cara, Inspector, when she took her ladyship's breakfast tray up."

Stokes arched a brow. "No one else?"

"No, sir." Jarvis was quite definite.

"Very well." Stokes looked down the table. "I will ask Miss Di Abaccio whether she saw the jewels—"

"Oh, I doubt she would have, Inspector."

Stokes glanced at the housekeeper; it was she who had spoken. "And you are?"

"Mrs. Jarvis, sir." She tipped her head toward Jarvis. "We've been butler and housekeeper to Lord Carisbrook for nigh on twenty-five years."

"I see. Why do you say Miss Di Abaccio is unlikely to have noticed the jewel case?"

"Because with the heavy tray in her hands," Mrs. Jarvis said, "she would make straight for the bed to set it down, and the dressing table is on the other side of the room in the opposite direction. She wouldn't have seen it either going in or coming back, not unless she peered that way on purpose, and her ladyship wasn't one to encourage Miss Cara in that sort of familiarity, if you know what I mean."

There were nods of agreement from all around the table. Not even Simpkins looked inclined to disagree.

"Very well." Stokes jotted, then closed his notebook and slipped it back into his pocket. "We will, of course, be conferring with Lady Carisbrook as to when she last remembers seeing the jewel case."

"One last question." Barnaby straightened and placed a hand on the table; it was the first time he'd spoken since they'd entered the room, and all eyes swung his way. In a swift survey, he met each pair of eyes, then asked, "Did any of you see, or hear, or do any of you know of anything that might, however distantly, have any possible bearing on what happened to the missing jewels?"

Stokes knew Barnaby's complex phrasing had been intentional—it made people think. It did not, however, usually result in exchanged glances, at least not of the sort the Carisbrook staff were presently casting—as if asking questions of each other.

Stokes, Penelope, and Barnaby—and Morgan—all waited, but in the end, no one volunteered anything.

Ultimately, Jarvis cleared his throat. "It appears, Inspector, that there's nothing more we can tell you regarding the emeralds."

Stokes suspected it would be more correct to say that there was nothing more the staff *wished* to tell them regarding the emeralds, but after a second's deliberation, he inclined his head. "Thank you." He pushed back from the table and rose; Barnaby, Penelope, and Morgan followed suit, which brought the staff to their feet, too. "We may well be back with more questions, depending on what else we learn, but if, in the meantime, anyone remembers something pertinent"—Stokes looked at Jarvis—"please send directly to me at Scotland Yard."

Jarvis bowed. "Of course, Inspector."

Stokes suppressed a disbelieving grunt and followed Barnaby and Penelope from the room. They climbed a short set of steps to the corridor that led to the front hall. Morgan had followed and joined them as they crossed to the front corner of the hall where Wilkes and the other men waited.

Before they'd reached him, Wilkes was shaking his head. As Stokes and the others halted, Wilkes reported, "Nothing. No sign of the case or the jewels anywhere, nor any sign of a break-in. Only places we haven't searched are the drawing room and study."

Stokes noticed a frown in Penelope's eyes. "What did you think of the staff's performance?"

Penelope blinked, then pushed her spectacles higher on her nose. "That they—the staff—clearly know more than they've told us, but I got the impression they don't believe Cara guilty of the theft."

"I have to agree that the staff know something they haven't yet shared," Barnaby said, "but I suspect that, whatever it is, they don't believe the person involved to be the thief."

Penelope was nodding. "They seem very loyal. If they did have an inkling of who took the jewels, I think they would say."

Morgan reported, "They're staunchly defensive of his lordship and the children—not so much with her ladyship, except for her hoity dresser. That said, none said a word against the lady, either."

"Hmm." Penelope's gaze grew pensive. "At this juncture, we have to consider that, for whatever reason, Lady Carisbrook herself has 'stolen' the emeralds."

"Indeed." Barnaby glanced at the closed drawing room door, then looked at Stokes. "Regardless, as you said, we're still very much in the early phase of gathering information. While Penelope and I see what Lord Carisbrook will tell us, why don't you see what you can extract from her ladyship?"

Stokes pulled a sour face, but grudgingly nodded. "Wilkes and Fitch —go with the Adairs and search the room while they distract his lordship. Morgan, stay here in case something happens. Philpott, you're with me—there shouldn't be so many places in a drawing room to search."

With nods, they parted.

Barnaby took Penelope's arm and steered her toward the study door. Jarvis and Jeremy had followed them into the hall; while Jarvis went to show Stokes into the drawing room, Jeremy knocked on the study door and, on hearing a muted "Come," opened the door for Barnaby and Penelope.

Following his wife into the room—a gentleman's study like many another, unremarkable in its conformity—Barnaby noted Franklin Carisbrook hovering uncertainly by the bookshelves near the window. His father was seated in one of three armchairs before the fireplace, more or less on the opposite side of the room.

The distance between father and son struck Barnaby as curious, although given the way Franklin continued staring at the door even after it closed, he seemed more concerned with Stokes—or perhaps his mother.

Lord Carisbrook heaved his bulk up from the chair to greet them. "Thank you for stopping by."

Penelope smiled reassuringly and, when Carisbrook waved her and Barnaby to the vacant armchairs, took the one nearest the fire, leaving Barnaby to sit in the other chair, at a slight angle to Carisbrook but still able to study his face.

Barnaby glanced at Wilkes and Fitch, who had halted just inside the door. "I regret the necessity, my lord, but the inspector needs this room searched, too."

"Heh?" Still on his feet, Carisbrook looked across and saw the two policemen, then realized what Barnaby was saying. His lordship waved and looked away, moving back to his chair. "Search as you wish. I'm sure there's nothing to be found, but by all means, look."

Barnaby nodded to the men, then sat.

After settling in his armchair, Lord Carisbrook glanced at Barnaby and Penelope, then cleared his throat and somewhat gruffly said, "While I understand what the inspector said, I wanted to ask if there truly is no way that we can't just drop this whole thing. Well, I mean to say, it's only jewelry, and it's patently obvious that the emeralds going missing has nothing whatsoever to do with dearest Cara."

From the corner of his eye, Barnaby saw Franklin, who had been watching Wilkes and Fitch commence their careful search, shift his gaze to his father. A puzzled frown overtook Franklin's expressive countenance; it seemed he couldn't understand his father's tack any more than Barnaby could.

"I understood," Barnaby ventured, "that the Carisbrook emeralds are rather valuable."

"Well, yes." Lord Carisbrook's color deepened. "But they are as nothing to Cara's well-being." His jaw firmed. "I would give up the emeralds rather than cause her distress. It's beyond ludicrous to accuse her of stealing them." His lordship met Barnaby's gaze and declared, "No matter what my wife imagines, I would happily take any oath that Cara is entirely innocent of this crime."

Barnaby exchanged a fleeting glance with Penelope, then evenly replied, "Sadly, once such an accusation is made, it must—as Stokes said—be proven either true or false."

"Indeed, my lord, that is the case." Penelope leaned forward, her gaze on his lordship's face. "Just think—no matter if Lady Carisbrook herself was to withdraw her accusation, suspicion of a sort would always hover over Cara. So as matters stand, the best way you and all others here can help Cara is to assist the inspector in determining exactly where the Carisbrook emeralds have gone and who removed them from this house."

Lord Carisbrook seemed to deflate, his pugnacious expression dissolving. He looked down at his hands clasped between his knees.

After another swift glance at Barnaby, Penelope said, "There's one point you might clarify for us, sir—we assume the emeralds weren't normally left in her ladyship's room."

"No, no." Lord Carisbrook had spoken distractedly, but then he seemed to focus on what Penelope was asking and raised his head. "Normally, of course, the emeralds are kept in the safe in here." He swung around and pointed to the wall behind his desk. "It's behind the painting."

At his lordship's wave, Wilkes, who was just straightening from the desk, turned and examined the right side of the painting, then released a catch and swung the framed canvas out to reveal a safe built into the wall.

"The emeralds are almost always in there," Lord Carisbrook said.

Wilkes swung the picture to the wall again, and his lordship turned to face Penelope. "However, as I'm the only one with the key, on those evenings on which my wife wants to wear the emeralds, she comes in before she leaves, and I take the case from the safe, hand the emeralds to her, and she dons them. Later, when she returns, as I'm usually in here by that time, she comes directly in and hands the jewels back, and I return them to the safe."

"I gather," Barnaby said, "that on this occasion that didn't occur because you were out of town."

"Just so." Lord Carisbrook sank back in his chair. "If I go down to Surrey—to Carisbrook Hall—and her ladyship wishes to wear the emeralds, I leave them with her until I return."

"In this instance," Penelope asked, "when did you take the emeralds from the safe?"

"On Friday morning, just before I left town. And if everything had gone as it usually did, Livia would have handed me the emeralds in their case when I came home." His lordship frowned. "She's usually as careful with them as I am."

"There's nothing to suggest that her ladyship was any less careful than usual," Barnaby felt forced to say. "I imagine that, over time, she'd grown accustomed to thinking the emeralds safe on her dressing table overnight."

"Indeed," Penelope said, "most ladies would think the same."

Barnaby caught the pointed look she sent him; while he could imagine several of the thoughts behind it, he didn't want to discuss them further now, not in front of his lordship.

Uncrossing his long legs, he said, "As that's all we have to share or ask at this moment, my lord, we should be on our way." He stood, and Penelope got to her feet.

His lordship rose more ponderously. He looked into Barnaby's face. "You will let me know of any progress, Mr. Adair?"

Reaching for his card case, Barnaby inclined his head. "We'll be sure to share whatever we can. Meanwhile"—he extracted a card and held it out—"if you think of anything pertinent, send either to Stokes at the Yard or, if you prefer, to us at Albemarle Street." He nodded at the card. "A message to that address will always find us."

Lord Carisbrook took the card, studied it, then looked at Penelope. "If I might ask…you will let me know of anything—anything at all—we might do to ease Cara's way. I'm concerned about how the poor child is bearing up through all this."

Sincerity poured from Carisbrook; genuine anxiety resonated in his tone.

Franklin, who had drawn nearer while they talked, also nodded earnestly.

Penelope reached out and squeezed his lordship's hand. "We'll let you know where she will be staying once that's decided."

"Thank you." His lordship bowed to them both. "You've been very kind."

With a gentle nod, Penelope led the way from the room.

As Barnaby passed Wilkes and Fitch, who was holding the door, the sergeant infinitesimally shook his head. Understanding that to mean that no sign of either the jewels or the case had been found in the study—confirming what they'd all expected—Barnaby followed Penelope into the front hall.

There, they found an impatient and clearly exasperated Stokes waiting for them. He looked at Wilkes. "Nothing?"

When Wilkes shook his head, Stokes sighed through his teeth. "Of course, that would have been far too easy."

As he turned toward the door, Penelope asked, "Just to be clear, no sign of a jewel case—even an empty one—was found anywhere?"

Stokes glanced at her, then at his men, all of whom shook their heads. "The answer appears to be no." He hesitated, then asked, "Is that significant?"

Penelope frowned. "I'm not sure, but it might be." She started for the door.

Jarvis, who had remained on duty to see them out, opened the door and bowed them through.

Once the door had shut firmly behind their party, Barnaby glanced at Stokes. "Did you get anything at all from that harpy?"

Stokes laughed. "No, but the epithet is appropriate. For most of the time, she treated me to a distempered harangue to the effect that Cara Di Abaccio was obviously guilty and I should simply cow her into telling us where the emeralds are now and then return them forthwith to her ladyship." As they stepped onto the cobbles, heading for the coach, Stokes added, "The way she carried on…it was as if she believed that stating her version of events loudly enough and often enough would somehow make it true." He tipped his head. "That said, the daughter—Julia—didn't seem anywhere near as convinced of Cara's guilt."

Barnaby arched his brows. "Interesting. But Cara did say she and Julia are close, and they are of similar age."

Ahead of Barnaby and Stokes, Penelope reached the coach, opened the door, and saw Hugo sitting beside Cara; he was holding Cara's hand and looking more lethally menacing than Penelope had ever seen him—enough, certainly, to remind her that, despite never having fought in any war, Hugo had spent a good decade in the cavalry.

Hiding a smile, she climbed into the coach. He truly did look as if he was fully prepared to charge into battle in defense of Cara Di Abaccio.

Luckily, Penelope seriously doubted violence would be required to lift suspicion's cloud from Cara's head; she was already convinced—albeit purely on instinctive grounds—that Cara was in no way involved in the theft.

After Stokes dispatched the other men back to the Yard, he, Barnaby, and Wilkes followed Penelope into the coach. They sat on the seat opposite, and briefly, Stokes summarized what little they had determined. "In short, the Carisbrook emeralds have disappeared. They are not in the house, and therefore the crime Lady Carisbrook reported has been substantiated and must be investigated." Stokes shot Barnaby a glance. "I don't need to describe the brouhaha that would ensue if it got out that jewel thieves were operating in Mayfair, taking jewels of this type, and the Yard wasn't expending every possible effort to find said thieves and get the jewels back."

Barnaby humphed. "Pandemonium wouldn't be the half of it, with calls to the commissioner to have every last policeman patrolling Mayfair's streets."

Penelope glanced sidelong at Hugo. "I believe we're all agreed that it's now imperative to focus our considerable talents on finding the emeralds. However, because of Lady Carisbrook's denunciation of Cara, it's even more vital that we identify the real culprit and so clear her name."

"Exactly!" Hugo said.

Cara's big eyes looked at them all in patent hope.

Regarding her, Barnaby stated, "We need to decide where it would be best for Cara to stay."

"My parents' house has plenty of room," Hugo said.

"True," Penelope replied, "but that won't wash. At least, not yet. We need somewhere...neutral. She can't just go from police custody to free in society. What's more, there's always the question of—" She broke off at a tapping on the carriage door.

They all looked out and saw Lord Carisbrook standing on the pavement.

Stokes swung the door open. "My lord?"

But Carisbrook's gaze had gone straight to Cara. "My dear Cara, I can't tell you how sorry I am about all this. If I could..." His lordship gestured weakly.

Cara's smile was swift. She leaned forward to say, "It's all right, Uncle Humphrey. I know this isn't any of your doing."

"Yes, but..." His lordship looked utterly wretched. He glanced at Penelope. "I truly don't know what to do." Then he looked back at Cara, and his face firmed. "I cannot apologize enough, but rest assured, my dear, that regardless of her ladyship's ridiculous claims, I will do everything in my power to put this right."

"If I might ask, sir"—Stokes caught his lordship's gaze as he glanced his way—"what do you think has happened to the emeralds?"

Lord Carisbrook blinked, then refocused on Stokes. "Inspector, I honestly have no idea. I am as thoroughly mystified as everyone else."

Immediately, his lordship returned his gaze to Cara, and his expression turned troubled. "My dear, as my ward, you really should return to the house, but in the circumstances, I would not subject you to the...the *vilification* that Livia might visit on you. I cannot be with you every moment of the day, so..."

Penelope spoke up, her tone bracing. "In the circumstances, with Lady Carisbrook as Cara's primary—and, indeed, sole—accuser, I have to inform you, my lord, that any notion of Cara returning to reside under your roof prior to this case being solved is entirely untenable."

The building tension in the carriage—from Cara, from Hugo, from Stokes, and even Wilkes—subsided.

Her gaze on Lord Carisbrook's earnest face, Penelope smiled sympathetically. "As you arrived, we were discussing where Cara should stay—and I was just about to point out that, as we don't know the motive behind this crime, it would be remiss of us to assume that Cara is in no physical danger."

Lord Carisbrook's anxious concern flared. "What about Grillon's? She would be comfortable there, and I would foot the bill, of course."

"That won't do." Hugo spoke with certainty and an absolute authority Penelope had not before associated with him. "Quite aside from any more nefarious danger, what about the newshounds? Once they hear of the charge, they'll be hot to learn all. They'll…well, hound her." Her hand still locked in his, Hugo met Cara's eyes while, to the others, he stated, "Cara can't be left defenseless."

"Indeed." Penelope pushed up her spectacles. She met her husband's gaze, and when, having understood her wordless question, he nodded, she went on, "Because of that and several other reasons, I would suggest that until we resolve this case to the commissioner's satisfaction, the safest and most appropriate place for Cara to reside"—she met Stokes's gaze—"a place that will satisfy the commissioner and any judge asked for an opinion, is with Barnaby and me in Albemarle Street."

Stokes blinked, but when Penelope—along with Hugo—looked at him challengingly, he nodded. "Yes, that will satisfy all the obvious quibbles and questions. Or at least, we can make it seem to."

Penelope cast her gaze over the other men, but no one argued. Finally, she looked at Cara and arched her brows. "I take it you won't be averse to spending the next few days at our house?"

Cara gazed into Penelope's eyes in a vain attempt to read her thoughts in the dark-brown depths—not an easy task at the best of times. Defeated, Cara tipped her head and regarded Penelope in something like wonder. In her faintly husky voice, Cara said, "I am a stranger accused of a serious crime, yet you would do this for me, welcoming me into your home?"

Penelope's smile was entirely spontaneous. She patted Cara's hand and explained, "Giving succor to the innocent is our favorite pastime."

CHAPTER 4

By six o'clock that evening, Penelope had settled Cara into one of the guest bedchambers in her and Barnaby's town house in Albemarle Street. She had also found time to send word to Violet and Heathcote Montague and to Griselda, Stokes's wife, informing them that the group had a new case to pursue and inviting them to gather at Albemarle Street with Penelope, Barnaby, and Stokes for dinner and discussion.

Initially, it had been Barnaby who had been drawn to solving crimes. His path had crossed that of Stokes several times, over several different cases, leading to a friendship and an undefined working partnership whenever Stokes's investigations involved members of the ton. Thus, when Penelope had stumbled upon disturbing disappearances among foundlings who should have come to the Foundling House, she'd known to approach Barnaby, and that case had also brought Griselda into Stokes's life. After Griselda and Stokes had married, followed soon after by Penelope and Barnaby, the foursome had worked together on several further cases, pooling their considerable resources and talents. And then, last year, their circle had expanded to include Heathcote Montague, renowned man-of-business to many of the great families of the ton, and Violet, now his wife. While Montague and the men in his office possessed unrivaled insight and expertise in assessing matters financial, Violet had proved invaluable with her ability to organize them all and keep track of the various threads that invariably surfaced during their investigations.

When the clocks chimed six, Penelope was in the drawing room, directing Hugo and James, her footman, in adding a love seat to the arrangement of armchairs and sofas situated before the hearth. "Just there." She pointed. "Between the ends of the sofas and facing the fireplace." The position would allow Hugo and Cara to sit side by side and join the group in discussing the disappearance of the Carisbrook emeralds.

Penelope and Barnaby's sturdy two-year-old son, Oliver, clung to Penelope's skirts and, along with Cara, who stood by the windows, watched the proceedings with open curiosity.

Hugo and James gratefully set down the love seat at the edge of the Aubusson rug. Hugo glanced at Cara, then walked to join her.

"If there's nothing else, ma'am?" James asked.

Penelope smiled. "Thank you—I believe we're ready for the evening."

At that moment, the front doorbell pealed. Oliver let out a joyful squeal and toddled off in a wobbly run for the door. Smiling indulgently—and expectantly—Penelope hurried after him. Oliver had insisted on coming downstairs to await the arrival of Megan, Stokes and Griselda's two-year-old daughter and Oliver's dearest friend.

Penelope caught up with her son and, laughing at his eagerness, steadied him through the door onto the black-and-white tiles of the front hall.

Mostyn, their butler, had already opened the door, admitting not only Griselda, Stokes, and Megan, along with Megan's nursemaid, Gloria, but also Montague and Violet, who was cradling their three-month-old son, Martin. Bringing up the rear was Hilda, Martin's recently hired nursemaid.

At the sight of Oliver, Megan shrieked, wriggled free of her father's arms, and rushed across to hug and be clumsily hugged by Oliver. Everyone smiled. As coats and bonnets were surrendered and taken, Penelope greeted her guests. Both she and Griselda crowded around Violet to admire and coo at Martin, who, for a wonder, was awake and lazily batted at their fingers.

Summoned by the noise in his hall, Barnaby, smiling, came walking out from his study as Hattie, Oliver's nursemaid, descended the stairs.

After several more minutes of extended greetings and fond exclaiming over the three children, the nursemaids gathered their charges and whisked them upstairs to the nursery.

The six proud parents watched them go, then the three ladies uttered identical sighs, exchanged glances, smiled, and at Penelope's all-encompassing wave, turned and headed into the drawing room.

Barnaby introduced Hugo and Cara to Griselda, Violet, and Montague, then everyone claimed what had become their customary seats—Penelope in the corner of one sofa closer to the fireplace, with Griselda beside her, Violet and Montague on the sofa opposite, Stokes in the armchair between Violet and the fireplace, with the second armchair, between Penelope and the fireplace, being Barnaby's habitual spot.

Penelope waved Hugo and Cara to the love seat. "This," she informed them, "has become our preferred way to approach our joint investigations. We spend the time before dinner reporting and reciting all we know—all the facts we've gathered to this point. Then once dinner is served, we go into the dining room and all mention of the case is suspended." She smiled determinedly. "We've discovered that the time spent discussing other things allows the facts of the case to settle and sort themselves in our minds. After dinner, we return here and focus on defining what we can deduce and what our best way forward will be—what trails there are that we might follow in order to identify our villain."

Violet had hunted in her capacious reticule, drawn out a notebook and pencil, and settled the book on her lap, pencil poised over a fresh page.

"And"—with a wave, Penelope indicated Violet's preparations—"Violet takes notes, which is invaluable in keeping us all on track."

"I've explained to Cara," Hugo said, "that as a group, you've solved several thorny cases over recent years."

"Indeed." Penelope inclined her head to Cara. "And you may be sure we'll get to the bottom of this one, too. Our aim is to find who took the Carisbrook emeralds and, thus, to exonerate you."

"You're getting ahead of yourself." Griselda smiled, taking any sting from her words. "Some of us as yet have no idea what the Carisbrook emeralds are."

"Good point." Penelope straightened in her seat. "Right, then. At present, the situation before us is this. Lady Carisbrook wore the Carisbrook emeralds to her Saturday evening's events. From memory, the parure consists of a very old necklace and earrings of large rectangular emeralds in heavy, ornate gold settings." Penelope arched a brow Cara's way. "Is that a reasonable description?"

Sitting rigidly upright beside Hugo, with her hands clasped tightly in her lap, Cara nodded. "Yes. They are as you say. Quite…" She searched for the right word.

"Ugly," Penelope ruthlessly supplied. "However, I suspect Lady Carisbrook sees them as an emblem of her status, and from what little I've seen and heard of her, she wears them frequently."

Cara nodded again. "I have only been in the Carisbrook house for the past four weeks, but from all I have seen, that is true."

"So," Penelope went on, "Lady Carisbrook returned to the Carisbrook town house in John Street at about half past one on Sunday morning. The butler, Jarvis, and the footman, Jeremy, saw the emeralds around her neck when she came in. She went upstairs to her room, and her dresser, Simpkins, confirmed that her ladyship removed the necklace and earrings, set them in their case—the usual black-velvet-covered affair—shut the case, and placed it on one side of the dressing table."

Penelope paused, then went on, "Simpkins left, and Lady Carisbrook went to bed. The next morning, at six o'clock, the household's tweeny, Missy, crept into her ladyship's room and tended and lit her fire. Missy didn't look toward the dressing table and can't say whether the jewel case was there or not. Subsequently, Cara here took up her ladyship's breakfast tray." Penelope glanced at Cara. "What time was that?"

"I was to knock on my aunt's door at precisely eight o'clock, as the clocks struck the hour," Cara said.

Violet looked up, puzzled. "Why didn't a maid take up the tray?"

Cara colored.

Hugo growled, "That was one of the nasty ways Lady Carisbrook attempted to, as she put it, keep Cara in her place."

Violet's gaze hardened.

Griselda humphed. "I can't say I'm feeling all that partial to Lady Carisbrook."

"Indeed," Penelope said. "I doubt any of us will feel much sympathy for her. However, to continue, Cara took in her ladyship's breakfast tray." Penelope fixed her dark eyes on Cara's face. "Did you, by any chance, notice if the jewel case was still on the dressing table?"

Cara shook her head sadly. "No. I didn't look in that direction at all."

Barnaby nodded. "The staff explained that the dressing table sits in the opposite direction to the bed and that unless you made a point to look in that direction, you wouldn't have noticed."

Violet had her head bent, scribbling in her book. "So what happened next?"

"Lady Carisbrook noticed the jewel case was gone." Penelope looked at Stokes. "Did you ask her when she noticed?"

Stokes had his own notebook open on his knee. "She said it was just a few minutes before she came downstairs and accused Cara in the breakfast parlor. Jarvis put the time at just after eight-thirty."

"So," Griselda concluded, "the last person known to have seen the emeralds is Lady Carisbrook herself, at about two o'clock in the morning when she climbed into her bed."

Barnaby and Penelope both nodded.

Montague, who until then had sat back and listened without comment, studied Barnaby's, Penelope's, and Stokes's faces, then asked, "What else do we know that's relevant?"

"Well," Penelope said, "the first thing that struck me as odd was that the thief, whoever they were, took the jewels in their case. The case is about nine inches long, five inches wide, and would likely be at least one inch deep." She glanced around. "That wouldn't fit in most pockets. The necklace and earrings by themselves, although heavy, would."

Barnaby narrowed his eyes. "The loose jewelry might have clinked. Perhaps the thief needed to be certain he wouldn't make the slightest sound."

Penelope nodded. "That's certainly possible, especially as it seems the jewels were stolen while Lady Carisbrook was in the room, but a jewel thief would still have got rid of the case as soon as he was out of the room rather than try to carry it. It would have no value in his eyes and would just make the jewels harder to conceal."

Stokes was tugging at his lower lip. "I agree. It is odd." He looked at Cara. "And surely if anyone within the household had intended to steal the jewels, they would have carefully extracted the necklace and earrings and left the case where it was. Who knows how much longer it might have been before Lady Carisbrook picked up the case and noticed the jewels weren't in it?"

"Judging from what Lord Carisbrook told us of what would normally have occurred," Barnaby said, "Lady Carisbrook would not have noticed until his lordship arrived home and she picked up the case to return it to him for placing in the safe."

In a small voice, Cara said, "I didn't know that."

Stokes looked at her and smiled one of his rare smiles. "Perhaps not, but you didn't have the jewel case in your room, nor had you hidden it anywhere else in the house, and you didn't have time to slip out and pass it on to anyone."

Cara frowned, then ventured, "Perhaps I had a…what is the word? An accomplice? And I tossed the case out to them through my bedchamber window. It faces—faced—the street."

Stokes's smile deepened. "I would take an oath the windows in your room haven't been opened since last summer—I checked." He held up a hand to stay Hugo's imminent protest. "And as Hugo and no doubt your uncle will point out, you haven't been in the country long enough to have made the right sort of contacts to pass on stolen items of this ilk." Stokes paused, then stated, "All in all, your uncle's description of her ladyship's accusation against you seems entirely justified. He labeled it preposterous, and preposterous it is."

"Forgive me for asking"—Violet bent an apologetic look on Cara —"but it needs to be asked. What on earth prompted Lady Carisbrook to make such a wild accusation?"

Penelope made a face. "I strongly suspect the answer has something to do with Cara outshining Julia, her ladyship's daughter. If I understood correctly, Lord Carisbrook insisted Cara join the family and that she goes with Julia to all social events. I can imagine that grated on Lady Carisbrook—who clearly feels no responsibility toward Cara, especially not at the expense of her own daughter. *However*, all that said, I feel there is more to it." Penelope looked at Cara. "Lady Carisbrook said something about Cara being the offspring of Lord Carisbrook's scandalous sister."

Cara elevated her chin and met Penelope's gaze. "My mother was Uncle Humphrey's younger sister, and she met and fell in love with an Italian painter—my father. My mother was adamant that she would marry her love even though her family wanted her to marry another—an older English lord. Mama and Papa eloped and went to live in Italy. That is the scandal." Cara shrugged. "Some see it as romantic, while others call it scandalous. But they were happy, and to them, that was all that mattered."

Penelope nodded. "Indeed. And it's hardly anything new, which is why I feel there is something still more behind her ladyship's animosity that we've yet to learn."

Silence descended.

Barnaby broke it. "To return to other things we know, one point that struck me about the jewels going missing was that them being left out on her ladyship's dressing table was a rare event. Normally, on returning from her evening's entertainments, Lady Carisbrook would hand the jewels directly to his lordship, who would lock them in the safe in his study. In general, the emeralds would not have been upstairs at all, but last night—or rather, early this morning—they were." Barnaby glanced at Stokes. "The only people who would have known that was what happened on the rare occasions when his lordship was from home were the staff."

Stokes nodded. "There's no chance at all that the emeralds were taken by some burglar who just happened to choose early this morning to visit her ladyship's room. Quite aside from there being no evidence of a break-in, nor any whispers of burglars operating in the vicinity, it's simply stretching credence too far."

"That would have been one very lucky burglar," Griselda observed.

"Which," Penelope said, "brings us back to the family and the staff." She regarded Cara, then asked, "Cara, do you think any member of the staff, or Franklin or Julia, might have taken the emeralds?"

Cara's eyes opened wide. "Oh no." She shook her head emphatically. "I cannot imagine it. The staff—they are all very kind and helpful. They are nice, almost like a part of the family, and I believe all have been with my uncle for many years." She spread her hands. "Why would any of them do such a thing?"

Stokes leaned forward. "Sometimes good people get into trouble and find themselves forced by circumstance into doing things they wouldn't normally do. Think of all the staff—have any of them seemed under pressure lately? Frowning, unhappy, short-tempered?"

Cara's brows knitted, but eventually, she shook her head. "I can think of no one who has behaved like that. Everyone seemed…content."

Penelope grimaced. "Lady Carisbrook also made that point—that the staff had all been with them for years and why would they turn to stealing now. Nevertheless, it's possible that knowing the emeralds would be left out over the early hours of Sunday morning proved too much of a temptation to someone in unexpected and urgent need."

Cara's head tipped up. "I cannot believe it of any of the staff." She frowned, then reluctantly added, "Not even the so-horrible Simpkins."

Penelope studied Cara's face, then hid a quiet smile and inclined her head.

Barnaby tapped his fingertips together. "We have yet to canvass the possibility that Lady Carisbrook herself has the emeralds."

All fell silent as they considered that.

Eventually, Penelope mused, "The supposed disappearance gave her an excuse to accuse Cara of a sufficiently serious crime to get her out of the house—and her ladyship did rush to notify the Yard before his lordship returned…" Penelope's voice trailed away, then she sighed. "Regardless, I'm having a hard time seeing her giving up her emeralds—which is what such a scheme would amount to—simply to achieve that." After a moment, she added, "Viewing matters from her point of view, it's hard to see the result being worth the sacrifice."

"True." Stokes stirred. "One other thing. We—Barnaby, Penelope, and I—would all take oaths that the staff know something they've yet to share, but whether whatever it is has any relevance to the emeralds going missing…" He shrugged. "Who knows?"

After several seconds of contemplation, Violet looked up from her notebook. "So what we have is that the Carisbrook emeralds, case and all, went missing from Lady Carisbrook's bedchamber sometime between the hours of approximately two o'clock and eight-thirty this morning, and everything points to the thief being a member of the household—either family or staff." Brows arched, she looked around at the others, but no one was inclined to disagree.

Then Penelope held up a finger. "The only member of the household who couldn't have been involved is Lord Carisbrook. He wasn't in town."

Stokes frowned. "We should note that, when his lordship arrived at his house just before we did in the early afternoon, he was horrified that his wife had called in the police. However, I can see multiple reasons why he would wish she hadn't, not least because of her accusation against Cara, his ward."

"So his lordship doesn't believe Cara is involved?" Griselda asked.

"Not in the least," Hugo stated.

Barnaby nodded. "None of the staff or other members of the family believe Cara was involved. Her ladyship appears a sole voice on that point. As for Lord Carisbrook's reaction, although not wanting the police to investigate the disappearance of a very valuable set of emeralds sounds strange, I suspect he would have been much more inclined to hire a private inquiry agent to pursue the emeralds rather than involve the police."

Penelope waved dismissively. "His reaction was totally understandable—gentlemen of his age and station abhor scandal of this sort. They see it as terribly tawdry."

The drawing room door opened to reveal Mostyn. He bowed to the company, then looked to Penelope. "Dinner is served, ma'am."

"Thank you." Penelope rose, and the others joined her. In a loose group, they ambled into the front hall and around into the dining room.

There, Penelope directed her guests to their seats. Normally, there were six places set, but with eight tonight, she placed Cara and Hugo at the middle on either side, facing each other, while Montague sat on her left and Griselda on her right, with Stokes to Barnaby's left and Violet on his right. Satisfied with her arrangement, Penelope slipped into her chair at the table's foot. "Now don't forget—no talking about the case."

Everyone grinned, then addressed themselves to the mock-turtle soup and, in between sips, exchanged comments on their children and households, on the comfortable minutiae of their lives.

As soon as the soup plates were cleared, Penelope turned to Cara. "Tell us about your life in Italy. Where did you and your parents live?"

Now significantly more relaxed in their company, Cara was happy to oblige. By dint of subtly leading questions, Penelope drew Cara into giving them a detailed picture of her life—up until her parents had fallen ill and, soon after, died. Cara confirmed that she'd initially been taken in by her father's family, but as soon as Lord Carisbrook had been informed of his sister's and her husband's deaths and that Cara was now his ward, he had written asking Cara to join his family in England and had made arrangements for her to travel with an English couple returning home after serving at the embassy in Rome.

Cara shrugged. "It was all made easy for me, and although my aunt does not like me, Franklin and Julia have been welcoming and kind, as has my uncle, of course."

Violet reached out and patted her hand. "You've done very well settling into a new country, and your English is polished even though it's not your native tongue."

Cara smiled shyly.

The main course was served, and once they'd all made decent inroads, Penelope turned her attention to Hugo. She caught his eye and remarked, "Your mother mentioned that you've given up the habit of smoking cheroots."

Hugo shuddered. "After that moment in the Fairchilds' garden, I haven't been able to take a cheroot between my fingers without seeing…" He blew out a breath. "Well, you know what I saw. You saw it, too."

Cara, however, opened her eyes wide at Hugo, clearly wanting to know.

Hugo shot Penelope a glance, but when she refused to come to his aid, he mumbled, "Smoking cheroots was a habit I picked up while in the army. Last year, at the first ball of the Season, I went out on a balcony to smoke one and tripped over a dead body."

Cara's eyes couldn't get any wider. She leaned forward. "Truly?"

Hugo nodded. "I don't recommend the experience."

"So"—Penelope artfully leapt in—"what have you been doing since? We all noticed you'd vanished from the ballrooms—did you hie into the country?" By "we" she meant the grandes dames and major hostesses with whom she was closely in league—a fact Hugo knew.

He eyed her but, unable to discern her ulterior motive, chose to take what seemed the easy way out and answer her question. "I went home to Wiltshire." He paused, then, as she'd hoped, looked at Cara and explained, "That's where m'father's manor is."

"What did you do there?" Cara was perfectly capable of asking her own questions. "Did you ride a lot? In Italy, we always think of English gentlemen as forever on a horse."

Hugo grinned. "Well, I was in the cavalry, so yes, I often ride, and the countryside around the manor is all gently rolling hills, so perfect for that." His gaze locked with Cara's, he paused for a heartbeat, then went on in a rush, "It's also good hunting country, and my father has kennels. I've always loved working with the hounds, and I realized—when I was down there last summer—that I wanted to breed them, more concertedly than my father has, although he's laid in excellent bloodlines on which I can build."

Barnaby threw in a comment, and Hugo—fired with zeal as Penelope hadn't before seen him—was off.

When Cara, hanging on his every word, put in, "You mean puppies?" Penelope sat back and grinned.

Griselda, beside her, caught her eye and, grinning too, winked.

The rest of the meal passed in an animated discussion of the very English obsession with breeding hunting hounds, largely led by Hugo, but with Cara also engrossed. The other three men were drawn in, caught by Hugo's enthusiasm. Montague was particularly interested in Hugo's intention of building a business based on the activity; as he said, if it could be done so successfully with horses, why not with hounds?

That observation enthused Hugo all the more.

Finally, with dessert served and consumed and the talk of hounds and hunting winding down, Penelope dabbed her lips with her napkin, then laid it aside and pushed back her chair. The sound drew the others' eyes.

She raised her brows at them. "Shall we return to the drawing room and the mystery of the emeralds?"

By general assent, they rose and filed back into the drawing room. With minds returning to the case at hand, they made their way to their previous seats.

Stokes sank into his usual armchair. As soon as the others had settled, he said, "Today being Sunday, I haven't yet reported this incident to the commissioner, but I will have to do so first thing tomorrow. Our summary"—he tipped his head to Violet—"will come in handy in that regard, but I would ideally like to lay before Sir Phillip a list of the avenues we consider worthy of pursuing. Given that, despite the lack of evidence to support her allegation, Lady Carisbrook has not withdrawn her charge against Cara—her husband's ward—I'm as certain as I can be that the commissioner will push for a thorough and rapid investigation." Somewhat cynically, Stokes predicted, "He'll want what he'll see as a tricky social situation resolved as soon as humanly possible."

"And," Penelope said, "in that, he's not wrong. The ton, let alone the news sheets, will have a field day with this—it has all the hallmarks of the sort of story the gossips love—and the longer the mystery remains unresolved, the worse the clamor will grow."

"So what can we surmise from what we already know?" Barnaby glanced around the circle, inviting speculation.

Montague frowned. "Would it be correct to say that Lord Carisbrook didn't seem overly concerned by the loss of the emeralds?"

Barnaby, Stokes, and Penelope all stared at Montague as they reviewed their exchanges with his lordship. Stokes looked at Barnaby and Penelope. "You two spoke with him more than I did."

Penelope met Barnaby's eyes. "At one point, his lordship did say that the emeralds were 'only jewelry,' which, when you consider what they must be worth, does, indeed, seem a little...well, dismissive."

"Yes—that's my point," Montague said. When the others transparently waited for further clarification, he briefly smiled and went on, "Your description of them, Lady Carisbrook's evident attachment to them, and the care normally taken to keep them secure all suggest that the emeralds are worth a small fortune. I assume they belong to the estate?"

Penelope said, "Well, they are known as the Carisbrook emeralds, so I expect that's the case."

"So the loss of the emeralds should be a significant loss of the estate's assets—if they belonged to her ladyship, that wouldn't be so, but if they are the estate's assets and they've vanished…well. Is Lord Carisbrook so flush with funds that a loss of that magnitude wouldn't concern him?"

Penelope frowned and looked at Barnaby. "I would have said the Carisbrooks manage well enough—they are certainly not paupers. But with three daughters in all—two already established and one as yet unwed—and two sons as well, and Lady Carisbrook is known to dress ostentatiously, meaning expensively, then I can't imagine there would be money to fling about."

Penelope turned to Cara. "Have you ever heard anything about the family's financial state?"

Cara looked uncertain, but then offered, "I don't really know much about such things, but…oh, about two weeks ago, I overheard Uncle Humphrey telling Aunt Livia that she needed to watch her expenses." She paused, then added, "Aunt Livia grew angry and stalked off in a temper."

Penelope nodded and looked at Montague. "Having to watch her expenses sounds about right."

His gaze on Montague, Barnaby said, "I can see where your mind is meandering, but perhaps you'd better spell it out for the others."

Montague inclined his head. Turning to Hugo and Cara, who had been listening intently to the exchanges, their expressions suggesting they were increasingly intrigued, he explained, "I've handled the finances of a great many estates in my time, and"—he shifted his gaze to Penelope's face—"I can think of many families of the ilk of the Carisbrooks who have found it expedient at some point to replace valuable stones such as the Carisbrook emeralds with the highest-quality fakes. Paste or, more recently, crystal. It's a common enough practice, and now that the fakes are more difficult to spot, certainly at a glance, for families in straitened circumstances, it's even more tempting, and of course, there's no crime involved."

Penelope put in, "Merely a sort of social sleight of hand, given they allow others to believe the stones are still real."

Stokes sat forward. "Are you suggesting that the reason Lord Carisbrook isn't overly exercised by the loss of the emeralds is because they're fakes?"

"That," Barnaby said, "would also account for his lordship's attempts to call off the investigation." He met Stokes's eyes. "He pressed us over the possibility when we saw him later. If the stones are fake, then from his point of view, the less noise made about the loss of the emeralds, the better."

"Hmm." Griselda shifted on the sofa. "While that might be true, until you get your hands on the emeralds, you won't be able to tell if they're real or not. And if I understood correctly, you believed Lord Carisbrook had other reasonable grounds for wanting to quash the investigation." She glanced at Cara. "And if the Carisbrook family have had to weather scandal in the past—such as with Cara's mother eloping with an Italian painter—then very likely his lordship would have a very strong antipathy to the thought of the family being embroiled in another scandal."

Penelope dipped her head in acknowledgment. "I could certainly see that being true."

Looking dissatisfied, Stokes slumped back in his chair. "Is there any way we can determine if the emeralds as they are now—the stones that were stolen—are real or fake?" He glanced at the others. "It makes a very real difference to the importance of this case."

After a moment, Montague offered, "It might be possible to learn if the Carisbrook estate has faced a financial crisis, although how far back the records might reach, I can't say." He glanced at Cara, then looked at Penelope. "I don't suppose you've heard of the family having any financial problems?"

"I haven't." Penelope looked at Cara.

Cara shook her head. "I know nothing about such things, and I doubt Franklin or Julia, or even Aunt Livia, would know, either. Uncle Humphrey is one to handle all matters to do with money quietly, without drama. He is very private in that regard."

Montague humphed. "Most men of his generation are." He looked at Penelope. "Do you have any idea how old the Carisbrook emeralds are?"

Penelope grimaced. "I've only glanced at them in passing, but given what I saw of the setting, I would say old—possibly Elizabethan."

Montague pulled a face. "I seriously doubt I can reach back that far, but I'll see what I can unearth." He looked at Stokes. "Regardless, it'll take a few days at least."

"I'll ask my usual contacts," Penelope volunteered. "One never knows what facts they might have tucked under their bonnets. If the Carisbrook estate faced a financial calamity within living memory, it's possible one or other of them will know." She glanced at Stokes. "There's a Cynster ladies' at-home tomorrow morning—a private one restricted to the family and connections. I'll ask if anyone there knows anything pertinent."

"It's possible," Griselda said, "that I might be able to find someone to shed light on that question—at least if our supposed financial crisis happened over recent years."

Violet looked up from her scribbling. "One of your contacts in the trade?"

Griselda grinned. "Exactly." She glanced at Montague. "If you want to learn the true financial state of any family in the ton, just ask the lady's modiste."

Stokes and Barnaby grinned, and Penelope laughed. "An excellent idea. Do you know who Lady Carisbrook's modiste is?"

"It is Madame Renee in Bruton Street," Cara said. "I have gone with Aunt Livia and Julia to have dresses made there, although mostly Madame makes for the likes of Aunt Livia." Cara gestured. "Big showy gowns with harsh colors."

Griselda nodded. "That sounds right, and as it happens, I know Renee quite well."

"I'll come with you," Violet said. "I confess I'm interested to learn of a modiste's view of her wealthy clients and what sort of information she might glean from her interactions with them."

"I was also going to suggest"—Griselda leaned forward to look at Barnaby—"that you might check with the family jewelers."

"Now there's a thought." Penelope looked at Cara. "Do you know who the Carisbrooks deal with?"

Plainly eager to assist in whatever way she could, Cara said, "It is a firm called Rundell, Bridge, and Company. On the road near the big cathedral—St. Paul's."

"They're in Ludgate Hill," Penelope confirmed.

Stokes was frowning. "But if the emeralds are so old—"

"It's not the making of them that you should ask about," Griselda said, "but the cleaning of them."

Penelope nodded. "A set of that style—very ornate—especially if worn often, and I believe Lady Carisbrook wore the emeralds regularly, would have to be cleaned fairly frequently." She glanced at Barnaby. "I have my sapphires cleaned by Aspreys about once a year, and I don't wear them all that often. Anyone with jewelry like the Carisbrook emeralds would have them cleaned by a reputable jeweler, most likely the family jeweler."

"*Except* if the stones are fake," Barnaby said. "In that case, the very last person to whom you would take such a set would be a reputable jeweler."

"At last!" Stokes was jotting in his notebook. "We might have a chance of learning something about these blasted emeralds."

"Meaning if Rundell, Bridge, and Company haven't been asked to clean the emeralds—indeed, haven't seen them…?" Penelope arched her brows.

"Exactly." Stokes finished scribbling and looked up.

Barnaby said, "While asking Lord Carisbrook if the stones are fake will almost certainly get us nowhere, we could ask his lordship which jeweler last handled the emeralds. Regardless of what his answer is, his reaction will be informative."

"As Livia Carisbrook has been wearing those emeralds frequently," Penelope said, "they would have to have been cleaned sometime within the last few years. And since they're so ornate, it's not simply a matter of washing them—you would need a jeweler to do even a passable job of it."

"Whoever of us next calls at John Street can ask Lord Carisbrook which jeweler he used—which one last saw the emeralds," Stokes said.

"Actually"—Penelope tapped her index finger to her lips—"I rather think we should independently ask Livia Carisbrook the same question. Just to see if we get two different answers."

"I like the way you think." Stokes was scribbling again, presumably making notes for his meeting with the commissioner. He paused, then looked at Cara. "There's one person in that household we haven't had even a few words with—your cousin Julia." He glanced at Penelope. "I really think one of us should speak with her, preferably alone, out of her mother's orbit."

"Indeed." Penelope pondered for a moment, then said, "Although the Season is under way, tomorrow night—Monday night—is usually relatively quiet. Major hostesses rarely hold their balls on a Monday. However, as Lady Carisbrook is attempting to marry off Julia, then I would expect her, with Julia in tow, to be out and about somewhere in the ton—she's not the sort to let moss grow under her feet." Penelope looked at Cara. "Do you know what event or events your aunt and cousin are planning to attend tomorrow evening?"

Cara tipped up her chin. "Yes, because I had to write the acceptance notes. Aunt Livia chose to go to a Lady Cannavan's soirée. She—my aunt—said that perhaps Julia would have a better chance of attracting the right sort of gentleman in a smaller, more select company."

Penelope smiled and looked at Barnaby. "We have an invitation. It appears we're going to make Lady Cannavan extremely happy."

Barnaby groaned. Then he shrugged. "I suppose it's better than having to weather a major ball."

Penelope patted his hand. "It'll be much quieter." She looked at Stokes. "And a much more likely venue in which I might manage to get Julia on her own."

"Good," Stokes said. "Ask her everything you can think of. We can't tell what she might know."

They all looked around at each other. "Nothing more?" Violet asked. When they all shook their heads, she held up her book and read, "So—Stokes is off to see the commissioner first thing, and then…?" She arched a brow Stokes's way.

"I believe I'll visit Rundell, Bridge, and Company," Stokes said, "and see what I can learn from them." Stokes looked at Barnaby and Penelope. "After that—after lunch—I think you two and I should have another session questioning the Carisbrook staff. This time, one by one."

Penelope nodded. "In the morning, I'll quiz the ladies at the Cynster at-home for all they can tell me about the Carisbrooks, the emeralds, and any financial problems the estate might have faced."

Violet pointed her pencil at Penelope. "Don't forget you have a directors' meeting at the Foundling House at one o'clock."

"Damn." Penelope wrinkled her nose. "I'd forgotten, but I can't miss that." She looked at Stokes. "Can we meet at John Street at three o'clock to take another tilt at the staff? Aside from all else, at that time, Lady Carisbrook should be out of the house."

Stokes nodded. "Let's make it three."

"And before we leave John Street," Penelope said, "Barnaby and I will contrive to ask Lord Carisbrook, and separately, her ladyship, assuming she's returned, which jeweler last handled the emeralds. Then later in the evening, we'll see if we can separate Julia from her overwhelming mama and encourage her to tell us anything she knows about this business."

"Meanwhile," Montague put in, "my associates and I will endeavor to see if we can turn up anything in the Carisbrook finances that might suggest a reason for the emeralds being substituted and sold."

"And Violet and I," Griselda said, "will choose our time and drop in on Madame Renee and see what she can tell us of the Carisbrooks."

"This is excellent." Violet was ticking off tasks on the list she'd made. "We're covering a lot of potential avenues quite quickly."

"Yes, indeed." Stokes studied the last note he'd jotted in his notebook, then he closed it, looked at the others, and smiled. "This is more than enough to keep the commissioner happy."

Penelope snorted. "You might point out that at least in this case, he doesn't have a dead lady and a murderer to expose."

Stokes chuckled as he tucked away his notebook.

Griselda glanced at the clock on the mantelpiece. "Great heavens—we've talked for hours!" She rose. "We really should get home."

Violet looked, too, and made a clucking noise. "Indeed. These meetings condense to just a single page of resolutions, but the talking to get to that eats up time."

They all rose. Barnaby tugged the bellpull, and when Mostyn appeared, Penelope sent him to summon the nursemaids. In a group, the six investigators ambled in Hugo and Cara's wake into the front hall.

"Given you and Barnaby are going to be busy tomorrow evening"—Griselda looked around at the others' faces—"perhaps we should plan to meet at Greenbury Street for dinner and discussion on Tuesday."

Everyone readily agreed.

"With any luck," Stokes said, "we'll have several definite clues to set our teeth into by then."

Penelope watched as Hugo accepted his coat and hat from Mostyn, then Hugo came to take his leave of her and Barnaby and exchange nods with the others, tendering his thanks for their help in clearing Cara's name.

Needless to say, despite Hugo's and Cara's transparent fascination with the way the six went about their collective enterprise, to Hugo's mind, the only thing that truly mattered was lifting all suspicion from Cara and restoring her to her rightful place.

While waiting for their children to be brought down, Violet and Griselda edged closer to Penelope, flanking her as all three watched Hugo exchange a few careful and conservative phrases with Cara.

"The way he treats her," Griselda murmured, "it's as if she's a porcelain princess."

Penelope smiled and whispered back, "She blushes like one, too."

By straining their ears, all three ladies heard Cara's hesitant response to Hugo's gallantry, then she drew in a breath and attempted—quite definitely—to deny there was any need for him to dance attendance on her...

Hugo merely looked at her. If anything, his jaw set more determinedly.

Then with one last bow, he turned, and Mostyn opened the door. With a general wave, Hugo clattered down the steps and strode away.

Penelope, Griselda, and Violet watched Cara—watched her continue to stare at the space Hugo had filled until Mostyn shut the door.

Then Cara sighed, turned, found a sweet smile, and thanked the six of them, sincerely and from the heart, for their championing of her cause.

The last in line, Penelope squeezed Cara's fingers. "Think nothing of it—it's what we're good at, and we enjoy the challenge, too. Now, off you go and have a good night's sleep. I take it you have everything you need?"

Cara confirmed she had, said another round of thanks, then raised her hems and went up the stairs.

On the landing, she passed the nursemaids—Gloria carrying a sleeping Megan slumped over her shoulder and Hilda with a bundled Martin cradled in her arms.

Watching Cara disappear along the gallery, Griselda murmured, "Why did she try to discourage Hugo? Over all the earlier hours, she and he seemed to be growing ever closer."

"Indeed." Penelope grinned. "I suspect that Hugo, at least, is falling head over heels for her. His mother has nearly despaired of him—I rather think she's going to be pleased. I must send her a note. But as to Cara's dissuading Hugo, if I read the signs aright, she's worried that any damage this business causes to her reputation will sully his. She's being noble in making every effort not to encourage him."

"That speaks well of her," Griselda observed.

"It does." Penelope continued to smile. "I have no doubt that her heart is in the right place, so to speak—especially when it comes to Hugo."

"Perhaps she thinks she isn't worthy of him?" Violet said.

Penelope pushed her spectacles higher on her nose. "If so, we'll have to teach her otherwise. As Lord Carisbrook's niece and ward, she's perfectly acceptable as Hugo's bride. And, of course"—she exchanged glances with Violet and Griselda—"collectively, we're going to ensure that, no matter what the solution to the puzzle of the Carisbrook emeralds proves to be, it won't in any way interfere with us guiding this budding romance to a successful conclusion."

"Just so." Smiling, Griselda reached out and took Megan from Gloria.

Stokes instantly appeared at Griselda's shoulder, checking that their daughter was still asleep.

With a grin and a nod of agreement to Penelope, Violet took Martin into her arms.

Mostyn had summoned the Stokeses' and the Montagues' carriages, and the families, with cloaks and hats donned and cuddling their sleeping children close, descended the steps. Barnaby and Penelope stood in their doorway and waved the carriages off.

Then Penelope looked up, met Barnaby's eyes, and grinned. "Once more, into the breach!"

Barnaby laughed, took her hand, and drew her inside, and Mostyn shut the door.

CHAPTER 5

Stokes's meeting with the commissioner went exactly as he'd hoped. Although Sir Phillip looked peeved at the prospect of a serious burglary in Mayfair hanging in the balance, he approved of Stokes consulting with the Adairs; that Barnaby's father, the Earl of Cothelstone, was one of the peers who oversaw the police force and was also a personal friend of Sir Phillip's was a source of continuing joy to Stokes. Sir Phillip concluded by grunting and telling Stokes to get on with it.

Stokes was very ready to comply. He jumped into a hackney and directed it to Ludgate Hill, but before the coach had traveled a block, he tapped on the roof and told the jarvey to detour via Albemarle Street.

Last night over dinner, Violet had asked if Cara had inherited her father's artistic talent, and although Cara had demurred, if Stokes had read Hugo's reaction correctly, she possessed superior drawing skills.

Regardless, her drawing had to be better than Stokes's ability to describe jewelry.

When Mostyn opened the door to Stokes, the majordomo smiled and informed him that both Barnaby and Penelope had already left the house. "The master thought a quick word with his father might be in order, and the mistress has gone to St. Ives House to consult with the ladies there."

"Luckily," Stokes said, surrendering his overcoat, "it's not either of them I need to see. Is Miss Di Abaccio downstairs?"

"Indeed, sir. She's in the back parlor with Mr. Hugo Adair. And, of course, Mrs. Montague."

"Naturally." Stokes hid a grin. He, Barnaby, and Montague had overheard enough of their ladies' comments in the front hall at the end of their evening to recognize that their other halves' interest in the case had expanded to include Hugo's and Cara's futures. With one shared glance, he and the other two had elected not to interfere. Furthering romances was what ladies did, after all.

He walked into the back parlor; a nicely proportioned room with long windows overlooking the back garden, the parlor doubled as Penelope's office.

Seated side by side on the damask-covered sofa, Hugo and Cara were discussing the offerings of various theaters revealed in a handful of playbills. They looked up as Stokes entered, as did Violet, who was perched behind Penelope's desk and appeared to be comparing Penelope's correspondence with her diary. Violet spent a few days each week organizing Penelope and the translations she undertook for various colleges and institutions up and down the country.

All three occupants of the parlor smiled at Stokes, then looked at him inquiringly.

He smiled at all three, then focused on Cara. "I hoped I would find you in, Miss Di Abaccio. My meeting with the commissioner went as well as I'd hoped, and I've been given a free hand to investigate this case as I see fit. I'm therefore on my way to visit Rundell, Bridge, and Company, as we discussed. However, I realized that my ability to describe the Carisbrook emerald necklace and earrings is likely to prove woefully inadequate. I wondered if I could prevail on you to make me a sketch of the set?"

Cara blinked, then her face lit. "Why, yes, Inspector." She bounced to her feet. "I will be very pleased to be of help." She stepped forward and gestured to the door. "If you will wait, I will fetch my pencils and paper."

Stokes bowed. "Thank you."

Smiling, Cara hurried past and whisked out of the door. A second later, the sound of her slippers running quickly up the stairs reached them.

Grinning, Stokes turned back to find Hugo gazing at the now-empty doorway, then Hugo raised his gaze to Stokes's face, and Stokes saw concern and an unvoiced query lurking in Hugo's dark-blue eyes.

"No one," Stokes stated, "not even the commissioner—who would dearly like to see the thief apprehended sooner rather than later—believes Miss Di Abaccio is guilty."

"Except for her loudmouthed aunt," Hugo replied.

Stokes inclined his head. "Except for her ladyship, but as matters stand, her unsupported stance is already reflecting more on her than on Miss Di Abaccio."

Hugo searched Stokes's face, then the tension thrumming just beneath his surface eased. "That's…good to know."

Aware of Violet watching their exchange, Stokes regarded Hugo for a second more, then, given that Hugo was there and showing no signs of shifting from Cara's side, Stokes yielded to impulse and said, "It occurs to me that until we resolve the question of who took the emeralds and why, it would be an excellent idea for Miss Di Abaccio to have a reliable watchdog by her side. Not just when she's outside but at all times through the day." Stokes paused for a second, then added, "I suppose I could delegate Morgan to guard her—"

"No need." Hugo met Stokes's gaze, his expression sober, serious, and utterly implacable. "I'm only too happy to oblige."

Stokes fought to hide his grin and inclined his head. "Very well. I'll leave that aspect in your hands."

He looked across the room at Violet, who, as Hugo was again watching the doorway, grinned widely and approvingly back. Stokes arched his brows. "Where's Martin?"

"Upstairs, playing with Oliver, Hattie, and Hilda." Violet set down one letter and picked up another. "Those girls have been a godsend."

Stokes nodded. "I don't know what we'd do without Gloria."

Pattering footsteps announced Cara's return. She swept into the room, beamed at them all, then returned to her place on the sofa, dumped a handful of pencils in her lap, retaining one in her fingers, and placed a sketch pad on her knees.

She bent over the pad. "The emeralds are—as Mrs. Adair said —quite ugly."

With quick, sure strokes, she created a sketch, at first bare bones, then filling in considerable detail of a necklace composed of what looked like medallions, each medallion formed from highly wrought gold wrapped around a large rectangular emerald. To Stokes's eyes, the result bordered on the hideous.

"And these are the earrings." Cara quickly sketched the matching earbobs—each made up of one medallion dangling from a shepherd's crook—on the same sheet of paper.

Cara sat back and examined her work. She bent again and added several tiny touches, then straightened, dropped her pencil into her lap, tore off the sheet, and handed it to Stokes. "There. That is the best I can do."

Stokes took the sheet and studied the sketch. Somehow, even without using colors, she had made the gold appear to be gold—even to glisten. There was perspective and depth to the items; he almost felt he could reach into the sketch and grasp the necklace. He looked at Cara—into her upturned face with its hopeful expression. "You truly are very talented."

She shrugged and looked away. "I just draw. It is easy."

Stokes felt his brows rise; he knew little about art, but even he could see that her talent was no minor thing. He folded the sheet carefully and slipped it into his pocket. "Thank you. This will help me greatly."

That made Cara beam again. "I am truly pleased to have been able to assist."

Stokes bowed to her. Straightening, he met Hugo's eyes and nodded, then at the last, raised his gaze to Violet and tipped her a smiling salute. "I'll leave you all to your day's endeavors."

With a general wave, he turned and left the room.

Seconds later, he quit the house. As he went quickly down the steps to where the hackney waited, he thought again of his suggestion to Hugo and felt his lips curve in a self-satisfied smile. Who said only ladies could matchmake?

Penelope hadn't known who she might find in the back parlor of St. Ives House that morning, but the instant she walked in and saw Lady Osbaldestone and Helena, the Dowager Duchess of St. Ives, ensconced in armchairs by the fire, she knew her visit wouldn't be in vain.

After the initial round of greetings, Honoria, Duchess of St. Ives and their hostess, fixed Penelope with a commanding look and arched her brows. "Well, my dear? Have you an inquiry for us to assist with?"

Penelope and, she suspected, all the others there viewed the queries she brought to such meetings as her contribution to the event—much like a superior form of parlor game. She pushed her spectacles higher on her nose—she really needed to get the bridge tightened—and swept her gaze over the interested faces now turned her way. "As it happens, a strange case fell into our laps just yesterday."

These ladies knew what they were doing when it came to secrets and the ton; without reservation, she gave them a précis of the disappearance of the emeralds, Lady Carisbrook's accusation against Cara, and what they'd subsequently learned and deduced.

After the inevitable exclamations died away, Penelope swept the gathering with her gaze. "What I would like to ask is, firstly, what any of you know about the Carisbrook emeralds and, secondly, what you can tell me of the Carisbrook family—the current members."

Heads bent close as the ladies whispered, then Lady Osbaldestone rapped her cane on the floor, drawing every eye.

"Helena and I," her ladyship declared, "both consider the emeralds quite hideous—so ridiculously overblown—but as far as either of us know, they've been in the family for generations."

Helena nodded. "I can remember the current Lord Carisbrook's grandmother wearing them in the days when I first came to England."

"So," Penelope said, "they've been around for a long time." She looked at the others. "I gather Lady Carisbrook—the current one—wears them frequently."

"At every possible turn," Caro Anstruther-Wetherby averred.

"Even when they clash horridly with the color of her gown," Patience Cynster confirmed.

"We can take it as read, therefore," Penelope said, "that the emeralds would be recognizable to many." She reviewed her questions. "Now, what about the current Carisbrook family?"

From various quarters came comments—confirmed by others—to the effect that her ladyship had a very firm notion of her own and her family's station. Several described incidents they'd witnessed that testified to her ladyship's often-sour disposition and her tendency to be overbearingly domineering to those of even fractionally less standing than her own.

"It's not so much a case of putting on airs *above* her station," Lady Osbaldestone explained, "as insisting to the nth degree on every last possible acknowledgment of her status. Of what is due to her by virtue of her birth and marriage."

"And," Honoria said, "she's been rigid in inculcating her children—the older three, at least—with the same attitude."

Others were quick to agree, citing examples of the pompous arrogance affected by her ladyship's older children.

"She was indefatigable in managing their lives up to and including their marriages," Celia Cynster, one of the older matrons, observed. "But as those three are very much made in her image, they fell in with her directions—well, to be perfectly accurate, I would say her directions paralleled their own."

Penelope was supplied with the older children's names and ages—the Honorable Gresham Carisbrook, now in his late thirties and married to a milksop named Hortense, the Honorable Millicent, now Lady Fletching, in her early thirties and married to Sir Herbert, and the Honorable Lucinda, Lady Collard, thirty and married to Sir Finlay.

"As for the younger children," Felicity Cynster said, "Franklin, who is in his late twenties, and Julia, who I think must be about twenty-three years old—I've only met them in passing, but they seem very different to their older siblings." Felicity met Penelope's eyes. "I would say they strongly favor their father rather than their mother. Regardless, both seem to chafe under her hand, which I don't recall being the case with the older three."

Jacqueline Debbington nodded. "Those two are certainly much...well, nicer young people, rather quiet and sensitive. One feels quite sorry for them having to cope with Lady Carisbrook as their mother."

Adding those insights to her own observations of Franklin and Julia left Penelope feeling that she was making progress in understanding the underlying family dynamics. "What about Lord Carisbrook?"

Silence reigned for several seconds, then Horatia Cynster, a redoubtable grande dame, stated, "A quiet, honorable gentleman. He's entirely unremarkable, and I've never heard a word said against him."

"Beyond the obvious question of why he married Livia Henry, as she then was," Celia said. "She was always a spiky character, but the marriage was arranged, of course."

"For money?" Penelope asked.

Celia frowned. "No—if anything, the Carisbrooks were wealthier than the Henrys. As I recall, it was more a case of both families agreeing it was a suitable match."

Before Penelope could frame her next question, Helena spoke. "As to Livia Carisbrook accusing her husband's niece of stealing her emeralds, understanding the earlier Carisbrook scandal might prove instructive."

All the other ladies swung to stare at Helena and Lady Osbaldestone.

"There was an *earlier* scandal?" Patience exclaimed. "I don't remember that."

"You wouldn't." Lady Osbaldestone folded her hands over the head of her cane. "It was before your time—before all your times, except for Celia, Horatia, and Louise."

Horatia nodded sagely. "Indeed—and quite a scandal it was."

Louise Cynster leaned forward. "It was Humphrey's—the current Lord Carisbrook's—younger sister, Margaret. Meg, as she was called. She was a beautiful girl, vivacious and charming—full of joie de vivre. The family wanted her to marry to their advantage—to an older widowed peer. The Carisbrooks had made up their minds, but frankly, no one could imagine a girl as lively as Meg settling down to a quiet life in the distant north—least of all, Meg herself."

Horatia shook her head. "A classic and entirely predictable case—Meg had met an Italian painter who had been invited to England to commemorate the Victory celebrations. He was dashingly handsome and also very talented. As I recall, although not titled himself, he was connected to one of the Italian contes, and of course, he and Meg fell in love."

Lady Osbaldestone snorted. "Naturally, when Meg stated she wished to marry him, her family would have none of it. They stood firm and whisked Meg off to the family estate in Surrey, thinking to put an end to her rebellion."

"What did Humphrey have to say to this?" Penelope asked.

Lady Osbaldestone's gaze grew distant as she apparently dredged deeper into her memories. After a moment, she said, "Most expected him to support the family line, but while he didn't speak against it, he didn't denounce Meg's wishes, either. Indeed, when she vanished from Carisbrook Hall, there was always a suspicion that Humphrey had had a hand in helping her run off with her Italian."

"They eloped?" Honoria was as intrigued by the story as Penelope.

"Indeed." Helena continued, "They were married in Italy with his family about them, and by all the accounts that filtered back through the years, Margaret and her Giovanni were ecstatically happy."

Louise nodded. "I clearly remember some of those who returned from their travels being quite put out that, far from reaping any retribution for denying her family's wishes and deliberately flinging her cap over the windmill, Meg gained only untrammeled happiness."

Lady Osbaldestone snorted. "Nonsense! It was true love, first to last, as anyone with a grain of sense could have seen. Meg was true to her heart and received her just rewards."

Everyone looked satisfied.

Penelope focused on Helena; she thought she understood the dowager's point in referring to the earlier scandal, but... "How do you see this old scandal impinging on the current situation?"

Helena met her eyes and seemed, as always, to see into her soul, then smiled faintly. "I suspect, my dear, that although she married Humphrey several years later, Livia is highly—indeed, one might say excruciatingly—aware of that scandal from the past. Livia did not marry for love. Her older children did not marry for love. And I'm sure she intends the two yet unwed to marry to benefit the family as well. However, one suspects that with her younger children, she is facing...perhaps we might call it the true Carisbrook character. A nicer, gentler nature that, perhaps, predisposes them to wish for love in their marriages."

Lady Osbaldestone put in, "Just because Humphrey married for the family's sake rather than his own doesn't mean he wouldn't have preferred to follow his own inclinations. But he was the title holder, so he did the expected thing and married Livia. However, his two youngest children are under no such pressure to marry to please the family."

"And now"—Helena sat back and spread her hands—"into this likely tussle of wills between mother and children over their right to marry as they please—for love—Cara is flung by Fate. Humphrey, I am sure, would have welcomed Cara with open arms—she is the only child of his beloved sister of whom he was sincerely fond. And so there is Cara, ensconced within the bosom of the family, a living, breathing reminder that marrying for love does not necessarily end badly."

"One relevant point." Honoria shifted on the sofa, drawing Penelope's attention. "Describe Cara."

Penelope thought, then said, "Glossy black hair in big, loose ringlets, large grass-green eyes, complexion pale but olive tinged, rose-red lips, and her features are what one might call alive. Vibrant and vivacious. Although in the circumstances, she's been understandably rather grave since we met her, I would say that normally, she smiles and laughs a lot."

"So she's attractive?" Felicity clarified.

"Exceedingly," Penelope confirmed. "She has a nicely rounded figure a little shorter than average, and on top of all that, she has the sort of confidence that catches gentlemen's eyes."

"And there," Honoria said, "is another strong motive for Lady Carisbrook to grasp any straw to get her niece-by-marriage out of her house. I've met Julia Carisbrook, and from your description, her cousin Cara will totally eclipse her."

Penelope nodded. "I got the impression Julia wasn't at all averse to being eclipsed."

"If her personality is as we surmise and her mother is constantly pushing her into the limelight, then," Patience said, "that's hardly surprising. Julia might well see Cara as a savior of sorts—or at least something of a social shield."

"Indeed." Lady Osbaldestone caught Penelope's gaze. "So now you know of several compelling reasons—familial, maternal, and indeed, personal—behind Livia Carisbrook's behavior toward her husband's niece."

Penelope inclined her head. "Thank you—all of you." She glanced around at the other ladies. "You've given me lots to think about and a much better insight into the family's inner tensions—which, I suspect, will be key to finding out what has happened to the emeralds."

She glanced at the clock, grimaced, picked up her reticule, and rose. "And now, I really must run—I have a directors' meeting at the Foundling House to attend."

"One thing." Imperiously, Honoria held up a finger. "In appreciation of our help, next time you join us, you must promise to bring Miss Cara Di Abaccio with you." Smiling, Honoria glanced at the others, then looked back at Penelope. "I believe I speak for us all in saying that we are now keen to make her acquaintance."

Penelope laughed, waved, and departed.

As she hurried out of the front door and down the steps to where her carriage waited, she reflected that no matter what poisonous rumors Lady Carisbrook thought to spread about Cara, with the likes of the ladies she'd just left in the St. Ives House parlor at Cara's back, Cara would be able to hold her head high in any company and simply ignore her ladyship's malicious slanders.

"As if they're beneath her." Penelope grinned at the irony. She accepted James's help, climbed into the carriage, sat, and turned her mind to the matters awaiting her at the Foundling House.

It was far later in the morning than Stokes had expected when he walked into the showroom of Rundell, Bridge, and Company. His hackney had got caught in a snarl of carriages in Fleet Street, and it had taken over an hour to get free; as there had been two badly damaged carriages involved, that he was an officer of Scotland Yard hadn't helped—he'd been recognized by the local constables, and they'd begged for his assistance.

He'd hoped to be early enough to avoid having to drag Bridge, the head jeweler, from his wealthy, usually aristocratic customers; instead, he had to hang back—pretending an interest in watch chains and doing his best to appear inconspicuous—until Bridge, unfailingly charming and attentive, escorted Lord Dundas and his lady from the shop.

Immediately he'd closed the door on his lordship, Bridge—John Gawler Bridge, who had become the head jeweler of the renowned firm on the original John Bridge's death five years before—turned and fixed Stokes with a direct and faintly impatient look. "How can I assist you, Inspector?"

Stokes had had occasion to consult Bridge before, and as Bridge knew of Stokes's association with several families who numbered among his most valuable clients, Bridge usually accommodated Stokes and his inquiries without fuss.

Bridge walked back to the other side of the long counter. He signaled to his assistant that the young man's help was not required, then turned to face Stokes as he halted on the counter's other side.

Stokes met Bridge's gaze. "Does this firm act as family jewelers to the Carisbrooks? Viscount Carisbrook of Carisbrook Hall."

Bridge nodded. "Yes." He plainly had no inkling of anything being amiss regarding the Carisbrooks' jewels.

"In that case"—Stokes pulled Cara's sketch from his pocket, unfolded it, and set it on the counter—"I need to know if you've ever seen these pieces."

Bridge studied the sketch for several minutes, then in an even tone, said, "Unless I miss my guess, these are the famous Carisbrook emeralds."

"They are."

"In answer to your question, no—we've never handled them."

Stokes frowned and caught Bridge's eyes as he raised his head. "Never?"

Bridge held Stokes's gaze, then lightly grimaced. "No—at least, not in my time. Trust me, I would remember them. Prior to that, it's possible the firm might have handled them, but all the workers from that time—those who might have worked with or even simply seen such jewels—are gone. Most have passed on." He studied Stokes's frown, then added, "And yes, now you've brought it to my attention, I do find it curious. We are the

Carisbrook family jewelers, and we've actively dealt with Lord Carisbrook and her ladyship over recent years, yet the emeralds have never been in our hands, not even to be cleaned."

Stokes studied Bridge's brown eyes. Although the man's expression and tone of voice gave nothing away, Stokes felt fairly certain Bridge was drawing the same conclusions he was. Stokes grunted. He looked down at Cara's sketch, then prodded it with one finger. "If we wanted to trace the jeweler who last cleaned these, how might we go about it?"

When Stokes looked up, Bridge was frowning. "Why not just ask Lord Carisbrook? Or her ladyship?"

"We will, but regardless of what they say, is there any way we might learn the answer ourselves?"

Bridge sighed and looked again at the sketch. "These are very old pieces. If they're being actively worn—say once or twice a month—"

"They are."

"—then we would recommend that the piece be brought in for cleaning and for the claw settings to be checked at least once a year." Bridge looked up. "A piece like this would absolutely scream to be cleaned if left untended for, say, three years. It would barely be wearable if left that long."

"Who could do the cleaning?"

"With a piece like this, with this degree of ornate working, only a reputable jeweler—someone with the right training and equipment—could do it properly."

Stokes drummed his fingers on the counter. "What if the set's been stolen?"

"If it has, I can assure you no reputable jeweler would touch it." Bridge nodded at the sketch. "It's too well known. Anyone in the trade—and that includes the less reputable side—would immediately recognize it." Bridge paused, then asked, "Has it been stolen?"

Stokes grunted and picked up the sketch. "Let's just say that it isn't where it's supposed to be." He folded the sketch and tucked it back into his pocket. "If it was stolen and you wanted to find it, where would you ask?"

"Is this a recent theft?"

"A day or so."

"In that case, Inspector, I would ask in the underworld. A set such as this is effectively worthless to the legitimate trade. A large part of its value lies in the whole set remaining as is—and therefore highly identifiable—and even if broken down, those emeralds would be a problem. They're cut in a very old style, and therefore, given their size, they'll remain distinctive." After a second's pause, Bridge added, "The more I think about it, the more certain I feel that the only way to look for your missing emeralds will be via your contacts in the underworld."

Stokes grimaced, then met Bridge's eyes and tipped him a salute. "That's what I feared, but it's useful to have your confirmation."

Bridge snorted and waved him off.

Stokes paused on the pavement outside the shop. Montague's hypothesis that the stones were fake and Lord Carisbrook knew of it was starting to gain weight. But… "If Gawler Bridge has never seen them, just how long ago were the stones switched?"

If the stones had been replaced by excellent fakes decades ago, how would anyone know? They assumed Lord Carisbrook would know of such a change, but had no proof of it.

And if the stolen emeralds were fake, then presumably not even those in the underworld would be interested in them.

Stokes straightened. "But if we accept that the emeralds have been stolen, then they've almost certainly been taken to some jeweler somewhere." Somewhere in the underworld.

Stokes stepped to the edge of the pavement and raised his arm.

A hackney swerved through the traffic and pulled up at the curb.

Stokes called up to the jarvey, "Chapel Court in the City."

He climbed in, sat, and consulted his fob watch. He had time to stop by Montague's office and send a message to Neville Roscoe. London's gambling king could undoubtedly point them to the best trail to follow—or at the very least, to the most useful jewelry fence to shake for information.

The bell over the door of Madame Renee's salon tinkled as Griselda, with Megan's hand firmly clasped in hers, led the way inside. Violet, carrying a swaddled and thankfully sleeping Martin in her arms, followed. They'd timed their appearance in the Bruton Street shop for two o'clock in the afternoon—a time when, during the Season, the ladies of the ton could be relied on to be at their lunchtime events.

Sure enough, the shop was deserted, but within seconds, a young girl came hurrying out from behind the heavy velvet curtain that shielded the rear of the shop. She took in Griselda's and Violet's clothes, and the children, and a faint frown formed on her face. "Can I help you, ma'am?"

Griselda smiled. "Please tell Madame Renee that the laces she's using are still second-rate."

The girl blinked, then looked horrified, but before she could speak, a woman with dark hair popped her head through the curtains. She stared at Griselda for a heartbeat, then her face lit. "Griselda!" Renee emerged—small, dark, and sprightly, exactly as Griselda remembered her. "Well, I never."

Beaming, Renee swept across the room, spread her arms, and did her best to envelop Griselda, who was significantly larger, in a ferocious hug. "It's been far too long, my dear, but I'm delighted to see you." After releasing Griselda, Renee looked down at Megan, who was clutching Griselda's hand. "And who's this?" Renee looked at Griselda's face, then back at Megan. "Oh my goodness! She's yours."

"Megan," Griselda proudly said. "You'd heard I'd married, hadn't you?"

"Yes, I had. To a handsome policeman, no less." Renee tipped her head. "Although I haven't seen him, I'd say she has the best of both of you. What a poppet!"

Renee crouched so she was on a level with Megan, hunted in her pocket, and drew out a mass of tangled ribbons. "Would you like to play with these?"

Megan smiled shyly, then looked up at Griselda. At Griselda's nod, Megan reached out and took the loose ball of ribbons.

As, absorbed, Megan turned the ribbon ball in her hands, Renee rose and smiled at Violet. "And who else have you brought me?"

Griselda introduced Violet. Renee—who was known to adore children but had never had any of her own—cooed delightedly over Martin.

Then Renee glanced at Griselda. "Bruton Street is a fair way from St. John's Wood. I take it there's a reason behind your visit?"

Griselda nodded. "Not that I wasn't thrilled to have a chance to call on you—I've watched your continued success from afar—but yes, there is a matter on which we'd like to pick your brains."

Renee turned to her assistant. "Mary, you'd better keep watch out here. Lady Hemmings isn't due until three o'clock, and I doubt anyone else will drop by, but still—better there's someone here."

The girl bobbed. "Yes, ma'am."

Renee held back the velvet curtain, then followed Griselda, Violet, and the children into what proved to be a luxuriously appointed fitting room. "This way." She stepped past and opened a door set so neatly into the side wall beside the curtain that it was well-nigh undetectable. "Welcome to my office."

The room beyond was small, neat, and airy, with magazines and catalogs stacked on shelves and in pigeonholes behind a simple desk. "Our workshop is upstairs." Renee waved them to two chairs set before the desk and moved to sit in the chair behind it. "But I assume the information you're after doesn't involve satins, laces, and beads."

"No, indeed." Griselda settled Megan on the floor beside her chair; the little girl was still fascinated by the tangled ribbons. Griselda straightened and met Renee's eyes. "We need to know...well, anything you care to tell us of Lady Carisbrook and the Carisbrooks in general."

Renee made an impolite sound. "Lady Carisbrook—she of the foul temper, overbearing ways, and complete disregard for the feelings of anyone even one rung below her social rank?"

Griselda grinned and tipped her head. "That's the one."

"Well, obviously, she's no favorite of mine, so yes, I'll tell you whatever I can." Renee arched her brows. "What, exactly, do you want to know?"

When Renee glanced her way, Violet said, "A question has arisen over whether, at some point in the recent past—ever since you've been modiste to her ladyship—you've had reason to suspect that the family might have been hard-pressed to pay your bills."

"I know what it's like to have ton clients," Griselda put in. Her lips quirked. "And I have to admit that since I married a police inspector, I've never had to chase one for payment, but everyone in our lines of trade has experienced instances when a customer is late paying, or says they've lost the bill, or..."

Renee nodded. "Such is our life." She paused, then said, "There was a time, several years back, when Lady Carisbrook was puffing off her two elder daughters at the same time—in fact, that period ran for nearly three years. The older one had already had her first and second Seasons, but hadn't taken, so her ladyship had both girls on her hands, and she and both daughters were frantically giving or attending party after ball after rout. It was utterly ridiculous the number of gowns the three of them went through in those years, year after year, but I daresay, in the end, the family considered the expense worthwhile—she got both girls married off well enough."

"When was this?" Violet juggled Martin and reached into her reticule and drew out her notebook.

Renee frowned. "It must have been at least five...possibly as many as seven years ago. I'll check my books in a minute, but the reason I remember it so clearly—well, quite aside from the ludicrous number of gowns—is that unlike the situation with most of my ladies, Lady Carisbrook doesn't pay her bills herself. I've always sent my bills directly to Lord Carisbrook, and it was he who came to see me when—I assume—her ladyship outran the constable."

Griselda blinked. "His lordship spoke to you about his wife's bills?"

"Yes, I know—not the usual way of things. But Lord Carisbrook was such a nice, kind gentleman, I felt quite sorry for him being married to her ladyship, and when he explained that his funds were somewhat stretched—given all the entertaining her ladyship was doing on top of all the gowns, bonnets, and such—and suggested a system of steady but smaller payments over time, I was happy enough to agree." Renee shrugged. "I own this building now, and given the number of ladies I supply, I could afford to be understanding. And regardless of her trying nature, Lady Carisbrook and her daughters have been a steady source of profit for me for the last decade, so it made sense to work with Lord Carisbrook if it meant his wife continued to come back."

"I can see that was a sensible move business-wise." Violet was jotting, then she looked up and met Renee's eyes. "Lady Carisbrook has another daughter she's currently taking about—Julia. Are her ladyship's bills in any danger of...ah, outdistancing the constable again?"

Renee chuckled, but shook her head. "Oddly enough, this time, with this younger daughter, Lady Carisbrook seems to be determined to do the minimum she can, at least with respect to young Julia's gowns. For herself, her ladyship has never stinted, and she continues to order new gowns more regularly than any of my other clients." Renee humphed. "With respect to her, I frequently ask myself just how many gowns a lady can wear in one year. To return to your point, however, given she's really only spending on herself, I doubt that my bills are causing Lord Carisbrook any sleepless nights."

Griselda and Violet exchanged glances, then Violet hmmed.

Renee got to her feet. "Let me look in my ledgers and find the exact year for you."

She was as good as her word, identifying the year of the Carisbrooks' financial stress as 1831. "Eight years ago," Renee said. "Further back than I'd thought."

Just then, the shop bell rang. All three women looked at the clock ticking on a shelf on the wall behind the desk.

"Almost three o'clock." Renee shut the ledger and set it back on the shelf. "That will be Lady Hemmings—she's almost always a trifle early."

Griselda gathered up Megan, tangled ribbons and all, and stood. Violet settled her notebook in her reticule and, hoisting Martin up, rose, too.

Griselda held out her hand to Renee. "Thank you for your help."

Renee frowned. "I forgot to ask—are the Carisbrooks in financial trouble?" She met Griselda's eyes. "Should I be wary of extending too much credit their way?"

Violet shook her head. "No—quite the opposite. We suspected the family had had a difficult time in the past, but that they overcame it. It's the past that concerns us. We've found nothing to suggest the family is in anything but sound financial health now."

"Good." Renee nodded. "I might thoroughly dislike his wife, but I like Lord Carisbrook."

Renee ushered Violet and Griselda into the salon, where a fussy lady was quibbling with the poor assistant. After exchanging a look with Griselda and Violet, Renee left them to find their own way to the door while she turned her attention to dealing with her customer.

Violet followed Griselda onto the pavement of the fashionable shopping street. Side by side, they walked toward the corner around which they'd left Griselda's small carriage. "What did you make of that?" Violet asked.

"Reading between Renee's lines," Griselda replied, "I would say that eight years ago, in 1831, Lady Carisbrook effectively beggared her husband."

"Hmm." Violet looked ahead. "And given the way his lordship's affairs are arranged, that means she beggared the Carisbrook estate."

CHAPTER 6

Hugo had wracked his brain to find an excursion that was suitable for him to escort Cara on alone and had hit on the latest exhibition of the Royal Academy, which was open to the public in nearby Burlington House.

With its adjacent arcade, Burlington House stood on Piccadilly a mere two blocks from the corner of Albemarle Street—an easy walk along well-populated streets.

He'd tentatively mentioned his idea to Mrs. Montague, half expecting her to disapprove. Instead, with her pen tapping on Penelope's blotter, Mrs. Montague had thought, then she'd called in Mostyn and consulted the experienced majordomo. After Hugo had agreed that there was no reason a footman couldn't trail along behind them—just in case of unforeseeable danger—both Mrs. Montague and Mostyn had smiled and, somewhat to Hugo's surprise, labeled his suggestion an excellent notion.

Now, with the midafternoon rush of visitors milling about them, Hugo stood with Cara on his arm and considered himself a lucky man. Cara's expression said she was delighted, fascinated, and thrilled—and, of course, given her absorption with the paintings and sketches displayed, she'd all but forgotten he was there. That meant he was free to gaze at her face, to drink in the intense appreciation of life that infused her features and attracted him as nothing and no one else ever had.

He indulged himself while indulging her and inwardly preened at having realized that art was the way to her heart.

Contrary to Hugo's assumption, Cara was very much aware of his gaze; the touch of it feathered over her senses, over her skin, like the gentlest caress. She should—perhaps—turn her head and frown at him and make him stop, but…standing before wonderful paintings while on his arm was currently her idea of heaven, and she was loath to mar it.

That said, beneath her joy at being able to feast her eyes on the artworks displayed and the pleasure she found in Hugo's company ran a darker, unsettling train of thought that insisted that what her silly heart had already started imagining and hoping for would never come to pass.

Within a day of her joining her uncle's household, her aunt had taken her aside, sat her down, and soberly explained what she had termed the facts of Cara's life. Namely that, as the daughter of a scandalous lady who had run off with a penniless Italian painter—Cara had bitten her lip and stopped herself from correcting her aunt; her father had been far from penniless—Cara could not hope to make what the English termed "a good match." Instead, she would have to be content with whatever gentleman her aunt could find for her after settling Julia. Her aunt had gone on to suggest that Cara should affect a retiring disposition until Julia was suitably established—if, that was, Cara wished for her aunt's support subsequently.

Her aunt had repeated her warnings several times since—sometimes with eyes blazing and her words hissed through her teeth.

Cara was still feeling her way in the partially familiar but in some ways strange arena of English society. She wasn't so naive as to believe everything her Aunt Livia told her, yet she remained unsure of what her place in the ton might be.

And now, close beside her, his steely arm beneath her hand, stood a gentleman who set her heart alight. Who, she sensed, might make her soul sing. Every moment she spent with Hugo Adair, every new little fact she learned about him, only increased her conviction that he might be…what her father had been to her mother.

Her father had seen the joy in her mother's soul and had seized her and set her free.

Hugo seemed to feel similarly about her…yet even though he didn't bear a title, he belonged to a noble family, and that family might frown direfully on any putative association with her, much as her mother's family had on her father's suit.

Cara simply didn't know how stable the ground on which she stood might be.

Indeed, in truth, she didn't even know on what ground she stood.

Just thinking about it left her feeling hopeful and cast down at the same time, and she truly didn't know which way to lean. Toward Hugo? Or would she be saving them both heartache if she forced herself to pull back from him?

"Hugo?"

Hugo snapped out of the reverie in which he'd been imagining the day on which he would take Cara into Wiltshire to see his parents' home, turned, and beheld Mrs. Jacqueline Debbington attired in a severe and highly fashionable gown and holding two of her children—the elder two, Hugo assumed—by their hands.

"Fancy meeting you here." Jacqueline—who Hugo knew was a close friend of Penelope's—quizzed him with her eyes, then she turned her gaze on Cara and, flicking free of her son's grasp, extended her gloved hand. "I'm Mrs. Debbington, and you must be Miss Di Abaccio. It's a pleasure to meet you, my dear."

Cara touched fingers and bobbed a curtsy. "I am pleased to meet you as well." Cara glanced at the children, then at the paintings surrounding them. "Do you often come here? Do the children enjoy it?"

"Yes." Jacqueline smiled. "They've had quite a lot of experience of exhibitions." She looked at her children. "This is Fredrick—he's seven—and this is Miranda, who is six."

Frederick dutifully made his bow, and Miranda bobbed a curtsy.

Cara smiled on them both. "You are very well-behaved children."

Frederick's eyes grew round, as did Miranda's, then Frederick blurted, "You're very beautiful."

Cara laughed delightedly and dropped Frederick a curtsy. "Thank you for the compliment, young sir."

Frederick had been prepared to be thoroughly embarrassed, but, reassured, he smiled easily back.

Jacqueline, too, was smiling, in her case, indulgently. She caught Hugo's eye. "I spoke with Penelope this morning. She mentioned you were keeping Miss Di Abaccio company—what an inspired idea to bring her here." Jacqueline included Cara with her gaze. "I hope you're enjoying the works, Miss Di Abaccio."

"Please, call me Cara." Cara returned her gaze to the large portrait she'd been studying. "I am particularly interested in the portraits…" She frowned, then looked at Jacqueline. "You are Mrs. Debbington? The wife of the so-famous Gerrard Debbington?"

Jacqueline laughed. "Yes, for my sins, I am, indeed, Gerrard's wife."

"So"—Cara looked at the children—"these are his children, and they are here to look on their papa's work?"

"Well, yes, but they're both more interested—as Gerrard is—in landscapes."

"Truly?" Cara looked surprised. Then her eyes widened. "Ah—now I have looked properly, I see you are the lady in Mr. Debbington's most famous portrait. Is that not so?"

Jacqueline nodded. "That was how we met. My father commissioned Gerrard to paint me."

Cara sighed. "It is a very lovely painting—I was lucky enough to see it once when it was shown in Florence. And now I understand why it has so much"—she gestured with her hands—"intensity. He was in love with you when he painted it."

Jacqueline regarded Cara shrewdly. "In the first throes, as it happens. You're very perceptive. Not many have seen that. Most simply see me and what the portrait reveals about me, not him."

"Ah, but I…" Cara broke off and amended, "My father was a painter, you see."

Jacqueline nodded.

Hugo was rather surprised she didn't question Cara further.

Instead, Jacqueline glanced around before returning her gaze to Cara's face. "This is the end of the exhibition for us. Have you finished, or are you just starting?"

"No." Cara smiled at the children. "This, too, is the last painting for us."

"In that case, might I suggest we all repair to the tearoom in the arcade next door?" Jacqueline looked fondly at her children, who promptly adopted pleading expressions. "If I don't get cream cakes for these two, my life will be a misery."

Cara looked hopefully at Hugo.

Jacqueline's look was a great deal more pointed; it warned him not to think of denying her, Cara, or the children.

Hugo managed a smile for all four. "Why not?"

Cara, beaming, joined the children in uttering a suitably muted cheer.

Hugo escorted his now-expanded party out of Burlington House and into the arcade. The tea shop proved to be half empty, and the children scampered to take possession of one of the round tables in the window.

Having glimpsed the footman who had been delegated to assist in watching over Cara as the man followed them into the arcade, Hugo decided the position was well enough. He didn't care if passing matrons noticed him having tea with Cara, especially not now Jacqueline and her children had joined them. Nothing could be more innocent than the picture they doubtless presented as pots of tea arrived and orders were taken for cream cakes and scones.

To Hugo's relief, it was a relaxed and comfortable interlude.

Jacqueline spoke to Cara of Italy; she and Gerrard had visited several times over the years, although they had never been to Sienna, where Cara's father and mother had lived.

"I do remember seeing several Di Abaccios in a gallery in Rome," Jacqueline said over her teacup. "Landscapes with quite wonderful brushwork."

Cara tipped her head from side to side. "My father loved the painting, but he never paid much attention to the business—that wasn't his love."

"Purely out of curiosity, did he leave you many paintings?"

"He tended to give his works away to family and friends, but I have thirty of his best canvases. They are on their way by sea and will be some months yet. I will have to find somewhere to put them—I'll have to ask my uncle where they might go."

Jacqueline shot a wide-eyed and rather intent look Hugo's way, but then, as if thinking better of whatever her point was, simply murmured in agreement.

A few minutes later, while Jacqueline was quizzing Hugo over what he was doing with his life and Cara was distracting the children and apparently succeeding wonderfully, judging by the way all three were giggling, Cara looked at Jacqueline and waved to get her attention. When Jacqueline arched her brows, Cara said, "I enjoy sketching faces—would it be all right for me to draw these two imps?"

Jacqueline smiled, glanced at her children, and waved. "By all means."

Cara pulled a sketch pad and her pencils from her large bag—Hugo had wondered at its size, but had assumed it was an Italian fashion—and after explaining to the children how she wished them to pose, happily settled to sketch.

"I heard from your sisters that you're proposing to expand your father's hound-breeding program." Jacqueline arched her brows. "Is it very different from breeding horses?"

Hugo found himself explaining in more detail than he had to anyone before, but then Jacqueline was an excellent listener. Later, he realized that she was also an excellent plotter, every bit as devious as Penelope.

But then the teapots were empty and the cakes all gone, and the children were eager to see what Cara had made of them.

Smiling, she set aside her pencil and tore three sheets from her sketch pad. "No," she admonished, as two pairs of greasy hands reached for the pages. "Your mama can hold them for you until you get home and wash your fingers."

Both children sat back, but strained to look at the creations as Cara handed them to Jacqueline.

"Oh." Jacqueline's eyes widened.

Cara blushed. "They are nothing, I know—not measured against your husband's talent. But they are just for the children to laugh at and remember this moment, you see."

Jacqueline looked at Cara, then back at the sketches she held in her hands. After a moment, her gaze still on the sheets, she said, "Would you mind, Cara, if we showed these to Gerrard?" She glanced at the children. "They'll wish to, of course."

Cara shrugged and smiled at the children. "The sketches are yours to do with as you please."

"Thank you, Miss Di Abaccio," the pair chorused.

Hugo had caught only the briefest glimpse of the sketches as Cara had handed them across the table; to his eyes, they had seemed very fine—expressive, which was an adjective he associated with Cara—but he wasn't any expert.

He had already paid their shot, so they gathered themselves, rose, and made their way out into the arcade and on to Piccadilly.

The footman hovered and, at Jacqueline's request, hailed a hackney.

Hugo helped Jacqueline and the children up, then stepped back and boldly retook Cara's arm as if he had the right to do so.

She made no demur, and after they'd waved Jacqueline and the children off, walked by his side as they covered the short distance along the busy thoroughfare, then turned in to the relative quiet of Albemarle Street.

After a moment of strolling along, Cara sighed.

"What is it?"

When she looked up, Hugo felt as if he was falling into the vivid green of her eyes, but then they clouded, and she faced forward. "Seeing all those paintings reminded me—I do miss my paints and easel."

"Where are they?"

"In the back of my armoire in my uncle's house."

Hugo slowed, then halted. "There's no reason we can't go and fetch them, if that's what you'd like?"

Cara blinked at him. She searched his eyes and confirmed he was in earnest. She'd expressed a wish for something, and he immediately offered to get her what she'd wished for…

In that moment, she fell—helplessly—just a little deeper in love with him.

He'd taken her to the exhibition, and for the past hours, she'd forgotten all about the difficulties of her situation. But those difficulties were still there.

Slowly, her eyes on his, she said, "Thank you for the kind thought, but it has only been just over one day. It was simply the sight of the paintings that made me wish to pick up a brush. But best I wait until this business with the emeralds is decided before I venture under the same roof as my aunt again."

He looked at her as if debating whether to challenge her decision or not.

She smiled, tightened her hold on his arm, and nudged him into walking again. "Truly, I would prefer not to run the risk of meeting Aunt Livia just now."

"That, I can understand." After a moment, he closed his hand over hers where it rested on his sleeve and, in a quieter tone, said, "But trust me, with Barnaby and Penelope—let alone Stokes and Montague and their wives—all working on the case, it won't be long before you have your paints, brushes, and easel again."

Three o'clock came and went, and Barnaby and Stokes still loitered on the pavement two houses up from the Carisbrook residence.

"It's not like Penelope to be late." Stokes's gaze was fixed on the northern end of the street.

"No." His hands sunk in his pockets, Barnaby leaned against the railings bordering the pavement. "There'll be some reason, but all in all, I suspect we'll do better to wait and have her with us when we go in."

Stokes grunted in reluctant agreement.

Barnaby mulled over what Stokes had reported of his interview with

Bridge. "Did Montague give you any idea of when we might hear back from Roscoe? Who best to ask about stolen emeralds shouldn't be hard for Roscoe to define."

"Let's hope for a quick reply." Stokes shifted. "If the Carisbrook emeralds aren't fakes and have fallen into some high-class fence's hands, we're unlikely to see them again."

"Not as that ugly necklace, anyway." Barnaby looked northward, too. "It'll be broken up, the stones removed, and the gold melted down faster than you can blink." A carriage turned in to the street. He recognized the coachman and straightened from the railings. "Here she is."

The carriage pulled up at the curb beside them. Barnaby waved the groom back and opened the door—and Penelope literally fell into his arms.

"Oh!" She blinked at him, smiled, then immediately her expression turned contrite. She looked past Barnaby's shoulder at Stokes. "I'm sorry I'm late—I couldn't get away from my sisters. Portia literally held onto my sleeve—they wanted me to agree to a new roster… Well, it took simply ages to go through it."

Barnaby grinned and set his wife on her feet. She didn't often get flustered, but as she huffed and straightened her gown and the small hat perched on her coiled hair, to him, she looked adorable. "We decided to wait for you before going in."

The look she cast him made it clear she hadn't imagined they wouldn't. Then she swung and faced the Carisbrooks' door. "Well, then—let's get to it."

She allowed Stokes to lead the way. Barnaby brought up the rear as they climbed the front steps, were admitted by Jarvis, and filed into the front hall.

After verifying that her ladyship was—as they'd hoped—out for the afternoon, Stokes requested an audience with Lord Carisbrook, and they were shown into the study.

His lordship rose to welcome them. After exchanging greetings, he fixed his gaze on Stokes. "Any news?"

"Sadly, no, but it's early days yet." Stokes saw no reason to mention his visit to Rundell, Bridge, and Company. "We're here"—he included Barnaby and Penelope with a glance—"to, with your permission, question the staff again. There are several minor matters we need to clear up."

"Of course, of course." His lordship waved expansively. "Ask whatever you wish. I'm sure all our staff will be happy to oblige." He looked toward the door where Jarvis had lingered. "Jarvis, please assist Inspector Stokes and Mr. and Mrs. Adair in whatever way they require."

"Yes, my lord."

With polite nods, Stokes, Barnaby, and Penelope turned to leave.

Lord Carisbrook reached out a hand to Penelope. "Mrs. Adair, I wonder… Cara—how is she?"

Penelope smiled reassuringly. "She's in good spirits. I believe Mr. Hugo Adair has arranged for Cara to meet with his sisters—Lady Guilfoyle and Lady Monk." She glanced at the clock on his lordship's desk. "Cara and he should be heading to Green Street shortly."

His lordship blinked, clearly taken aback. "Oh, good." Then his expression brightened, and he smiled. "Very good." He inclined his head to Penelope. "Thank you, Mrs. Adair. Cara is clearly in good hands."

With a final nod to his lordship, Stokes led the way out. He paused in the front hall and arched a brow at Barnaby and Penelope, but when they merely stared back at him, he turned to Jarvis, who had followed them from the room and stood waiting, as instructed, to render all assistance. "We need to speak with all the members of the staff, this time one by one, in private."

Jarvis thought, then offered, "Mrs. Jarvis's room would be best for your purpose. Who do you wish to speak with first?"

Stokes glanced at Penelope. This time, she responded. "Her ladyship's dresser."

Jarvis inclined his head. "If you will come this way?"

He preceded them through the green-baize-covered door at the end of the hall, into the short corridor that led to the servants' hall. A few paces along the corridor, Jarvis opened a door to the left and ushered them into a small square room, modestly but comfortably furnished with a dresser, two armchairs angled before a small fireplace, and most pertinently, a simple desk with a mismatched selection of straight-backed chairs.

"Will this do?" he asked.

"Admirably." Penelope set her reticule on the dresser, then turned to survey the desk and chairs.

Stokes looked at Jarvis. "Simpkins?"

"I'll send her along immediately." Jarvis bowed and withdrew.

Penelope directed Barnaby and Stokes in arranging the three most comfortable chairs behind the desk. She selected a simple wooden one with no cushion and placed it facing the desk. "There. Our stage is set."

She bustled around to claim the chair at one end of the row of three. Stokes sat in the central chair, with Barnaby on his other side.

They'd barely settled when a tap fell on the door.

At Stokes's "Come in," Simpkins appeared. She shot them a wary, measuring glance, then closed the door and, at Stokes's wave, approached the desk.

Penelope nodded at the single chair. "Sit, please."

Like most staff, Simpkins wasn't comfortable sitting in the presence of her betters; she sank rather carefully onto the seat, arranging her skirts tightly about her legs, then clasping her hands in her lap.

Stokes had laid his open notebook on the table before him; he kept his gaze on it. "We need to verify exactly who was in this house in the early hours of Sunday morning, between the time Lady Carisbrook returned and the time she realized the emeralds were missing."

"I've already told you all I know." Simpkins's tone was decidedly snippy.

Barnaby arched his brows. "Is that so?" His tone suggested he wasn't impressed by Simpkins's attitude. "Because we should point out that, as matters currently stand, you are one of only two staff members who could have taken the emeralds."

Simpkins bristled. "I didn't take them. What would I want with such things?"

"We really don't know," Penelope countered, "which is why we would like you to think very carefully about whether anyone else could have entered her ladyship's room between the time you left and the time the tweeny—Missy—went in to lay the fire in the morning."

Simpkins frowned. "But Miss Di Abaccio—"

"Went in later," Stokes cut in. "Yes, we know. But at this point, we want to confirm that no one else—no one else at all—had access to that room and the emeralds."

They had no evidence that there had been anyone else, just the odd behavior of the staff and the unlikelihood that any of the four people currently on their list—Lady Carisbrook, Simpkins, Missy, and Cara—was the thief. But they'd often found, especially when dealing with a diverse group such as the staff of a house, that simply pressing hard on one possible point would cause someone to stumble and reveal where the real clue lay.

Simpkins all but glowered and repeated, "I've told you all I know."

All three of them pressed her in various ways, but the most clarification they got from her was "No one else came into the room while I was with her ladyship, and when I left, I didn't see anyone else on that floor or on the stairs or anywhere about."

Finally, Stokes dismissed her. After jotting down various points in his notebook, he saw that Penelope's head was tipped, her gaze fixed on the door through which Simpkins had gone. "What did you think?" he asked.

Penelope frowned. "I think she's telling the truth about not seeing or knowing of anyone else being there, but I got the distinct impression she's worried that there might have been someone—someone we don't yet know about—who went to her ladyship's room during the critical hours."

Barnaby nodded. "I agree—Simpkins doesn't know, but she suspects."

"Right, then." Stokes consulted the list of the staff Morgan had made for him. "Let's leave the Jarvises for now and go on down the list."

They spoke next with the senior footman, Jeremy. He pointed out that he hadn't been summoned to that part of the house at any time during the evening in question. The same was true for the parlor maid, Helen, and the upstairs maid, Abby. Henderson, his lordship's valet—a quietly spoken, very neat individual—was vague and could tell them nothing; as he explained, with his lordship away, there was no reason for him to be on that floor.

Julia's maid, Polly, had been waiting in Julia's room when her mistress, along with Lady Carisbrook and Franklin, had returned to the house. "Miss Julia's chamber is on the same floor," Polly admitted, "but it's right away at the end of the wing. At night, you can barely see her ladyship's door from Miss Julia's."

While they questioned her, pressing her to remember anything she'd seen or heard, especially on quitting Julia's room and descending to the servants' hall, Polly shifted and squirmed, but ultimately, told them nothing.

Penelope stared at the door after Polly had left. "Again," Penelope said, "she isn't lying and truly doesn't have anything factual to tell us. But there is something—something they're all hiding!"

Barnaby's expression had hardened. "We're not asking the right question."

"Would that we knew what the right question was." Stokes considered his own impressions. "The staff are staunchly loyal, and I get the feeling that's to the family as a whole. They don't want to lie—not even Simpkins—but they're going to do their damnedest to avoid telling us anything they think might damage the family."

Penelope nodded. "Lord Carisbrook and the children, certainly, and because anything regarding her ladyship will, by association, reflect on his lordship, she's protected, too."

Stokes inclined his head. After a moment, he went on, "It's perfectly possible that whatever they're hiding has nothing to do with the emeralds, but…"

"They might be wrong." Barnaby glanced at Stokes. "We still need to know."

Stifling a sigh, Stokes consulted his list. "Next up is the under footman, Henry."

Henry proved to be an earnest lad hoping to work his way up to butler. "Eventually, obviously." He blushed, pressing his hands, palms together, between his knees.

"So," Stokes said, pretending to read from his notebook, "between the hours of two o'clock and eight-thirty on Sunday morning, did you see anyone on the first floor, either near or going into or coming out of her ladyship's room?"

"No." Henry's reply was confident and clear. "I didn't see anyone."

Penelope frowned. "But you were on the first floor during those hours?"

Suddenly, Henry looked conscious. He had the sort of countenance best described as open; no matter how hard he tried, he couldn't hide his emotions. "Ah…well…yes." The last word came out on a squeak. He stared at Penelope as if she'd transformed into a dangerous being.

"What took you to the first floor?" Barnaby drew Henry's startled attention.

"Ah…" Henry's features blanked, then, hesitantly, he offered, "Lady Carisbrook rang…and I went up."

"Just to be clear"—Stokes used his calmest, most matter-of-fact tone—"this was after she returned home and went up to her room?"

Henry gulped and nodded. "Jeremy had already gone to bed, so I went up."

"And what," Penelope asked, "did her ladyship want?"

"She…ah…asked me to deliver a message, ma'am."

"To whom?" Penelope inquired.

Henry stared, then shifted his gaze to Stokes, as if seeking rescue, but all he met was Stokes's steady and utterly implacable gaze. Henry swallowed again and squeaked, "It was for Mr. Franklin."

"And did you deliver the message?" Barnaby asked.

Henry's head bobbed. "Yes, sir."

"What was the message?" Stokes brought Henry's gaze back to him.

Henry met Stokes's eyes, then rubbed his palms along his thighs. "Her ladyship wanted to speak to Mr. Franklin. Straightaway."

"And did Mr. Franklin go to her ladyship?" Stokes's voice had turned stern.

His eyes wide, Henry shook his head vehemently. "It's like I said—I didn't see anyone near or going into or coming out of her ladyship's room. I swear I didn't."

"So what happened when you gave Franklin the message?" Penelope leaned forward, her attitude one of all reasonableness. "What did he do?"

"He thanked me and waved me off," Henry said. "I left and went downstairs, and I didn't see anybody on the way."

Penelope stilled for a second, then leaned over to look at Stokes's list of the staff. "Does Mr. Franklin have a gentleman's gentleman?"

"No, miss." Henry had sucked in a breath and was calming. "His lordship's valet, Henderson, does for Mr. Franklin as needed."

"I see." Penelope exchanged a brief glance with Barnaby. That was another indication that the Carisbrooks might not be as well-to-do as they appeared.

Stokes considered his notes. "So you, too, entered Lady Carisbrook's room that night. While you were there, did you see the jewel case on her dressing table?"

Henry frowned, clearly thinking back, then shook his head. "I can't say that I noticed, sir. I just looked straight ahead like we're told to."

Stokes faintly grimaced. He paused, then asked, "Is there anything you haven't told us of what you saw or did while on the first floor of this house during those hours?"

Henry swallowed, but his gaze had steadied. "No, sir."

Stokes inclined his head. "You may go."

Henry escaped.

Once the door had shut behind him, Stokes glanced at Penelope, then at Barnaby. "It sounds as if we'll have more questions for Franklin, and for her ladyship as well."

"Hmm." Penelope frowned. "But later." She waved to the door. "Let's continue on with the staff. There's something niggling at the back of my brain—it'll surface eventually, but for now, let's make sure there's nothing else the staff have carefully omitted to mention."

Stokes rang a small handbell and, when Jarvis stuck his head around the door, asked to see the cook next. Mrs. Smollet had nothing at all to tell them—apparently she and the scullery maid, Peggy, were tucked up in their beds the whole time. "We get to bed early because we're the first up."

Peggy confirmed that, as did Missy, the tweeny.

They were all exceedingly gentle with Missy, who appeared terrified that she'd be browbeaten into saying more than "I don't know anything, miss. I didn't see anyone about. It was only me, creeping about, laying and lighting the fires."

As Missy rose to leave, Penelope looked up. "Please send Polly in again."

Missy blinked, but bobbed and slipped through the door.

Stokes angled a questioning look at Penelope.

She smiled tightly. "I just remembered a question we forgot to ask."

Once Polly—now even more nervous over having been summoned a second time—had subsided onto the hard chair, Penelope smiled reassuringly and asked, "Before, we spoke of when you were on the first floor around the time Miss Julia and her ladyship returned to the house." Penelope smoothly continued, "Let's talk, now, of when you went up to Miss Julia's room in the morning. What time was that?"

Polly's eyes went wide. She whispered, "I always go up at seven-thirty, ma'am."

Penelope nodded. "Did you see anyone else in the corridor or on that floor on your way up and back?"

"No, ma'am." Polly's hands were in her lap, her fingers gripping tight.

"While you were in her room, did Miss Julia leave the room at any time?" Stokes asked.

Polly hesitated, then her chin firmed. "No, sir."

Penelope narrowed her eyes on the maid. "Polly..."

Polly caught her breath and looked as if she might cry. After a second's fraught silence, she blurted, "I don't know where she was—she wasn't in her room when I got there, but I can't say she was in her ladyship's room. I don't know!"

The last was a wail, but when Penelope simply blinked and sat back, Polly gulped in a breath and, gradually, quieted.

After a moment, Penelope nodded. "All right. So you went up to Miss Julia's room at seven-thirty. You saw no one else wandering about along the way. But when you entered Miss Julia's room, she wasn't there." Penelope paused, then asked, "I presume you waited until she returned?"

Polly nodded. "Yes, ma'am. She came in…must have been about five or so minutes later."

"Was she carrying anything?" Barnaby asked.

Polly blinked and shook her head, plainly not registering the implication. "No. She just came in, sighed, and plopped down on her dressing stool, and I started doing her hair."

"Did she often go to see her mother at that time of the morning?" Penelope asked.

Polly waggled her head. "I wouldn't say often, but sometimes, when Miss Julia wanted to know something about where they were going that day or what her ladyship wanted her to wear, Miss Julia would go in around then. Her ladyship likes to wake about then and lie in before her breakfast tray arrives at eight." Polly shifted, looking supremely uncomfortable. "But I can't say as where Miss Julia actually was that morning. I didn't ask, and she didn't say."

"No matter." Penelope smiled. "We'll ask, and then we'll know."

After a glance at Stokes, she dismissed Polly.

The instant the door closed behind the maid, Stokes, scribbling in his notebook, said, "Now we're getting somewhere." He glanced at Penelope. "That was a good catch."

Penelope tipped her head at Barnaby. "It was one of those questions we hadn't asked."

Stokes looked at what he'd written. "Do we continue with the staff or, instead, speak with Lady Carisbrook, Franklin, and Julia?"

"Lady Carisbrook and Julia, and most likely Franklin as well, will still be out," Penelope said. "Let's be thorough and get through all the staff."

Stokes agreed. "Other than the Jarvises, who are unlikely to have been upstairs during the relevant period, we've only the coachman, groom, and stable boy yet to interview, and it's unlikely they can tell us anything of what happened during the early hours of Sunday morning."

That prediction proved true for the coachman, Wills, and the groom, Cobb. The pair had rooms in the house, accessed via the rear stairs; after driving Lady Carisbrook, Franklin, and Julia, to their Saturday-evening entertainments, then returning them to the house, the men had taken the coach into the mews, unhitched and stabled the horses, then pushed the carriage into the coach house, closed the door, and retired to their beds. "Saw nothing and no one along the way," Cobb confirmed, "other than Jarvis, who was waiting downstairs to let us in and lock up after us."

They called in Willie, the stable boy, more for completeness's sake and so he didn't feel left out.

A bright-eyed urchin of about twelve, he sat on the chair, swung his legs, and informed them he was training to be a groom.

Penelope smiled. "Do you sleep in the attics with the others?"

"Oh no, ma'am. I sleep in the loft above the horses so's I can keep an eye on 'em."

Stokes looked up, thinking to cut the interview short and move on to more likely subjects—namely her ladyship and her children—but Barnaby, smiling indulgently, said, "We've been asking all the others if, last Saturday night between two o'clock when her ladyship, Miss Julia, and Mr. Franklin came home and eight in the morning, they saw anything out of the ordinary."

Willie tipped his head and scrunched up his face. "Well, I s'pose the gent ain't exactly ordinary—he's not about every night."

Stokes blinked. Penelope sat up, while Barnaby froze.

"What gent?" Barnaby—remarkably gently—asked.

"There's a gent what comes visiting every so often—always at night, mind, in the dark and late." Willie's bright eyes passed from face to face. "I only knows about him 'cause he leaves his horse in the stables. Opens the door, calm as you please, and walks his horse in, ties it up, then he goes out and shuts the door. He'll be gone for a while—I can't rightly say for how long—but eventually, he'll come back, take his horse, and off he goes." Willie paused, then offered, "I thought I was dreaming him, first few times, but the droppings I found in the mornings meant he and his horse were real."

In a fascinated tone, Penelope asked, "And the man was here—or at least, left his horse in the stable—this past Saturday night into Sunday morning?"

Willie paused, thinking back. "Not last night, but the night before?" When Penelope nodded, Willie grinned. "Aye—he came that night."

"After her ladyship had returned to the house, obviously." Stokes scribbled madly, then shot a look at Willie. "When the man came, was it a long time after Wills and Cobb had put the horses away and gone?"

Willie wrinkled his nose. "Can't say, really, 'cause I'd fallen asleep. I'm almost always asleep when he comes."

"Have you ever seen him well enough to identify him?" Penelope asked. "Even if he doesn't light a lantern, there'd be moonlight some nights."

But Willie shook his head. "Nah. By the time I wake up and lift my head to look, all I ever see is his back, whether he's leaving his horse and going out, or taking his horse and riding away."

In an even tone, Barnaby asked, "Have you told Wills and Cobb about this man and his visits?"

"Oh, aye—I mentioned him right off, the first time. They thought I was bamming them the first few times, but once they saw the dung, they spoke with Jarvis, and they all decided it was something we didn't rightly need to make a fuss about. The gent never did any damage or made any bother, so there wasn't anything we needed to worry about." Willie shrugged. "He just uses our stable to shelter his horse. It's not a big thing."

Stokes exchanged looks with Barnaby and Penelope, then Barnaby looked at Willie and asked, "You say you've never seen him well, yet from the first, you've labeled him a gent. Why?"

Willie wriggled on the chair, then pulled a face. "Sort of the way he walks and his outline—the shape of his clothes."

"And, perhaps, the quality of his horse?" Penelope, her eyes on Willie, arched a cynical brow. "I find it difficult to believe you didn't—at least on one night—slip down and take a closer look at the man's horse."

Willie blushed and glanced at Stokes and Barnaby. When all they showed him was mild interest, he nodded. "Aye, I did, once. Fine beast he was, sixteen hands at least, with a glossy coat and good conformation."

"The saddle and bridle?" Stokes asked.

"Best quality," Willie replied, "but not new. Well-worn and comfortable, I'd say."

Stokes read what he'd written in his notebook, then raised his gaze to Willie's open and innocent face. "Thank you, Willie. You've been a great help. The gentleman who visits might have nothing at all to do with the missing emeralds, but you were right to tell us of him. That's exactly the sort of thing we need to know."

"And," Penelope said, bestowing a warm smile on Willie, "we'll make sure no trouble comes your way because you told us."

Willie bobbed his head. "Thank you, miss. Sirs." He looked at Stokes and Barnaby. "Can I go now? I need to muck out the stalls."

Stokes nodded, and Willie all but scampered out.

His expression unreadable, Barnaby tapped a finger on the table. "I think it's time we spoke again with the senior staff—all those whose business takes them above stairs."

Stokes grunted an assent and rose. "We'll see them all together and find out what they'll deign to tell us now."

Penelope, the light of battle in her eyes, led the way out.

Five minutes later, after a few words with Jarvis, she and Barnaby flanked Stokes as he stood at the head of the long table in the servants' hall and, slowly, let his gaze travel around the table, passing over the faces of the staff members summoned to stand about it.

This time, no one sat.

"As you're all aware, we've been endeavoring to assemble a list of all those who, for whatever reason, entered Lady Carisbrook's room between the time her ladyship returned there after her evening's entertainments and the time she raised the alarm regarding the emeralds' disappearance." Stokes glanced around the table again, then stated, "We originally had on our list Lady Carisbrook, Simpkins, Missy, and Miss Di Abaccio. We've now learned that we can add to that list Henry the footman, Mr. Franklin Carisbrook, Miss Julia Carisbrook, and possibly, an unknown gentleman who was known to be in the vicinity of the house at the time."

To a man and woman, the staff were now staring at the table, none of them willing to meet Stokes's eyes.

Stokes sent his weighty gaze around the bowed heads. "It appears I need to warn each of you that not volunteering information that might have bearing on a case such as this is, in itself, regarded as a crime. Obstructing justice is frowned on by the police force and the magistrates."

Several of those around the table stiffened.

From beside Stokes, Barnaby said, "Withholding information also risks unnecessarily prolonging the investigation, to the detriment of the Carisbrook family."

"And," Penelope added, her tone severe, "the longer the emeralds are missing, the less likely it is that they will be recovered."

Glances were shared around the table, then Jarvis cleared his throat and raised his head. "It appears, Inspector, that we have, perhaps, been somewhat less forthcoming than we might have been, but please understand that this is not a situation with which any of us are familiar."

Stokes inclined his head. "We appreciate that, which is why we've returned to clarify your statements in light of our more recent discoveries."

The tension around the table eased a notch. Others looked up, glancing at Stokes, Barnaby, and Penelope.

"Perhaps," Stokes said, studying his notebook, "we could start with Lady Carisbrook's summons to Mr. Franklin." Stokes glanced around the table. "Did Mr. Franklin respond and visit her ladyship in her room?"

Jarvis straightened to attention. "I can confirm that I sent Henry upstairs when her ladyship rang, but I didn't learn of the summons to Mr. Franklin until Henry returned downstairs."

Jeremy, the senior footman, cleared his throat. "I'd already gone to bed, but I couldn't sleep, so I came downstairs for a nightcap. I was on the back stairs going up again—this was after Henry returned and told us her ladyship had summoned Mr. Franklin to her room—and I saw Mr. Franklin in the corridor, heading toward her ladyship's room, but I can't tell you if he went inside."

Stokes was jotting. He nodded, then looked up. "Anyone else?"

Henderson pursed his lips, then said, "I was putting away some of his lordship's linen in his dressing room, and when I came out, I saw Mr. Franklin. He was walking away from her ladyship's door, heading toward his room." Briefly, Henderson met Stokes's eyes. "I didn't think anything of it."

Mildly, Stokes nodded. "Did you continue upstairs or return downstairs?"

"Upstairs," Henderson said. "I was on my way to bed."

Barnaby glanced at Jeremy. "Did you notice if Jeremy was back in his room?"

Henderson blinked myopically. "I can't say I noticed…no, wait. His door was shut—I remember that."

Jeremy was nodding. "I was in my bed by then—I heard you go past."

"How long would you say it had been," Penelope asked, "between when you saw Franklin in the corridor and the time Henderson passed your door?"

Jeremy frowned. "Ten minutes? Fifteen? Something like that. I was almost asleep."

Stokes nodded. He scanned his notes. "Good." He raised his head and looked around the table. "We now have a reasonably complete timeline of events up to Franklin Carisbrook leaving his mother's room." He paused, then asked, "To the best knowledge of everyone here, did anyone else venture into her ladyship's room prior to Missy, the tweeny, going in at six o'clock?"

He looked around, as did everyone else. No one spoke up, and no one looked even vaguely conscious.

"Right, then," Stokes continued, "that brings us to Miss Julia Carisbrook, who we now know was out of her bedroom at seven-thirty." Stokes surveyed the staff. "Does anyone have any information as to where she was?"

Abby, the upstairs maid, shifted nervously and cast a frightened glance up the table—toward Penelope rather than Stokes. "I was carrying towels up to the linen press—it's on the first floor close by the back stairs—and I saw Miss Julia leave her room, go down the corridor, and go into her ladyship's room." Abby paused; when no one criticized her, her confidence grew, and she earnestly added, "I've seen her do that before, about that time of a morning, so thought nothing of it." She glanced at Jarvis. "But I suppose I should have said."

"At least you've spoken now," Stokes said. "Do you know what time that was?"

Abby blinked and looked helplessly at Mrs. Jarvis. "I couldn't say, sir."

Mrs. Jarvis obliged. "It was nigh on quarter past seven when I sent you upstairs with the towels, so it'd be just after then."

"Thank you." Stokes looked at his jottings, then nodded. "That's very much better. We've covered the movements of all those we know to have been involved. Now"—he swept his gaze over the assembled staff—"we have one more potential player to account for. The mystery gentleman who occasionally leaves his horse in your stable." He paused to decide exactly how to phrase his question, then asked, "Did any of you see him, or hear anything, or gain any inkling at all that he was in this house that night?"

Silence fell. The staff looked at each other, but no one spoke.

Then Penelope said, "Can any of you be certain he *wasn't* in this house at some time during that night?"

Jarvis looked at her with something akin to relief. "No, ma'am—you've put your finger on our problem. None of us"—he gestured around the table—"have ever seen this gentleman either inside or outside the house. Only Willie has ever even glimpsed him. But it's simply impossible for us to say he wasn't here." Jarvis glanced around the table again, then said, "However, I believe the answer to the inspector's question is no. None of us saw or heard anything of any mystery man inside the house that night."

All the staff around the table looked at Penelope, Barnaby, and Stokes, agreement with that statement written on their faces.

Stokes noted it and nodded. "Very well. For the moment, that's all the questions we have." He tipped his head to Jarvis and Mrs. Jarvis. "Thank you for accommodating us."

Jarvis half bowed and came to accompany them to the front hall.

Once past the servants' door, Stokes halted in the lee of the stairs—just as the doorbell pealed. Jarvis excused himself and made for the front door. A second later, shrugging on his coat, Jeremy hurried past, on his way to assist Jarvis.

Barnaby and Penelope had halted with Stokes. While all three waited to see who had arrived, Barnaby murmured, "Our mystery gentleman is plainly intent on keeping his visits secret, and I suspect we can guess why, but it's perfectly possible he's visiting some other house along this row. The Carisbrook stables might simply be the most convenient in which to leave his mount."

"And"—Penelope pushed her spectacles higher on her nose—"if he truly wanted to conceal his destination, using a stable that belonged to another house might, from his point of view, also be wise."

Thinking of the staff's responses regarding the mystery gentleman, Penelope tried to remember what reaction Simpkins had had...and realized she couldn't recall seeing Simpkins around the table. But they'd asked for all the upstairs staff, so Simpkins should have been there. Penelope frowned and, in her memory, started working her way around the table, trying to locate the uppity dresser.

Jarvis had opened the door. Lady Carisbrook swept inside, with Julia trailing her.

The sight distracted Penelope; she remembered the questions they had for her ladyship. She grasped Barnaby's arm. "Why don't you two go and ask Lord Carisbrook about the emeralds while I tackle Lady Carisbrook."

She wasn't surprised to get no argument from either Stokes or Barnaby. Leaving them to find his lordship—who was no doubt ensconced in his study—she glided forward to do battle with her ladyship.

Julia had surrendered her bonnet to Jeremy and now hurried toward the stairs. Penelope got the impression Julia wanted to avoid her—that she was embarrassed, possibly over Cara's treatment. With nothing more than a regal nod, Penelope let Julia escape; she had bigger fish to fry.

The instant Lady Carisbrook had spotted her, her ladyship's lips had pinched, but as Penelope approached, Lady Carisbrook inclined her head, albeit with wary reserve. "Mrs. Adair."

"Lady Carisbrook. As you're aware, my husband and I are assisting Inspector Stokes with his investigation. We have a few questions, and it might be best were I to put them to you." Penelope allowed her lips to curve, but she wasn't actually smiling. "If we might appropriate your drawing room?"

Tight-lipped, Lady Carisbrook turned and led the way.

Penelope bestowed a smile on Jarvis as she passed him and, with a nod, indicated that he should close the door behind her.

Lady Carisbrook swept across the room to an armchair by the hearth and subsided into it with an agitated rustling of her skirts. Penelope opted to sink gracefully onto the sofa across from the armchair. The light from the windows at her back fell on Lady Carisbrook's face, illuminating every line and unforgivingly revealing every shift and nuance of expression.

Although she had met Lady Carisbrook in passing, this was the first time Penelope had conversed with her ladyship.

Her expression already peevish, Lady Carisbrook tugged at her gloves. "Has there been any progress in locating my emeralds?"

"I daresay there has been, but at this point, there are several other matters we feel it necessary to address."

Penelope had expected her ladyship to badger her further, but the look Lady Carisbrook threw her was…almost frightened. Surprised, Penelope replayed her words…and the notion that the mystery gentleman was her ladyship's lover—something they had all wondered, but had yet to articulate—took firmer hold.

Penelope hesitated, but then decided it would be to her advantage to capitalize on her ladyship's uncertainty. "Among other things, we need to know more about the emeralds themselves. We understand the set is very old. Is that correct?"

Her gaze locked on Penelope as if watching a potentially lethal snake, her expression wooden, Lady Carisbrook nodded. "I've been told that the parure was created in the sixteenth century."

Penelope inclined her head. "In that case, we'll need the name of the jeweler who last cleaned the set."

A scowl passed over her ladyship's face. "I'm afraid I can't help you. My husband insists on taking care of everything to do with the emeralds."

Penelope inwardly blinked; clearly, the care of the emeralds was a sore point. "Very well. To move on to the last known sighting of the emeralds—you returned to your room in the early hours of Sunday morning, removed the necklace and earrings, set them in their case, shut it, and left it on your dressing table."

When her ladyship nodded, Penelope asked, "Did you see—by which I mean, consciously lay eyes on—the case at any point thereafter?"

Lady Carisbrook frowned. After a moment, she stated, "No."

Smoothly, Penelope continued, "We understand that, subsequent to the time when you last sighted the jewel case, Simpkins was moving around your room until you dismissed her."

"Yes, of course."

"Then you called for a footman and dispatched him with a summons to your son and, subsequently, spoke with Franklin."

This time, her ladyship's agreement was significantly longer in coming, but eventually, she said, "Indeed. I spoke with my son for several minutes over matters of a personal nature arising from his behavior during the evening."

Penelope adopted an understanding smile. "We assume that, after your discussion with Franklin, you retired to your bed."

Somewhat to Penelope's surprise, a faint smile touched her ladyship's thin lips—more a lightening of expression than a true softening—then Lady Carisbrook responded, "Indeed."

"Moving on to the morning, the next person we have entering your room is the tweeny, Missy, who came in and lit the fire."

Lady Carisbrook, more confident now, inclined her head.

"And then, we understand that your daughter, Julia, came in to speak with you."

Lady Carisbrook blinked; it appeared she'd forgotten her daughter's visit. "Yes. She did. She asked about the day's engagements."

Penelope nodded. "And then, at eight o'clock, your niece Cara delivered your breakfast tray to you." Penelope opened her eyes wide. "It seems rather odd that your husband's ward should need to assist in a household such as this, but apparently, that was the case."

She felt not a single iota of guilt for the flush that suffused her ladyship's face. More, she waited, her unvoiced question hanging in the air, until Lady Carisbrook felt forced to acknowledge the point with a strangled "That's correct."

"I see." Penelope made sure her tone conveyed that she truly did see all. Then she straightened and briskly summarized, "From what we've ascertained and confirmed to this point, any one of seven people might have removed the jewel case containing the emeralds from your dressing table."

"Seven?" Lady Carisbrook looked taken aback.

"Indeed." Penelope ticked their potential suspects off on her fingers. "Simpkins, Henry, Franklin, Missy, Julia, and Cara." She waited while Lady Carisbrook took that in, then added, "And, of course, yourself."

Her ladyship's eyes flew wide. "What?"

Penelope allowed her lips to curve and rose. "You must have realized that accusing someone of removing a case of jewels from your room while you were present would mean that your own name would be on the list of suspects."

With that, she inclined her head. "Thank you for your time." She turned and glided to the door, but paused before she reached it and looked back to say, "Incidentally, although she no longer resides under this roof, you will, no doubt, be glad to hear that Miss Di Abaccio is presently in the company of Lady Guilfoyle and Lady Monk, who, I believe, are making arrangements to take Cara to the theater tomorrow night." She refrained from adding that, that evening, Cara would be sitting down to dinner with, among others, the Earl and Countess of Cothelstone.

She was too far away to make out the expression in her ladyship's eyes, but when, after a farewell dip of her head, she left the room and was closing the door, she thought she heard a muted screech.

Stokes and Barnaby were waiting in the hall. Stokes waved her to the front door, which Jarvis promptly opened.

"Anything?" Barnaby took her arm and steadied her down the steps.

"Nothing as to any jeweler," she replied, "but I did verify our list of suspects. Lady Carisbrook admitted all had been in her room—and she also confirmed that she has no firm recollection of the jewel case being on her dressing table after she set it there."

"That's useful." Stokes halted by her carriage.

He waited while Barnaby helped her in, then both men followed and sat, Barnaby beside her and Stokes facing them.

"So what did you learn from his lordship?" she asked. "Did he give you the name of the jeweler who last cleaned the emeralds?"

"No." Stokes looked less than impressed.

Barnaby leaned back. "He claimed that it had been so long since they were last cleaned that he couldn't remember, but that he would check to see if there was any mention of it in his accounts."

"And I checked with Bridge," Stokes said. "No one presently with the company has sighted the set, but Bridge confirmed that it should need cleaning about once a year."

She looked from Stokes's dour expression to her husband's severe one. "So the likelihood of the emeralds not actually being emeralds increases another notch."

Stokes grunted in agreement. "However, I still need to find the wretched things—the commissioner will expect a result, fake stones or not."

Barnaby made a derisive sound. "In a way, it's the principle of the theft—famous jewels taken from a house in Mayfair—rather than the actual damage done that the police are expected to address."

"As far as the emeralds are concerned, our hopes now rest with Roscoe," Stokes said. When Penelope looked her question, he explained he'd already sent a message.

"Well," she said, "if anyone can help you locate the set, it's Roscoe."

"On another note," Barnaby said, "we asked after Franklin—it would have been nice to speak with him—but apparently, he left late yesterday to stay with friends and isn't expected back until this evening." He shifted on the seat to better see Penelope's face. "What did you make of her ladyship?"

Penelope rapidly replayed her moments with Lady Carisbrook, then grimaced. "Hugo was right in calling her a pompous tartar, and Cara will do much better out from under her wing. But her reaction to my questions was curious." She met Barnaby's eyes. "I would take an oath there's more going on in that household than just a set of missing jewels."

After a moment of staring into Barnaby's blue eyes, Penelope pulled another face and admitted, "I sincerely hope that at the soirée this evening, we can manage to steer well clear of Lady Carisbrook. Being forced to exchange pleasant platitudes with such as she is guaranteed to ruin our evening."

CHAPTER 7

After waving Cara and Hugo off to a quiet family dinner with Hugo's and Barnaby's parents, Penelope and Barnaby grasped the chance of enjoying a quiet family dinner of their own—in the nursery, along with a smiling if sleepy Oliver.

When, eventually, after tucking their somnolent son into his cot, they headed down the stairs, Penelope glanced at Barnaby. "It's a pity we decided to attend this soirée. Given all that we learned today and what the others might have unearthed as well, having to wait another day before we can share our findings is…well, annoying."

Barnaby smiled. He closed his hand about one of hers and gently squeezed. "Impatient as always." She threw him a narrow-eyed look, which he pretended not to see. "Nevertheless, we need to hear Julia's version of events." A second later, he met Penelope's eyes. "It would be helpful if you could also draw her out on the other relationships in that family."

She arched her brows. "You're not planning to be there when I speak with her?"

He allowed his chagrin to show. "Sadly, no. She'll speak more freely to you alone." With another, this time fondly amused, look, he added, "Don't forget, you're a youngest daughter, too."

She widened her eyes. "You're right—I'd forgotten she and I share that distinction."

"Now I've reminded you, I'm sure you'll use it to our best advantage.

You might also ask her if Franklin's returned to town. He's another we need to catch up with."

"True." Penelope walked beside Barnaby into the back parlor, where they planned to while away the next hour or so until it was time to climb into their carriage and venture out on tonight's investigative foray. Absentmindedly strolling to her desk, she said, "I wonder if, as in many larger families, Julia, as youngest, will prove to be the quiet but observant type."

That hope was high in her mind when, two hours later, she and Barnaby walked into Lady Cannavan's drawing room, occasioning as intense a stir as Penelope had foreseen. She and Barnaby were both connected to many of the premier families in the ton, and their involvement in investigations over recent years had only increased the ton's interest in them. However, as neither was fond of the social whirl, they tended to appear only at events hosted by a select group of family and friends, thus denying the wider ton the opportunity to draw close and claim acquaintance.

Consequently, Lady Cannavan beamed as she welcomed them gushingly to her home and preened as, after exchanging the usual pleasantries, they walked into the large room to mingle with her other guests.

As Lady Cannavan was not one of the premier hostesses, Penelope had feared that she and Barnaby would know few of her ladyship's guests, but luckily, several of the Cannavan connections who had been prevailed upon to attend were nodding acquaintances; there were just enough of them to provide cover as she steered Barnaby on a circuit of the room.

They spotted Lady Carisbrook among the crowd, with Julia in her shadow, but passed by with nothing more than polite nods—receiving an exceedingly stiff acknowledgment from Lady Carisbrook in response.

Since marrying Barnaby, Penelope had mastered the art of appearing politely interested in all about her while inwardly pursuing quite different thoughts. As they passed between two groups of guests, she smiled at Barnaby and murmured, "This is going to be more difficult than I'd thought."

His expression deceptively mild, Barnaby replied, "Because Lady Carisbrook has chosen to bruit the loss of the emeralds far and wide?"

Penelope nodded, severe disapproval peeking through her gracious veil as she glanced between guests to where Lady Carisbrook was dramatically expostulating to an inquisitive circle of matrons and young ladies. "I suppose I should have guessed she would use the incident to make herself interesting. I just hope she has sense enough not to accuse Cara publicly—although I gather from Hugo she's already done that once, on the porch of St. George's, no less."

"Given the way the Adairs—and all our connections—are closing ranks around Cara, I don't believe you need to be overly worried on that score." Taking her elbow, Barnaby steered her on. "Instead, turn your mind to this—given that our connection to Stokes and investigations such as this is widely known, how are you going to approach Julia without drawing the attention of every last gossipmonger here?"

Drawing her gaze from the spectacle of Lady Carisbrook and her hangers-on, Penelope cast him a wide-eyed look. "Obviously, I'm not going to approach Julia at all—not openly." She cast one last glance at Julia, all but literally shrinking into her mother's shadow, then summoned a smile for the next knot of guests. "But the instant Julia heads for the withdrawing room, I'm going to have to move fast."

Understanding her intention, while Barnaby steered her through the guests, stopping here and there to chat, but sliding away before anyone could focus on their involvement in criminal investigations, he used his height to keep a distant eye on Julia Carisbrook. He fervently hoped that some distraction would magically occur to cover Penelope's necessary retreat; sadly, when the moment came and Julia slipped away from her mother's side, heading for the drawing room door, and no diversion offered, he swallowed a long-suffering sigh, nudged Penelope, then seized on a leading question from an older gentleman as to how he and Penelope spent their time these days to capture and hold the attention of everyone in their group by replying, "Well, our association with Inspector Stokes of Scotland Yard continues to prove…diverting."

Their history with Stokes and his investigations gave Barnaby plenty of fodder with which to entertain his now-eager listeners. Although doubtless they hoped he would move on to describing their current endeavors, they were nevertheless keen to hear of past investigations; sacrificing himself on the altar of distraction, he glibly related just enough to whet their appetites and keep all attention fixed on him while Penelope slipped away in Julia's wake.

In the hall outside the drawing room, Penelope found a footman who directed her to the withdrawing room; Julia Carisbrook wasn't the sort of young lady to have made for any other destination. Sure enough, Penelope found Julia seated in what appeared to be glum dejection on a stool in the room set aside for female guests. Glancing around and seeing only a supremely disinterested maid standing, eyes vacant, in a corner, Penelope thanked the gods for smiling on her enterprise and briskly walked forward; with a rustle of fashionable skirts, she sat on the stool facing Julia.

Julia blinked, then recognized Penelope. "Oh! You're Mrs. Adair." Animation returned to Julia's features. She leaned forward and asked, "Can you tell me anything of Cara? About how she's getting on?"

As with her father, Julia's concern was transparently genuine.

"Cara is well." Penelope paused, then added, "I suspect she's missing you and his lordship, and possibly Franklin as well, but Hugo Adair is… well, more or less courting her, so she has that to distract her."

"Oh." Julia sat back, but there was nothing beyond relief in her face. "I'm so glad. I know she's drawn to him. I hope she can…find her way to happiness."

But what of you? The words leapt to her tongue, but Penelope had sense enough not to utter them—at least, not yet. Instead, she said, "As you know, my husband and I are assisting Inspector Stokes in investigating the disappearance of your family's emeralds, and we need to clarify several points with you." The sounds of other ladies approaching reached Penelope's ears. "I rather suspect," she said, "that you'll be more comfortable answering our questions without your mother or anyone else looking on, so might I suggest"—she rose and urged Julia to her feet—"that we find somewhere a little more private in which to converse?"

Julia looked uncertain. "Mama will expect me back soon."

"She's rather absorbed talking to others at the moment, and this won't take long."

Julia seemed to come to a decision. "All right." She followed Penelope to the door, then waited with her while four other ladies, chatting gaily, entered the room. After following Penelope into the corridor, Julia asked, "Where should we go?"

No stranger to the layout of town houses, Penelope found a small parlor at the end of the corridor. It was unlit, but the curtains had been left wide, and sufficient light pooled on the window seat to make it a perfectly viable interrogation spot.

Once she and Julia were settled on the cushions, facing each other, Penelope said, "The first point we need to confirm is that on Sunday morning at about fifteen minutes past seven o'clock, you went to your mother's room to speak with her."

Julia blinked and nodded. "Yes. That's right. She…rarely tells me which events she's accepted invitations for. She likes me to come in and ask every morning, and then she tells me which gown to wear and whose attention I should try to engage."

Penelope already knew she disapproved of her ladyship's managing ways; she suppressed her instinctive reaction and asked, "Did you happen to see if the jewel case containing the emeralds was still on your mother's dressing table?"

Julia frowned, clearly wracking her memory, but then shook her head. "I can't say. I didn't look at Mama's dressing table—it's on the other side of the room to the bed."

Penelope nodded. She captured Julia's gaze and said, "You have to understand that, along with everyone else who ventured into your mother's room between the time she came home and when she raised the alarm, including your mother herself, you are on our list of suspects." When Julia recoiled, Penelope held up a staying hand. "That doesn't mean we're accusing anyone—merely that we have to look into what each of you did around that time. Apropos of that, after your mother accused Cara, I assume you stayed indoors until you went to church, and after you returned to John Street, you remained there until your papa arrived and Inspector Stokes and my husband and I appeared."

Clasping her hands in her lap, Julia nodded. "Yes, that's right."

Penelope fixed her with a direct look. "Do you have any notion of who might have taken the emeralds?"

"No!" Vehemently, Julia shook her head. "And it's quite wrong for Mama to have said Cara took them. Cara would no more have done that than I would. I mean, what use are the emeralds to us? We couldn't possibly want to wear such awful things, and neither of us would have any idea of how to sell them."

Penelope tipped her head in agreement.

Julia gripped her fingers tightly. "I should have spoken up—I know I should have. But Mama is so…" She grimaced and gestured.

"Indeed." It was hard to fault Julia for not standing up to her overbearing mother. Penelope rapidly reviewed what they knew, then asked, "We know your mother called your brother into her room after you all got home that night. We haven't yet had a chance to speak with him, but do you have any idea what that exchange was about?"

Julia looked reticent over speaking of her brother's affairs, but then her courage firmed, and she offered, "I don't think Franklin would mind me saying that Mama has strong views about which young ladies Franklin should be spending his time with."

"And Franklin hasn't been falling into line?"

Julia nodded. "I imagine Mama wanted to…upbraid him over that."

"I've met your mother. I suspect she would have made her point rather forcefully." When Julia didn't respond, Penelope went on, "Our final question concerns a mystery gentleman who leaves his horse in your family's stable on certain nights." She kept her eyes trained on Julia's face. "Do you know anything at all about him?"

Julia's expression blanked. Then she swallowed and shook her head. "No. I don't know anything about him."

But you know that he exists. Penelope frowned. She would swear Julia's words were not a lie. "How do you know—"

"I must go." Julia all but leapt to her feet. "I've been away from Mama for far too long."

Penelope quashed the impulse to seize Julia and wrestle her back down to the window seat.

Julia turned to flee, then paused and looked back. "Please—will you tell Cara that, of course, not one of us thinks she took the emeralds, and we're sorry Mama acted as she did, but Mama keeps us on a tight leash, so it's difficult to get away…" Julia gestured. "I wouldn't want Cara to think we're turning our backs on her."

Reading Julia's distress easily enough, Penelope inclined her head. "I'll pass the message on."

"Thank you." Julia whirled and hurried to the door.

Penelope watched her go, then, thinking over their recent exchange, followed more slowly.

Barnaby all but wilted with relief when Penelope returned to his side. He quickly brought his retelling of one of their old cases to an end—to the disappointment of the small crowd who had gathered about him—and when Penelope intimated that they needed to get on, he gladly took her elbow and steered her directly to their hostess.

They took their leave and, minutes later, sat wrapped in the comforting shadows of their carriage. As Phelps, their coachman, tooled the horses through the Mayfair streets, Barnaby glanced out at the passing streetscape, then turned to Penelope. "So what did you learn?"

She leaned companionably against his arm. "Several things." After a moment, she went on, "Just before I rejoined you, I spent a moment observing Lady Carisbrook. I saw Julia return to her mother's side, but her ladyship didn't really notice. That said, she noticed me."

Penelope paused, then said, "I'm getting the distinct impression that, in spite of all the lovely attention the theft of the emeralds is directing her way, Lady Carisbrook seems increasingly uneasy. I think she's genuinely anxious about the emeralds—the longer they're gone, the more she fears she might not get them back, and I suspect they mean a lot to her, not purely because of their monetary worth but as a social symbol she feels naked without. On top of that, I'm sure she never imagined that accusing Cara of the theft would result in such a fraught situation—one that has pitfalls for her. I would even go so far as to say she truly believed Cara had taken the emeralds—possibly because she couldn't imagine anything else. I wouldn't style her ladyship as an imaginative person."

Barnaby humphed. "She strikes me as the product of a rigidly conventional and antiquated upbringing."

"Indeed. But her ladyship aside…" In a few short sentences, Penelope outlined all she'd extracted from Julia, concluding with, "I know we have to consider the possibility that the mystery man visits some other house, rather than the Carisbrooks'. However, Julia knew of his existence before I spoke of him. I would stake my sapphires that our mystery man does, indeed, venture into the Carisbrook house, yet Julia was speaking the literal truth when she said she didn't know anything about him."

Barnaby grunted. "Another candidate to add to our suspect list."

The carriage slowed and drew up outside their house. Barnaby opened the door and handed Penelope down, and they walked into the warmth and soft lamplight of their front hall.

After surrendering her cloak and his greatcoat to Mostyn, hand in hand with Penelope, Barnaby climbed the stairs. As they always did on returning at night, they headed for the nursery to check on Oliver.

As usual, Barnaby propped his shoulder against the frame of the open door and watched Penelope as she leaned over their sleeping cherub and gazed down at Oliver with such naked love that it never failed to—just for an instant—stop Barnaby's heart.

He—and, he was quite sure, everyone else who knew her well—had wondered how Penelope would cope with motherhood. How she would juggle the demands of her eclectic but powerful intellect with the emotional and physical demands of being a mother. But she'd met every challenge and—to no one's real surprise—had triumphed in creating a fluid balance that satisfied all sides of her personality, the maternal as well as the intellectual.

Her success had supported his own interests, his own life's desires, on every plane. On oh-so-many levels, they were a perfect team.

Naturally enough, given their characters, now that they'd conquered thus far, they'd turned their minds to further expansion. To the next challenge.

They'd been flirting with the notion for several months.

When, with that glorious Madonna-like smile still illuminating her face, Penelope bent and pressed her usual goodnight kiss to Oliver's golden curls, then straightened and came to join Barnaby, he reached for her hand and stepped back from the doorway. He waited until she'd closed the nursery door, then, with her hand clasped in his, turned and walked with her along the corridor to the stairs that would take them to their bedroom on the floor below.

Neither said anything, not until they'd entered their room, shut the door, and Penelope had walked to stand before the uncurtained window. She looked out at the night, but Barnaby felt certain her mind remained in the nursery above.

He halted behind her, slid his arms about her slender waist, and drew her back against him. Bending his head, he pressed a kiss to her temple. "Should we have another child?"

They'd skirted the subject several times, but until now, he'd never been so blunt.

As usual, her mind seemed to be following the same track as his; she wasn't the least disconcerted.

After a moment, she replied, "I had wondered if there would be… well, room in our sometimes-busy lives. But here we are, once more immersed in an investigation, yet with all the people we've surrounded ourselves with—such excellent friends as well as excellent staff—we're managing almost without effort. Certainly with no extra or unexpected effort. On the domestic and familial fronts, everything's rolling along and falling into place as it should without any fuss or bother, much less strain. So yes."

She turned within his arms, raised hers, and draped them around his neck. She captured his gaze and said, "I really wasn't sure I—we—would ever get to this point, but Oliver is over two years old, and he's happy and contented, and I adore him and being with him, and you do, too." She continued in a rush, "And I do think he would like a brother or sister, and indeed, his life and ours won't be complete—or as complete as they might be—without another child."

Barnaby felt a rush of joy fill him and let it infuse his expression.

He watched as Penelope mentally stepped back—he could now follow the direction of her mind virtually without thought—as she considered again what she'd just said. She'd let her emotions speak, let her instincts and impulses guide her tongue, and now needed to take rational stock. But he was confident that would only strengthen her resolve—her commitment to, hand in hand with him, taking this next step toward enlarging their family.

Then she blinked, focused on his eyes, and smiled. "Oliver and his generation—any more we might be blessed with and all the others, too—stand at the heart of it, after all. They're the reason we do as we do."

Her smile was one of joy and decision, and she pressed closer, tightening her arms about his neck as she stretched up, offering her lips.

He bent his head and accepted her invitation, kissing her long and deep. Letting passion rise slowly, as they preferred, letting it swell and broaden and fill them.

They chose the route of established lovers, taking their time to savor, letting this moment, that caress, stretch, tightening their nerves notch by notch, ultimately building to dual climaxes that shattered their senses and stole their breaths and left them gasping, hearts thundering, minds fragmented, and souls united, irrevocably joined amid the rumpled sheets of their bed.

Later, when they'd recovered sufficiently to climb between the sheets and slump in each other's arms, Penelope murmured, "I might hope for a girl to even things up as Oliver grows older."

One palm gliding slowly, soothingly, up and down her spine, Barnaby thought, then offered, "A little girl like you..." Might be more than he could handle. "Another boy might distract him more."

"Hmm." Penelope settled her cheek on his chest. "A valid point. Luckily, it's not something we get to decide."

Barnaby realized that, now they'd embarked on their new venture, the jackpot of life was, one way or the other, going to make their lives even more interesting. Regardless... Smiling, he dropped a kiss on Penelope's curls, then relaxed into the pillows. "God willing, sometime in our future, we'll get to add another crib to our nursery."

And he would continue to see Penelope with her Madonna-like love shining in her face for many, many nights more.

~

A thunderous knocking on the front door jerked Barnaby from a deeply sated slumber. He half sat up, listening.

Beside him, Penelope blinked awake, then frowned. "That has to be Stokes."

Jaw setting, Barnaby tossed back the covers. "Something must have happened."

The sun had risen, the day had dawned, but it couldn't be that late.

Barnaby shrugged into his dressing gown while Penelope scrambled into a nightgown, then thrust her arms into a frilly peignoir. After belting his robe, he threw open the door and strode down the corridor with Penelope rushing after him.

James, their footman, was approaching along the corridor; he saw them coming and stepped aside. "Inspector Stokes, sir. With urgent news."

Barnaby nodded. He reached the head of the stairs and started down, Penelope on his heels.

Stokes was pacing like a tiger in the front hall; he looked up and saw them. Immediately, he said, "Simpkins—Lady Carisbrook's dresser—is dead."

"How?" Penelope demanded as she and Barnaby stepped onto the hall tiles.

"I don't yet know. Apparently, she was found on the back stairs with a broken neck." Stokes's gaze shifted from Penelope's face to Barnaby's. "But that's only half the excitement. The Carisbrook emeralds have reappeared."

"Good God." Penelope stared.

His expression showing satisfaction that they were as stunned as he, Stokes nodded. "Indeed."

Barnaby stirred. "Give us ten minutes, and we'll come with you."

"I don't have ten minutes to give, not if we want to preserve the scene." Stokes met Barnaby's eyes. "I'll go and hold the fort. Join me there."

With a crisp nod, Barnaby agreed. Stokes saluted him and strode for the door, which Mostyn was already opening.

Grim faced, Barnaby turned to see Penelope rushing back up the stairs.

Taking the stairs two at a time, he followed.

~

On reaching the Carisbrook residence, Barnaby and Penelope were immediately led by a stricken Jarvis to the first half landing on the back stairs. There, they found Stokes crouched over Simpkins's lifeless body.

Barnaby and Penelope climbed up. Leaving Penelope on the lower flight, Barnaby stepped carefully over Simpkins's splayed limbs onto the higher flight and looked down at the body.

After observing that Simpkins had fallen on her back, facing squarely up the stairs, and that her eyes were still open, staring straight ahead, Barnaby glanced at Penelope, then looked down the stairs to where Jarvis stood in the open doorway that connected the tiny foyer at the bottom of the stairs with the servants' hall. Many of the staff were clustered behind Jarvis, shock on every face.

Penelope took Barnaby's hint and turned and addressed Jarvis. "You may close the door. We'll call if we need you."

Jarvis bowed, faint relief in his face. "Yes, ma'am."

He shut the door. The stairwell was reasonably illuminated by light falling through a skylight high above. Penelope turned back to the body and Stokes. "Odd that she fell that way."

"Indeed." Stony faced, Stokes reached for Simpkins's head, which was propped at an angle fully perpendicular to her shoulders and spine. "The wall broke her fall—and the impact with it broke her neck." He grasped Simpkins's jaw and tried to move her head, but couldn't—not easily. "Rigor is already setting in." He shifted, raised Simpkins's hand, then bent her arm. "But it hasn't yet reached her extremities."

"So," Penelope said, "she died between approximately three and six hours ago."

Stokes nodded and rose. "It's reasonably cool in this stairwell, so I'd say at least five or six hours ago."

"The early hours of the morning." Barnaby met Stokes's eyes. "What was she doing on these stairs, fully dressed, at that hour?"

Stokes tipped his head. "That's one question we'll ask."

Penelope stepped up one more stair. She studied Simpkins's face, then looked up, past Barnaby, to the top of the steep flight of stairs. "She fell backward—straight back from the top of the stairs. She didn't try—or didn't have time—to grip the bannister or twist about, as she would have if she'd stumbled." She looked at Stokes. "Could she have been flung?"

Stokes grimaced. "That's possible, but I've checked under her nails, examined her hands and arms, and there's no evidence I can see that anyone touched her."

Barnaby, too, was wrestling with devising a scenario that would account for what he could see. "If she'd been struggling or fighting with someone, she wouldn't have fallen like that. It's as if she got to the top, then simply tipped back and fell." He glanced at Penelope. "What are the odds of a maid of her experience missing her footing and simply falling down the stairs?"

Penelope thought, then said, "If she'd stumbled and fallen, trying to save herself but failing, I might have accepted that as possible. But falling like this? It's hard to credit."

Stokes grunted, then waved them down the stairs. "That young tweeny, Missy, was the one who found the body. Let's have a quick word with her and leave her to recover."

Penelope turned and started to descend. Stepping off the last stair, she looked at Stokes as he joined her. "You said the emeralds had been found —were they on Simpkins?"

"No." Stokes met her eyes. "They were discovered by her ladyship in her room."

Penelope's eyebrows rose to significant heights. "Really?"

Stokes reached past her to open the door. "Obviously, we'll be reinterviewing her ladyship."

He opened the door and led the way into the servants' hall. Although plates and pans continued to rattle, most of the staff were either seated about the long table or standing uncertainly around it. All looked up as Stokes, Penelope, and Barnaby came to stand at the head of the table—just as they'd stood the day before. The memory popped into Penelope's mind and left her with another question she made a mental note to ask.

Mrs. Jarvis was sitting beside Missy, a motherly arm around her, and Abby, the upstairs maid, sat close on Missy's other side, patting the hand Missy wasn't using to dab at her reddened eyes.

Stokes glanced at Penelope. She read his plea and stepped forward. "This must have been a horrible shock for you, Missy." When the girl glanced up at her through tear-drenched eyes, Penelope let reassurance seep through her sympathy. "All we need you to do is tell us what you did this morning. What time did you get dressed?"

Missy stared at her, then hiccuped and whispered, "Just before six, ma'am. Then I came down the attic stairs—they reach the upper corridor just beside the top of the back stairs. I turned in to the back stairs…and then I saw her. I didn't know what to do. I just stared for a time, then I went back up to the attics and found Mr. Jarvis, ma'am."

Penelope shifted her gaze to Jarvis; he was standing behind his wife.

Jarvis cleared his throat and said, "Missy told me what she'd found, and I left her upstairs with Mrs. Jarvis. I took Jeremy, who was just getting up, with me and came down to see…"

Stokes shifted. "Did you—or anyone else—touch the body?"

Jarvis looked shocked. "No, Inspector…well, we didn't need to, it being so obvious she was dead."

Stokes nodded. "Good. So what did you do next?"

Jarvis explained how they had got Henderson up, and he had woken Lord Carisbrook, and after his lordship had come and—from the top of the stairs—viewed the body, his lordship had dispatched Henry to Scotland Yard.

The Yard had then sent to St. John's Wood to summon Stokes. To Penelope's mind, that accounted for the timing well enough.

"In coming down this morning," Barnaby said, "did any of you use the back stairs?"

"No, sir. None of us wanted…" Jarvis hauled in a breath and pulled himself together. "In the circumstances, we all used the main stairs."

"Very good," Stokes said. "So Simpkins is lying exactly as she fell—as she was when she was found by Missy, then viewed by Mr. Jarvis."

There were nods all around.

"Right, then." Stokes scanned the staff's faces. "We know Simpkins died in the small hours of the night. Yet she was fully dressed in what appear to be her usual clothes. Had she gone upstairs to bed and later got up or…?"

"No, sir." It was Mrs. Jarvis who spoke. "I was the last to see her last night. She was sitting there"—Mrs. Jarvis nodded to the other side of the table—"sipping a mug of cocoa as she often did. She was often the last up." Mrs. Jarvis paused to draw in a breath. "I left her sipping and went upstairs to bed—Jarvis had locked up and gone up ahead of me. I'd stopped to check on how much flour we had in the pantry."

Stokes was scribbling in his notebook. "You're sure everyone else—all the rest of the staff—were upstairs by then?"

"Yes, sir. I'm sure I was the last one up, barring only Simpkins."

Barnaby stirred. "I assume this was after all the family were abed?"

"Yes, sir," Jarvis said. "They'd all come in and gone to their rooms sometime before."

"Mr. Franklin returned as expected?" Stokes asked.

"Indeed, sir. He arrived just before dinnertime, sat down to the table with the rest of the family, then he went out again, but he returned a little after twelve, not long before her ladyship and Miss Julia, and went straight to his room. His lordship had gone out, too, but he'd already returned and retired by then."

Stokes nodded, finished writing, then looked around at all the staff. "From what each of you knows of the family's movements, do you all agree that was what happened?"

There were nods all around.

Stokes paused, then asked, "Did any of you come downstairs after Mrs. Jarvis had gone to bed, but before Missy came down in the morning? Even if you didn't see Simpkins?"

"No, sir" came from all directions, along with much shaking of heads.

Stokes slipped his notebook into his pocket. "Thank you. That's all for now—"

"Actually," Penelope said, "I have one minor question." She looked around at all the faces. "Yesterday, when we gathered here later in the afternoon after we'd interviewed you all separately, was Simpkins here?"

Frowns abounded.

Jarvis ventured, "She should have been."

Hesitantly, Polly, Julia's maid, put up her hand. When everyone looked at her, she swallowed and said, "I think…that is, I know that Simpkins stayed upstairs. Jeremy came and told us to come down, but when I looked into her ladyship's room, Simpkins said she had better things to do. She didn't come down."

Stokes glanced at Penelope and arched a brow.

She gently nudged him toward the door and nodded to Polly. "Thank you."

Stokes looked at Jarvis. "The men from the morgue should be here shortly. If you would keep everyone else away from the stairwell, they'll remove the body with as little fuss as possible."

"Thank you, Inspector." Jarvis turned to his troops and clapped his hands. "Come now, everyone. We still have a household to run."

Penelope led the way up the steps, along the short corridor, and into the front hall. She paused in the lee of the stairs. Barnaby halted beside her.

Joining them, Stokes asked, "What was that about Simpkins?"

"She wasn't there when we asked about the mystery gentleman."

Penelope narrowed her eyes. "While everyone else vowed they had never seen him—and we believed them—Simpkins didn't say any such thing."

"Ah." Barnaby nodded. "I see."

"Hmm." After a moment, Stokes shook himself. "We need to speak with his lordship. I assume he'll be in his study."

They set off to cross the hall, but as they passed the foot of the stairs, they heard heavy, ponderous footsteps descending and turned to see Lady Carisbrook coming down.

They halted, surprised by the signs of shock and sadness that ravaged her ladyship's normally haughty and reserved countenance. She looked haggard and had plainly been crying; she clenched a bunched handkerchief in one hand.

She saw them and gestured weakly with the jewel case she held in her other hand. "I found them." She dragged in a breath and continued to descend. "They were in my dressing table drawer. I don't often open it and hadn't thought to look..." On a weak sigh, she concluded, "They must have been there all along."

Penelope cast a sharp glance at Stokes, then stepped forward to meet her ladyship at the bottom of the stairs. She held out a hand. "Could we see?"

Without so much as a blink, Lady Carisbrook surrendered the jewel case—a black-velvet-covered case exactly as described. "I was just bringing them down so Humphrey could put them back in the safe." As Penelope opened the case, her ladyship gustily sighed again. "Such a wretched end for Simpkins." Her voice quavered as she added, "I'm sure I don't know how I'll go on without her."

With that, Lady Carisbrook retreated behind her handkerchief.

Barnaby stepped up to look over Penelope's shoulder at the necklace and earrings neatly displayed on a bed of black silk. They were, as Cara had intimated, quite hideous—the settings overly large and ostentatiously ornate.

Penelope raised one hand and wiggled her fingers. Under her breath, she murmured, "The loupe. I saw you slip it into your pocket."

Barnaby swallowed a grunt. He glanced at Lady Carisbrook, then looked farther up the hall at Jarvis and Jeremy, who had emerged to take up their usual stations. "Perhaps," Barnaby said, "we should repair with her ladyship to the drawing room."

Penelope followed his gaze to Jarvis and Jeremy and nodded. "Yes. Perhaps we should."

Stokes signaled to Jarvis. "Please inform his lordship that we'll await him in the drawing room."

Jarvis bowed and headed for the study. Jeremy went to open the drawing room door.

With another sigh, Lady Carisbrook stumped off the stairs and led the way. Still carrying the emeralds, Penelope followed, with Barnaby beside her and Stokes bringing up the rear.

Lady Carisbrook made for her usual armchair and slumped into it. Penelope sat on the sofa, laid the open jewel case in her lap, and held out her hand to Barnaby.

He dug in his pocket, pulled out his jeweler's loupe, and dropped it into her palm.

Penelope lifted the emerald necklace from its bed, put the loupe to her eye, and examined several of the stones. After laying the necklace in her lap, she examined first one earring then the other, before handing necklace, earrings, and loupe to Barnaby.

She looked at Stokes, but didn't say anything.

Barnaby carefully examined several stones in the necklace, then raised his head and met Penelope's eyes. They exchanged a long look, then Barnaby slipped the loupe back into his pocket and glanced at Stokes before transferring his gaze to Lady Carisbrook. "I'm sorry to be the bearer of further bad tidings, Lady Carisbrook, but these stones are not, unfortunately, emeralds at all."

"What?" Lady Carisbrook rocked back in her chair; her eyes widened until they resembled saucers. "What did you say?"

Barnaby handed the necklace to Penelope, who set it into the case. "The stones, as such, are crystals. Not paste, but also definitely not emeralds."

"But...but..." Stupefied, Lady Carisbrook stared at them.

Stokes frowned at Penelope and Barnaby. "So were the jewels stolen, the emeralds switched for fakes, and then the jewels put back?"

Penelope arched her brows. "And was the act of the jewels being returned in any way linked to Simpkins's odd death?"

Barnaby inclined his head. "Good point."

"Odd death?" Lady Carisbrook was struggling for breath. "What was odd about it? I thought it was an accident."

Her ladyship's voice had risen to a pitch that threatened imminent hysterics.

Stokes—along with Penelope and Barnaby—was relieved when the door opened and Lord Carisbrook, followed by Franklin and Julia, walked in.

While shock and worry showed in all their faces, Simpkins's death had clearly not affected them to anywhere near the same degree as it had Lady Carisbrook.

"What's that?" Lord Carisbrook stumped to a halt beside Stokes. "Surely, Inspector, Simpkins's death was an accident. I thought it obvious that she'd fallen down the stairs."

Stokes inclined his head. "She did, sir, but one has to ask why she fell. Until we can answer that to the coroner's satisfaction, we can't declare the cause of death."

"Ah." Lord Carisbrook nodded. "I see. You need to cross your t's and dot your i's. Just so."

Penelope chose that moment to shut the jewel case; it closed with a distinctive *snap*, drawing Lord Carisbrook's gaze.

His lordship's face cleared. "Ah—found the bally things, did you? Where were they?"

Penelope glanced at Lady Carisbrook, but her ladyship was still grappling with her emotions. Leaning forward, Penelope handed the jewel case to his lordship. "We understand her ladyship found the case in the drawer in her dressing table."

Lady Carisbrook gestured weakly. "They must have been there all the time."

"No," Stokes said. "They weren't." When the Carisbrooks all looked his way, puzzlement in their faces, he went on, "We searched her ladyship's room on Sunday afternoon, and at that time, the case wasn't in that drawer nor anywhere else in this house."

Penelope watched all four Carisbrooks blink, their expressions displaying varying degrees of confusion.

Stokes and Barnaby were watching closely, too. At Barnaby's nod, Stokes went on, "Given the sequence of events, we must now entertain the possibility that the jewels were stolen, the stones replaced with fakes, and that the jewels being subsequently returned to her ladyship's room in some way led to Simpkins's death."

Absolute silence and looks of muted horror greeted Stokes's statement.

After several moments of staring silence, Lord Carisbrook breathed, "Good Lord." He blinked, then focused on Stokes. "You can't be serious."

Stokes dipped his head. "Unfortunately, my lord, that's one avenue we will now need to pursue. It may, of course, come to nothing."

Lady Carisbrook shook her head. "I can't think…"

Julia shifted and, without a word, sank onto the end of the sofa opposite Penelope.

Lord Carisbrook glanced at Julia, then at his wife, then turned to Stokes and Barnaby. "This is all so shocking, Inspector—not at all what we expected on waking this morning, even with the news of Simpkins's demise." He gestured with the jewel case. "The jewels turning up, then the emeralds being fakes, and now this connection to Simpkins falling…" He blew out a breath, then shook his head as if he'd run out of words.

Penelope glanced at Lady Carisbrook, then at Julia, and last of all at Franklin, who had remained a few feet behind his father, but looked equally stunned and all at sea. Penelope caught Barnaby's gaze and rose. "We'll leave you, my lord." With an inclination of her head, she farewelled her ladyship. "You've all had a shock—several shocks—and have much to take in."

Lord Carisbrook shook himself to attention. "Yes…yes. Thank you, Mrs. Adair. It's all…" His lordship gestured with one hand, then let it fall. "Overwhelming."

Penelope led the way from the room. After murmuring their good-byes, Barnaby and Stokes were quickly on her heels. The three exited the house and walked toward where the Adairs' carriage waited.

They'd just reached it and paused, intending to confer, when the patter of running footsteps had them looking south along the pavement.

A loping figure raced toward them. Barnaby recognized Davies, one of the runners from the Yard.

Davies pulled up, snapped off a salute along with a grin, and handed Stokes a folded note. "Arrived first thing at the station, sir. Sergeant Wilkes said as you'd want to see it straightaway."

Stokes unfolded the note, scanned the contents, then looked at Davies. "My thanks to Wilkes and to you as well. You can return to the station." He nodded a dismissal, and with another grin, Davies turned and took off again, his very long legs eating up the yards.

"Who's it from?" Penelope asked the instant Davies was out of earshot.

"Jordan Draper, Roscoe's right-hand man," Stokes replied, "in response to Montague's request regarding who to ask about stolen emeralds."

Penelope frowned. "But we have the emeralds back...except they're now fakes, so we still need to speak to those in the underworld about the Carisbrook emeralds."

"Indeed, we do." Stokes folded the note and slipped it into his pocket.

"And?" Imperiously, Penelope made a "keep talking" gesture.

Stokes glanced at Barnaby, but knew better than to attempt to refuse. "Jordan suggests we speak with a certain Gentleman George, who at ten-thirty sharp, we'll find waiting to speak with us on a bench in Chatham Square."

Barnaby slid his hands into his coat pockets. "That's at the northern end of Blackfriars Bridge—on the edge of the jewelers' district."

Stokes kept his gaze on Barnaby and arched his brows. "Coming?"

"Of course." Barnaby—along with Stokes—looked resignedly at Penelope.

To Barnaby's surprise, his wife continued to frown in an absent-minded fashion. Eventually, he asked, "Are you going to come with us?" He couldn't imagine she would turn down the chance of meeting the sort of high-class jewelry fence Roscoe would have steered them to, especially given the item to be discussed was the Carisbrook emeralds.

Penelope refocused on Barnaby's face, then grimaced and proved she could still surprise him. "I would love to, of course, but I have a previous engagement that I believe I must keep."

Both he and Stokes blinked at her.

Airily, she waved them off. "I'll have to leave Gentleman George to you, and having remembered that engagement, I really must be off." She looked up at their coachman. "Home, Phelps."

Stokes recovered from his shock and leapt to open the carriage door.

Barnaby dutifully helped her inside.

She sat, and still amazed, he shut the door, stepped back, and nodded to Phelps.

Barnaby and Stokes stood side by side and watched the carriage drive off.

After several seconds, Stokes rumbled, "Not even for a villain named Gentleman George?"

"Apparently not."

"Do you know where she's off to?"

"No, I don't." Turning to Stokes, Barnaby shook his head. "I'm relieved on the one hand, while on the other, I'm not reassured in the least."

CHAPTER 8

Several hours later, with the sun nearing its zenith, Penelope strolled the lawns of the Hestley estate, which lay down along the river toward Richmond.

She was feeling exceedingly virtuous, her metaphorical halo gleaming. In order to facilitate the budding romance between Hugo and Cara, she'd given up the chance to meet a criminal fence by the name of Gentleman George; she felt sure such a sacrifice would make her mentors proud and place the entire Adair family in her debt—if they ever heard of it.

Sadly, she wasn't about to breathe a word about consorting with villains—much less one called Gentleman George—to any but her trusted co-investigators.

Nevertheless, warmed by an inner glow, she glided over the sward with her parasol tipped at precisely the right angle above her head.

Lady Hestley was rather younger than Penelope had supposed, and those invited to her ladyship's al fresco luncheon were much of an age with Cara. Although Penelope had yet to celebrate her twenty-seventh birthday, as Cara's chaperon, she found herself relegated to the company of the other duennas, many significantly older than she.

Regardless, buoyed by the sense of doing her duty, she kept her social smile in place and consented to listen to the older ladies' comments while, along with the other younger folk, Cara and Hugo chatted, laughed, and transparently enjoyed themselves.

Eventually, one matronly lady, a Mrs. Makepeace, leaned closer to Penelope and inquired, "Who is that lovely young lady you're watching over, dear?"

Penelope smiled. "She is lovely, isn't she? Her name is Miss Cara Di Abaccio—she's Lord Carisbrook's niece and his lordship's ward."

"Oh! The Carisbrooks." Mrs. Makepeace smiled indulgently. "I know Mr. Franklin Carisbrook quite well. He's often at events such as this, although he isn't among her ladyship's guests today."

"I see." Penelope's instincts were twitching. She cast around, then ventured, "I haven't had much to do with Franklin Carisbrook, but, of course, Cara is his cousin."

Mrs. Makepeace nodded. "In that case, I'm sure Franklin will be wanting to introduce Miss Di Abaccio to his intended—Miss Lilibeth Ives. Miss Ives is a close friend of my charge, Miss Heather Byrnes, so, of course, we've all watched the romance unfold. So very affecting. We're all agreed"—Mrs. Makepeace's wave included all the gossiping chaperons—"that it's definitely a case of true love."

"Indeed?" Slowly, Penelope nodded. "I can certainly see how that might be." And she truly could. She pushed up her spectacles and looked around. "Is Miss Ives here today?"

"No, sadly, the Iveses had a prior engagement, and Franklin wasn't expected, either…" Mrs. Makepeace lightly shrugged. "But Lilibeth is a quite unexceptionable young lady—her father is one of the curators at the British Museum, you know, and her mother was a vicar's daughter. Although Heather—my niece—is a sunny, good-natured girl, Lilibeth has a degree of quiet strength as well as a sort of beauty that is very restful. One can easily see why she caught Franklin's eye."

Penelope glanced at Mrs. Makepeace, then at the other ladies avidly talking around them. "Am I to take it that, in general, the match is viewed as appropriate by all those here?"

"Oh, indeed, my dear Mrs. Adair." Mrs. Makepeace smiled as sunnily as her niece. "We're all waiting to hear that Franklin and Lilibeth have set a date for their wedding." Mrs. Makepeace leaned closer and lowered her voice conspiratorially. "Heather told me that Franklin has already spoken to Mr. Ives, and the Iveses couldn't be happier. All that remains is for Franklin to gain his father's approval, and as Franklin is his lordship's second son—and with his older brother married with sons of his own—no one imagines there'll be any great difficulty there."

Mrs. Makepeace straightened. "We're all looking forward to hearing wedding bells."

Penelope managed to keep her smile appropriately bright and encouraging, even while, inside, all she could think was: *Oh, Franklin. What a battle you've taken on.*

Yet as the afternoon wore on, more and more snippets of information and observation slipped into place—into the mental jigsaw she was forming of what had gone on and was still going on in the Carisbrook household.

She chatted and idly exchanged comments while, with the other chaperons, she followed their charges down to stroll along the riverbank—and all the while, her mind churned as she remembered the discussion Lady Carisbrook had forced on Franklin, and Julia's comment about Franklin's refusal to look at the young ladies his mother pushed his way, and that Franklin had gone on Sunday afternoon to visit a friend's family in Richmond and had stayed overnight.

What odds he had visited the Iveses?

Penelope refocused on Hugo and Cara as, several yards ahead, they laughed, talked, and less and less shyly, responded to each other—and, Penelope knew, shared their hopes and dreams. This was what courtship should be, and while in her own case, she had never needed any encouragement, not all young ladies were as confident and self-driven as she, and not all gentlemen were as single-minded as Barnaby.

Some young ladies and gentlemen needed encouragement—needed to be given a nod and a smile and the chance to find happiness.

Lady Carisbrook, Penelope suspected, didn't understand that, or if she did, had shut her mind to the concept and, instead, had embarked on a quest to manage her children's lives for her own social gain.

As Penelope stood and watched love unfold between Hugo and Cara, she acknowledged the significance of what her mentors had always maintained: that this, too, was a part of her duty—hers as much as it was theirs—to foster the relationships that, as the years rolled on, would strengthen their families by laying down the bedrock on which those families stood.

Love was that foundation—that true bedrock of family life.

Apparently, Franklin Carisbrook had found his way to that realization without his parents' help.

The question that thought left Penelope facing sent a chill sliding through her. Did Franklin's pursuit of love have anything to do with the missing emeralds and Simpkins's death?

~

It was past four o'clock in the afternoon before Barnaby and Stokes finally ran the individual known as Gentleman George to earth. Their original directions to the bench in Chatham Square had proved to be only the first in a series of steps that, ultimately, had brought them into the East End, to the Bully Boy tavern off Stepney Green.

Impatience riding him, Stokes led the way inside. Barnaby followed. They stopped just inside the door and scanned the dimly lit space, then Barnaby spotted the man they'd been told would be waiting; he was unmistakable, being close to the size of two men combined, and was seated on a bench in the front corner.

Barnaby nudged Stokes and, with his chin, directed his friend's gaze. "Gentleman George, at last."

Stokes looked, grunted, and headed toward the table behind which George sat. Stokes pulled out a chair and sat opposite. Barnaby drew out the second chair and set it a trifle farther back and to the side—allowing him to keep a watchful eye on the rest of the tavern's patrons.

George noticed and smiled faintly. "No need to be on guard—no harm will come to you while you're with me."

Despite it being a tavern, George wasn't drinking. In the circumstances, neither Stokes nor Barnaby wanted a drink, either, and the barmaid, after one glance their way, didn't bother to approach.

"So now, I've been told I oughta help you gents with your inquiries." George looked at them through surprisingly clear hazel eyes. "So let's have your questions, then."

Without further ado, Stokes said, "We want to know about a certain set of jewelry—a necklace and earrings, in gold, and set with large rectangular emeralds."

George nodded. "Thought it might be that."

Stokes arched his brows. "You know of them?"

George eyed Stokes for a full minute, then glanced at Barnaby, before returning his gaze to Stokes's face. "Roscoe's requests ain't ones to turn down, so I reckon it can't hurt to tell ye that a party came to see me Sunday—late afternoon, it was. Later than this. The gent said as he was wishful of pawning the emeralds in that bloody great necklace, and the earrings, too."

Stokes drew out and unfolded Cara's sketch of the parure. "These the ones?"

George took the sketch, glanced at it, and nodded. "Good likeness. Yes, that's them." He handed the sketch back and looked at Stokes. "But the stones were already fake."

Stokes opened his mouth, and George pointed a finger at him. "Don't ask me if I'm sure. I've been in this business since before you was born, and those stones…they were pretty much the best fakes I've ever seen, but fakes they were." George sat back. "I told the gent straight up I could offer him something for the gold, but the stones were near worthless."

"You gave the necklace back?" Barnaby asked.

George nodded. "Not much use to me—it'd have to be melted down as it was."

"And this gent took it back," Stokes said.

"Aye—he was shocked to begin with. Shocked to his back teeth, I'd say. But once that wore off and he accepted I knew what I was telling him, he was right cast down. You could see it clear as day—written all over his face."

Stokes glanced at Barnaby, then looked back at Gentleman George. "I don't suppose this gentleman gave you a name?"

George laughed. "Nah—they never do."

Stokes nodded. "In that case, can you take a stab at describing him?"

Barnaby wished he'd had Cara do sketches of all the males in the Carisbrook house. Sure enough, as George's description unfolded—dark hair, pale complexion, a gentleman's clothes but not showy, medium height, medium build—it became increasingly clear that the so-called gent could have been any one of a thousand such gentlemen in London.

When George finished, Stokes stared at the fence, then in a resigned tone, asked, "Would you be willing to identify the man—to pick him out of a line of several men?"

George shook his head. "Not even for Roscoe will I do that—very bad for business, you see."

Stokes sighed and nodded.

"One more thing you might be able to tell us," Barnaby said, "given your undoubted expertise."

George showed his teeth.

Barnaby grinned back and asked, "Can you give us any indication of how long ago the fake stones were put into the necklace?"

George blinked. He frowned, then stared at the scarred tabletop and sucked his teeth. After several long minutes, he raised his head and looked at Barnaby. "Just my opinion, mind, but from the look of how settled the stones were in the setting—which is an indication of how long they've been undisturbed—combined with the type of crystals used, I'd say the fakes were put in some years back. Possibly six or more years ago."

Barnaby and Stokes exchanged glances, then Barnaby inclined his head to George. "Thank you. Despite not being able to help us with identifying the gentleman, you've nevertheless been a great help."

George looked curious, but curbed the impulse to ask questions and just nodded. But as Barnaby and Stokes pushed back their chairs and rose, George said, "Seeing as I've been such a help to you, it'd be a help to me if you'd pass on your satisfaction to Roscoe—just to let him know I held up my end. Never hurts to stay on his good side."

Stokes's lips curved wryly. "Done. We'll pass on a few good words."

Barnaby tipped a salute George's way and followed Stokes out of the tavern.

They paused on the pavement, and Stokes met Barnaby's eyes. "So the emeralds have been fakes all along—that puts quite a different slant on things."

Sobering, Barnaby nodded. "It does, indeed, and in more ways than one."

They gathered in Greenbury Street that evening, with everyone bubbling with something to tell. Stokes and Barnaby were the last to arrive; at six o'clock, they walked in to discover their wives and Montague on the floor, playing a rowdy game with Oliver and Megan with Martin smiling and babbling, looking on from the safety of Violet's lap.

Having halted in the doorway to take in the view, Stokes and Barnaby, both grinning, went forward to join the fray.

Their wives surrendered their positions, retreating to sit on the sofa and an armchair and smile indulgently on their husbands' antics.

After a moment, Griselda sat back and looked at Penelope. "Where are Hugo and Cara this evening?"

Penelope smiled smugly. "Before I left, I saw them off to Hugo's sister's house for dinner with her family, along with the family of one of his other sisters, and then the adults are making up a party to go to the theater."

Violet exchanged a glance with Griselda, then asked, "Is there likely to be any…well, nastiness, given Lady Carisbrook's regrettably public accusation against Cara? I imagine there are many who've heard her ladyship's views by now."

Penelope inclined her head. "Undoubtedly, but I suspect the majority who've heard of the emeralds' disappearance are awaiting further confirmation—her ladyship isn't well regarded. But with the ton in mind, this afternoon, I sent word to the Adairs—all of them in town—that the necklace had been returned to the Carisbrooks' house overnight, and as Cara has been with us constantly throughout, there's no possibility that she had had any hand in that."

Her eyes gleaming behind her spectacles, Penelope stated, "I believe that news will be taken as permission for the family to forge ahead in their quest to encourage Hugo and see him appropriately settled. Cara's the first young lady he's shown any real interest in, and the family has quite taken to her. His mother is delighted and, along with his sisters, is busily engineering Cara's acceptance into the ton. If Hugo fails to come up to the mark, it won't be for lack of familial support."

Griselda laughed. "It sounds as if poor Cara won't know what's hit her."

Violet smiled. "When I was chaperoning them yesterday, I got the impression Cara's greatest difficulty is believing her luck."

"Speaking of luck"—Penelope jiggled her knees—"I gather we've all been visited to some degree. It sounds as if we've a lot to share."

"You're right, and time's getting on." Griselda glanced at the men and the children, then rose and crossed to the bellpull.

The nursemaids arrived and took the children, now flagging, off to be tucked up to sleep. The three men rose and settled into armchairs, then at Penelope's suggestion, Stokes summarized what he'd learned since they'd met on Sunday evening—his visit to Rundell, Bridge, and Company, his detour to Montague's to send a request to Roscoe, then the gist of what he, Barnaby, and Penelope had stumbled on during their interviews with the Carisbrook staff.

"A mystery man who might be wandering around at night and who no one there has actually seen…" Violet widened her eyes. "It's the stuff of Gothic novels."

Stokes grunted. "That's something I could do without. Nevertheless…" He continued, detailing the events of their morning's summons to the Carisbrook residence, where they'd found Simpkins dead and the jewels returned to her ladyship's dressing table drawer. "There's no evidence either way to say whether Simpkins was pushed or simply missed her footing and fell, although with a maid of her experience…it's stretching credulity to say she stumbled and somehow fell backward in the way she did—falling straight back down the stairs. And then the emeralds turned up in a place in which we know they hadn't been thirty-six hours before, and on top of that, the stones were fake."

Griselda frowned. "Did the family—any of them—react oddly to being told the emeralds weren't genuine?" She looked from Stokes to Barnaby, then at Penelope.

Barnaby shook his head. "Not oddly enough to point to. I would have said all were shocked and stunned by the news."

He glanced at Penelope, who nodded. "They were…flummoxed. We didn't get anything useful from them."

"So," Montague said, "were the emeralds already fakes, or were they stolen, replaced by fakes, and the necklace returned?"

"And was Simpkins falling to her death on the same night the jewels turned up again a coincidence or linked?" Violet said.

Stokes shifted. "I don't like coincidences at the best of times. Regardless of the lack of evidence of foul play in Simpkins falling, I'd take an oath the two have to be linked in some way—that the jewels going missing and Simpkins's death will prove to be connected."

"I concur." Barnaby looked at the others. "Subsequently, Stokes and I followed Roscoe's lead and learned several interesting things about the emeralds and where they've been."

"And I," Penelope declared, "went to a garden party near Richmond and—entirely unexpectedly—learned that Franklin Carisbrook is leading something of a social double life."

Stokes and Barnaby both focused on her, but before they could speak, Penelope waved at Griselda, Violet, and Montague. "But before we get to what we learned today, we should catch up with the information you three have managed to ferret out."

Violet and Griselda exchanged a look, then Violet reported, "Griselda and I went to visit Madame Renee, the modiste in Bruton Street who has supplied gowns to Lady Carisbrook and her daughters for many years."

"I've known Renee since we were girls," Griselda said, "and when we asked whether she'd ever had reason to suspect that the Carisbrooks were short of funds, she told us of a time eight years ago when her ladyship had her two older daughters on her hands at the same time and was somewhat desperately trying to get them wed."

Violet eagerly added, "According to Renee, her ladyship was entertaining lavishly, too—and she had that from Lord Carisbrook himself, when he came to see Renee about her ladyship's bills—"

"Which," Griselda triumphantly stated, "he was having difficulty paying!"

Violet looked at Montague. "His lordship approached Madame Renee, and they agreed on a schedule to pay off the debt. Renee said his lordship adhered to the plan, and the debt was paid off as arranged."

"She had nothing but good to say of his lordship," Griselda added, "but her view of Lady Carisbrook is no more favorable than the others we've heard."

"And how is Lady Carisbrook's spending now?" Penelope asked.

"Apparently, she's still profligate over her own gowns," Griselda replied. "Renee said she orders gowns more frequently than any of her other ladies. But that's all for herself—she isn't spending on Julia as she did with her elder daughters."

Penelope arched her brows cynically. "From what I've seen of her, Julia Carisbrook would still rank as well turned out."

Montague had been staring at the carpet and tugging at his lower lip. Penelope and Violet both regarded him fondly, then Penelope prompted, "Clearly, Montague, you've something to report."

He looked up, blinking, then smiled somewhat sheepishly. "Indeed. I was testing whether Violet's and Griselda's information fits, and I think it does. I had a chat—purely social, so to speak—with his lordship's man-of-business. I gather that the Carisbrook estate has always been...modest is the word that springs to mind. The family has always scraped by—they've had just enough, but extravagances were beyond their reach."

Stokes grunted. "That doesn't fit well with Lady Carisbrook's activities eight years ago."

"No, indeed." Montague went on, "The family has no meaningful debts, but the estate also has no accumulated capital—no investments. They rely on the income from the estate itself, and that's been the case for decades. As far as his lordship's man was aware, there's never been an issue—not since his lordship came into the estate on his father's death more than twenty years ago."

"Hmm." Penelope pushed her spectacles up on her nose. "Correct me if I err, but what his lordship's agent has confirmed is that any excessive spending would have—should have—plunged the Carisbrook estate into a debt the estate wouldn't have been able to pay off."

Montague nodded. "Given there was no extra income at any time over the years, that would be my supposition, too."

Violet said, "But we know Lady Carisbrook ran up monstrous bills that his lordship couldn't pay."

"So," Barnaby said, "where did his lordship get the funds to cover his wife's debts?"

Stokes frowned. "It's tempting to assume he sold the emeralds and used the cash for that purpose." He glanced at Montague. "I'm assuming Lord Carisbrook's man-of-business would have known nothing of that?"

Montague nodded. "No reason his lordship couldn't have accomplished such a sale without anything showing up anywhere, financially speaking." He glanced at Griselda and Violet. "In such cases, the only firm evidence would come from suppliers with bills paid that the estate shouldn't have been able to meet."

"Quite," Barnaby said. "And that the emeralds in the Carisbrook parure were replaced with fakes eight years ago matches what Stokes and I—eventually—learned from Roscoe's Gentleman George. Even more to the point, George was the fence approached on Sunday, late in the afternoon, by a gentleman hoping to sell the Carisbrook emeralds."

"George had to disappoint them both—himself as well as the gentleman," Stokes cynically said, "by telling the gentleman that the stones were fake."

The others stared at them. "Who was the gentleman?" Penelope demanded.

Stokes grimaced. "Would that life were so easy. The description George gave us would fit half the gentlemen in London—dark haired, neatly dressed, average height and build."

"And, of course," Barnaby put in, "we have zero chance of convincing George to formally identify—much less testify against—a man who approached him as a client."

Somewhat to Barnaby's surprise, Penelope was looking at him with a light in her eyes that suggested she'd made some revelatory connection. "Did George tell you what the gentleman did after George had informed him that the emeralds were worthless?"

Stokes—who was also eyeing Penelope with interest—replied, "Apparently, the gentleman looked shocked, then cast down. George told him he could get something for the gold, but the gentleman declined and took the necklace back."

Penelope smiled intently, as if that somehow confirmed something.

Barnaby caught her eye. "Your turn—you're the last to report, and you've clearly learned something relevant."

She smiled swiftly at him—a different sort of smile—then glanced around at the others. "I believe we're all clear, at least in our minds, that Lord Carisbrook sold the emeralds eight years ago to pay for Lady Carisbrook's excessive spending over the years she had their two older daughters to establish." When the other five all dutifully nodded, she went on, "And while I agree that, in the wider sense, George's description is of little use in identifying the gentleman who brought him the necklace, we know that description matches Franklin Carisbrook. What I learned this afternoon—the information that quite literally fell into my lap while chaperoning Hugo and Cara at Lady Hestley's garden party—is that, apparently unknown to all others in his family, Franklin Carisbrook is unofficially engaged to a Miss Lilibeth Ives, the daughter of a curator at the museum."

Silence fell as the others digested that news, then Stokes stirred. "You're suggesting that, in order to marry his Miss Ives, Franklin Carisbrook stole the emeralds hoping to sell them and…" Stokes frowned. "What? This Miss Ives doesn't sound like the sort to countenance setting up house on ill-gotten gains, and I strongly doubt her family would encourage that, either."

Penelope nodded. "I'm fairly certain Franklin hadn't really thought beyond the immediate outcome—he's apparently already gained Miss Ives's parents' blessing, and in doing so, I suspect he would have… inflated his capital, so to speak. Everything I heard suggested that he is sincerely attached to Miss Ives. Therefore, given what we know of the situation with his mother, and that his lordship doesn't, it seems, interfere with her ladyship's managing of their children, then it's not hard to imagine that Franklin might have felt desperate enough to take the emeralds, try to sell them, and then—presumably—persuade Miss Ives to marry him while cutting himself off from his family." Penelope arched her brows. "Perhaps he thought to elope and flee the country." She looked around at the others. "Love does prompt people to do the most desperate things."

They all knew that for fact.

"If that's true," Violet observed, "then Lord Carisbrook having already sold the emeralds saved his son from committing a crime now."

Stokes half laughed. "That's true. And as Lord Carisbrook owned the emeralds, they were his to sell, so no crime there, either."

"But," Barnaby said, and his somber tone drew all eyes back to him, "we're then left with the prospect of Franklin Carisbrook returning the emeralds to the drawer in his mother's dressing table." He looked around, meeting his friends' eyes. "Did Simpkins see him? Was that the reason she ended up dead on the back stairs?"

Penelope met Barnaby's eyes, her expression now as grim as his. "Indeed. Did Simpkins see Franklin, did he realize, and then feel he had to silence her?"

Stokes looked from Penelope to Barnaby, then straightened and sighed. "First thing tomorrow, it's back to John Street for us."

CHAPTER 9

The following morning, together with Penelope, Stokes, Wilkes, and Morgan, Barnaby walked into the Carisbrook front hall at a minute past nine-thirty, the earliest he and Penelope had deemed appropriate for their purpose; they hadn't wanted to find the family about the breakfast table or to risk Franklin going out.

Stokes asked if Franklin was in and, after being assured he was, asked to see him.

Jarvis glanced at Penelope, who faintly arched her brows, prompting Jarvis to suggest they wait in the drawing room while Jeremy fetched Mr. Carisbrook.

Penelope inclined her head and led the way into the room. Barnaby followed. He heard Stokes instruct Morgan to check in the servants' hall to see if any of the staff had remembered anything relevant to the investigation; in reality, Morgan would be keeping an eye on the back door to make sure Franklin didn't think to slip out that way and avoid them. Then Stokes, with Wilkes at his back, walked into the drawing room, and after Jarvis had bowed, withdrawn, and shut the door, the four of them looked at each other, then moved to the positions they felt would serve them best in the interview to come.

Wilkes retreated to stand along the wall beside the door, making himself as inconspicuous as possible. He drew out his notebook and pencil and stood ready to take down any information their interviewee let fall.

Barnaby crossed to stand behind the chaise on which Penelope had chosen to sit. From that spot, along with Penelope, he would have an unimpeded view of anyone coming through the door.

For his part, Stokes ambled, but finally came to rest to one side of the hearth.

Stokes settled, and they waited. The clock on the mantelpiece continued relentlessly ticking.

After several minutes, Penelope swiveled to study the clock, then looked at Stokes. She was about to comment when the door opened, drawing their eyes.

Franklin entered, openly wary. He glanced at them all, then shut the door, drew in a fortifying breath, and came forward. "Mr. and Mrs. Adair." He halted and half bowed in their direction, then raised his gaze to Stokes's unreadable face. Franklin swallowed, his Adam's apple bobbing, and inclined his head. "Inspector. You wished to speak with me?"

"Indeed." Stokes didn't suggest Franklin take a seat, but as Stokes's lips parted on his first question, the drawing room door opened again.

They all looked, Franklin turning to do so. Barnaby could almost hear Stokes cursing as Lord Carisbrook came in, followed a heartbeat later by Lady Carisbrook, already frowning. Julia Carisbrook slipped through the door last, concerned curiosity in her face.

His lips thinning, Stokes cast an eloquent look at Barnaby.

Almost imperceptibly, Barnaby shook his head. This was the family's home; Stokes couldn't order the rest of the family out.

Seated before Barnaby, Penelope stirred and shot a look at Stokes.

From the way Stokes—having caught Penelope's glance—relaxed and merely watched as the newcomers joined Franklin in staring uncomprehendingly at Stokes, Barnaby guessed Penelope's look had suggested that, now the whole family had chosen to attend, it would be wisest to allow the situation to unfold as it would—to reveal whatever reactions might surface.

Lord Carisbrook didn't sit but took up a stance by Franklin's shoulder; he folded both hands over the head of his cane and leaned heavily upon it. "What's this all about, Inspector?"

Stokes hesitated, then replied, "We have several questions, my lord." Stokes gestured to the chairs and sofa. "Perhaps you and your family should sit, my lord. This might take a little time."

Lord Carisbrook humphed, but after a glance at his wife, who drifted to claim her usual armchair beyond the end of the sofa, his lordship walked to the armchair opposite the sofa and closest to Stokes, leaving Franklin to sit in its mate, opposite Penelope.

Julia Carisbrook appeared to be having second thoughts about the wisdom of having followed her family into the room; she elected to sink onto a straight-backed chair beside a small round table beyond the armchair her brother now occupied.

Stokes waited until everyone had settled, then looked at Franklin. "If you would, Mr. Carisbrook, can you tell me where you went after you left this house on Sunday in the late afternoon?"

Franklin paled. He shifted in the chair, glanced briefly at his mother, then at Stokes. "I went to visit a friend who lives near Richmond."

Penelope glanced from Franklin to Lady Carisbrook in time to see her ladyship direct a direful frown at her son.

Stokes inclined his head. "Indeed." He waited until Franklin looked back at him to ask, "But before you headed out to Richmond, did you go anywhere else first?"

Franklin stared at Stokes, then his expression wavered, as if he could no longer maintain the façade he'd been clinging to. After a further moment of studying Stokes, Franklin gave a short sigh. "As you're asking, I assume you know that I did."

When Stokes didn't reply, Franklin glanced at Barnaby.

Barnaby tipped his head, acknowledging that Franklin had guessed correctly.

Franklin dragged in a huge breath, straightened, and squared his shoulders. In the tone of one getting a weight off his chest, he stated, "I went to the East End to see a man about…selling the emeralds."

"What?" Lord Carisbrook swiveled to stare at his son.

"You?" Lady Carisbrook jerked upright like a marionette whose strings had been tugged. Her eyes flared. "*You* stole my emeralds?"

To say her ladyship was shocked would have been a grave understatement.

Before his mother could recover the use of her tongue, Franklin set his jaw. The glance he threw her was as unforgiving as granite. "Yes, I did. That night, you called me in and railed at me as if I was a child. You told me who I was to marry—a young lady of your choosing, not mine. You refused to listen to a word I said—whenever I've tried to talk to you of my feelings, you've ridden roughshod over me. I was so…*furious* that when I turned to leave and saw the jewel case lying there, I picked it up and walked out."

"One point." When Franklin glanced at him, Stokes asked, "Where were the jewels when we searched the house?"

"Initially, I had them in my room, then when Mama raised the alarm and I realized the police might come and search, I hid them under my coat and moved them to the study. By the time your men came to search the study, I'd slipped them under my coat again, then once you'd all gone, I took them back to my room."

Stokes nodded. "Then later on Sunday, you took them to a fence in the East End."

"Yes." Franklin turned to look at his father. "But they were already fakes—crystals and not real emeralds at all—so I couldn't get anything for them."

Lord Carisbrook stared at his son, his expression uncomprehending more than anything else.

Franklin's lips turned down, then he raised his gaze to Stokes's face and went on, "I suppose you want to know what happened next. After I'd learned the emeralds were...not what I'd thought, I went down to Richmond as I'd planned." He drew breath and continued, "When I came home on Monday, early in the evening—just after seven o'clock—Mama and the others were already in the drawing room. I had the emeralds in their case in my satchel. I went upstairs to change, and on the way, I stopped in Mama's room and put the jewel case into her dressing table drawer." He glanced briefly at Lady Carisbrook. "I thought she'd imagine she'd just forgotten to look there."

Penelope saw Stokes glance across the room at Wilkes, confirming that the sergeant was busily scribbling in his notebook.

Then Stokes looked at Franklin. "You put the jewel case back into the drawer at just after seven o'clock—not later?"

Franklin frowned. "No. As I said, it was just after seven o'clock—you can check with Jarvis that was when I came in."

Stokes arched his brows. "You're sure you returned the jewels then?"

"Yes!" Franklin's frown deepened. Confused, he studied Stokes's face, then spread his hands. "It was the obvious moment to put them back—I was the only one on that floor. At that time, virtually everyone would be downstairs, and as it was Monday, I didn't know whether Mama would be going out or not. If she'd stayed in, I might not have had another chance, not that evening, not such a certain one, so I seized the moment and put the jewel case back." He paused, then added, "The case was burning a hole in my pocket, as they say. I didn't want to keep it a moment longer than I had to."

Stokes studied Franklin through narrowed eyes.

Behind Penelope, Barnaby shifted and, keeping his voice light, asked, "Did you see Simpkins while you were slipping into or out of your mother's room?"

Glancing at Barnaby, Franklin blinked. "No. I didn't see her at all."

"But did she see you?" Stokes's voice took on a more aggressive note. "Unknown to you, had she spotted you? Did she approach you later that night and speak to you about what she'd seen?"

Franklin reared back, his face a mask of dismay. "No! I didn't speak with her at all! In fact, I didn't set eyes on Simpkins after I returned to the house."

Lady Carisbrook was breathing heavily, outrage pouring from her. "Stuff and *nonsense*!" Puffing up like an agitated hen, she focused her ire on Stokes. "This is entirely beyond bounds, Inspector! You cannot conceivably believe that Franklin had anything to do with Simpkins falling down the back stairs! It's perfectly obvious that she simply missed her footing. Her death is regrettable, but it has nothing whatever to do with the crime your investigation is supposed to be concentrating on—namely, who stole my emeralds! That is the issue here—that Franklin took them, learned they were fake, and subsequently returned them is not the point. That's not the crime, and your distraction with that matter is blinding you to what is!" Lady Carisbrook had worked herself into a fine state. Eyes blazing, chin setting pugnaciously, she swept the gathering with a scorching glare. "Someone has stolen my emeralds and replaced them with fakes!"

A seething silence held for five seconds.

Then, "It was a necessary economy," Lord Carisbrook calmly said.

His wife looked at him. "What?" Lady Carisbrook stared at her husband while her brain caught up with her ears, then her gaze turned baleful. Her voice had lowered several octaves when she ground out, "What have you done with my emeralds?"

Penelope looked at Lord Carisbrook. To, she suspected, everyone's quiet amazement, he appeared wholly unperturbed by his wife's histrionics.

"It's quite simple, Livia." Across the intervening space, he met her gaze levelly. "If you recall, eight years ago, you outran the constable several times. I warned you about overspending, but you refused to listen to a word I said and continued to spend money as if it grew on trees." He considered his wife for a moment, then added, "As if we were far wealthier than we were, which I suspect is nearer the mark. You drove the estate to the point where selling the emeralds seemed the only way..." His lordship straightened, and his features hardened. "It *was* the only way—you'd left me no other. And, after all, the emeralds belonged to the estate—they were never yours in the sense of ownership. However"—his lordship dipped his head toward his wife—"as I was aware how much stock you placed in the parure, rather than simply sell it—and then endure the scenes you would doubtless have enacted me—I had the stones removed and replaced with passable fakes."

For several seconds, Lord Carisbrook regarded his wife, who was now goggling all but apoplectically. Unmoved, he continued, "I sold the emeralds to pay for your extravagances, my dear. I wasn't about to allow you to beggar the estate and sink it and the entire family into penury merely to support your profligate ways."

Dead silence greeted his lordship's pronouncement.

Penelope looked from one face to the next—from his lordship to Lady Carisbrook, to Franklin, and back again—eager to note every reaction; they hadn't yet learned anything regarding Simpkins's death.

Finally, Lady Carisbrook dragged in a massive breath, her bosom rising like a balloon inflating. Her fists clenched as if she was literally holding onto her temper, then in a voice so deep it was almost a growl, she grated, "How long?"

Penelope blinked, amazed—and then not at all amazed—that of all she might have asked, that was Livia Carisbrook's first question. Of course it was.

When, his expression suggesting that he, at least, was not at all surprised by his wife's tack, Lord Carisbrook faintly arched his brows and didn't immediately reply, her voice vibrating with suppressed emotion, Lady Carisbrook demanded, "For how long have I been parading through the ton with my head held high while wearing worthless fakes?"

By the end of her question, her voice had risen to a near shriek.

Impassive and unbending, Lord Carisbrook replied, "Really, Livia, I would have thought the answer obvious. It was eight years ago that you brought that on yourself."

Teeth gritted, fists clenched, Lady Carisbrook screwed her eyes tight shut, tipped back her head, and let out an unladylike shriek of utter fury.

Lord Carisbrook ignored the spectacle entirely. Instead, he turned to study Franklin.

When, eschewing the unedifying sight of his mother, her eyes still closed and her fists still clenched, her head bowed, biting her lip and drumming her feet on the rug, Franklin turned and met his father's gaze, his lordship reached a hand toward his son. "What I don't understand is why you needed the money, my boy. I would have thought your allowance enough—you've never been a spendthrift." When Franklin didn't immediately reply, Lord Carisbrook leaned closer and lowered his voice. "Are you in debt? Is that it?"

"No." His gaze locked with his father's, Franklin shook his head. "That's not it at all. I…"

Watching avidly, Penelope thought: *This is it.* The moment—one of those pivotal moments in a life—when Fate gave a man a chance to grasp his future. If he had the courage.

After a further moment of studying his father's face, Franklin glanced briefly at his mother, then he drew breath, looked back at his father, and declared, "I'm determined to marry Miss Lilibeth Ives. She's the daughter of Mr. Colin Ives, who is the principal curator at the British Museum. The Iveses are a perfectly respectable family." The sharp glance Franklin threw his mother—as if daring her to gainsay him—suggested she frequently and vociferously had.

Franklin returned his gaze to his father and, his tone and his expression growing stronger, more definite, continued, "No matter what Mama or you decree, I'm going to marry Lilibeth. I thought to use the extra money together with what I've saved to convince Lilibeth to marry me and leave for America." He cast another swift glance across the room. "It seemed the only way."

Dragged from her fit of temper—the most appalling fit of temper Penelope had ever witnessed—by the horrifying prospect of her son marrying, as she saw it, beneath her, Lady Carisbrook was gulping in air. Now she spluttered, "*Not* a curator's daughter! No—it's simply not acceptable!" Sadly for her, she was all but breathless, and her words were weak.

One glance at Lord Carisbrook confirmed that his wife's words had little impact on him.

Heartened by what he saw in his father's face, Franklin gestured at his mother. "You see?"

Lord Carisbrook consented to consider his wife for a second, then nodded—surprisingly decisively. "Indeed, I do. But marrying in some havey-cavey fashion is not the answer, my boy." He met Franklin's eyes. "I'm sure, if we put our heads together—and perhaps have a chat with the Iveses—we'll be able to manage a solution much more acceptable to all involved." His lips gently curving, his lordship added, "We're not flush with funds, but neither are we paupers, my son."

Franklin's expression was a sight to see; dawning hope had never been so clear.

Prompted by her ladyship's continuing mutterings about the unsuitability of curators' daughters, Penelope raised her voice sufficiently to reach his lordship. "I have it on excellent authority, my lord, that Miss Ives is a well-mannered, pleasant, and altogether admirable young lady."

Lord Carisbrook smiled and inclined his head. "I would expect no less of the young lady Franklin has chosen."

From her position beyond Franklin, Julia—who until then had remained mute—asked, "Franklin—is your Miss Ives the young lady I met at the Tolwhistles' garden party last week?"

Turning to look at his sister, Franklin nodded. "Yes—that was her. You spent some time speaking with her."

Julia nodded, a smile breaking across her face. "I liked her—she was nice."

The siblings shared a smile.

Penelope smiled herself. Franklin had more supporters than he'd supposed.

Barnaby's fingers brushed her shoulder, and she looked up at him. He met her gaze, then looked at Stokes and tipped his head toward the door.

Penelope turned to see Stokes nod. She rose, interrupting the low-voiced conversation that had sparked between Franklin and Lord Carisbrook; both men hurriedly got to their feet.

Ignoring Lady Carisbrook, Penelope held out her hand to his lordship. "Thank you for your time, my lord." To Franklin, she directed an encouraging nod, but held back any words of congratulations; they hadn't resolved the issue of Simpkins's death, and until they did, Franklin remained a suspect.

Lingering suspicion clearly preyed on Stokes's mind, too. He nodded formally to his lordship. "At this point, my lord, we have no further questions for you or your family. Regarding the emeralds, all has been explained to my satisfaction. However, Simpkins's death requires further investigation. In light of your son's information, we would like to question your staff once again. Rest assured we'll do our best to speedily determine how it was Simpkins came to fall."

"Thank you, Inspector. I am content to leave the matter in your—and Mr. and Mrs. Adair's—clearly capable hands."

Barnaby had come around the sofa to stand with Penelope and Stokes. His lordship half bowed to them, then glanced to where Franklin and Julia were now quietly talking. "I must admit that, as I'm sure you can appreciate, I was initially concerned as to what your investigations might uncover. But now"—his lordship spared a harder glance for his wife, sitting isolated, her attention turned inward and a sour and petulant expression on her face—"it seems that your revelations have come not a moment too soon."

Lord Carisbrook turned back to them and smiled in his gentle, benevolent way. "Thank you for facilitating a catharsis that I hope will be a turning point for us." By "us," it was clear he meant Franklin, Julia, and him. As Penelope saw it, Lady Carisbrook's place in their future was going to be very much up to her ladyship. Lord Carisbrook continued, "And as for finding out what happened to Simpkins, we owe her that much. By all means"—his lordship waved, encompassing his house—"Inspector, Mr. and Mrs. Adair, investigate as you see fit."

~

Stokes, Barnaby, and Penelope took his lordship at his word; leaving Wilkes in the front hall and dispatching Jarvis and Jeremy ahead of them, they made their way directly to the servants' hall.

In the corridor before they reached it, Stokes halted and turned to Barnaby and Penelope. He met their gazes, then said, "I still can't see writing Simpkins's death off as an accident."

Barnaby slid his hands into his pockets and, understanding Stokes's direction, stepped into the role of devil's advocate. "You said the police surgeon confirmed there was no bruising or other indication that she'd been pushed, and no evidence of any fight, either."

"True," Penelope acknowledged. "But I, too, find it impossible to believe that a maid of Simpkins's experience, who had spent all her life going up and down such stairs, would have marched to the top of that flight and then forgotten where she was and just stepped back."

Stokes nodded. "And it's a narrow stairway, which makes it all the more surprising she didn't grab at the railing to save herself—anyone would. If she had, she'd have twisted and fallen on her side, not straight down on her back. She didn't stumble—she must have literally stepped straight back, as Penelope said."

"So let's say she did that," Penelope went on. "Exactly as our evidence says she did. She marched to the top of the flight—those stairs are steep as well as narrow, so until she reached the top, she would have been looking down, managing her skirts. She reached the top and paused or halted, raised her head, and looked—then she stepped straight back and fell." Penelope met Barnaby's eyes, then looked at Stokes. "So what caused her to step back? There had to be something." Penelope widened her eyes. "Did someone leap out at her?"

Stokes nodded decisively. "That's it—that's what's bothering me. That's what we need to learn."

Barnaby nodded, too. "Indeed." He looked down the corridor and waved. "Let's get to it."

Stokes led the way. They entered the servants' hall to find all the staff seated around the long table, and Constable Morgan, as usual, jollying them all along. As before, the head of the table had been left for them. Stokes halted with Penelope on his right; Barnaby moved behind him to take up station on his left while Morgan went to stand opposite, at the table's foot.

Stokes looked around the table, allowing his gaze to touch each face, then stated, "We need to revisit the train of events that occurred in this house from the time Lady Carisbrook returned to it in the small hours of Sunday morning." He paused, then went on. "We now know that Lady Carisbrook took off the emeralds, laid them in their case, shut the case, and left it to one side of her dressing table. Subsequent to that, she called Mr. Franklin Carisbrook into her room, and in leaving the room, he took the emeralds with him." A soft gasp came from several throats; Stokes ignored it and rolled on, "Mr. Carisbrook had the emeralds with him when he left the house later on Sunday. Subsequently, when he returned to the house on Monday evening, he brought the emeralds back."

Stokes focused on Jarvis. "Mr. Carisbrook says you can vouch that he arrived just after seven o'clock on Monday evening."

His expression impassive, Jarvis nodded. "Indeed, sir. His lordship, her ladyship, and Miss Julia were already in the drawing room, awaiting dinner. Mr. Franklin went directly upstairs to change. He came down shortly afterward and joined the others in the drawing room."

Stokes nodded. "How long was he upstairs?"

Jarvis frowned. "Perhaps ten minutes. Not much longer. Just enough time to change."

And to replace the emeralds in his mother's room, but not time enough to have any meaningful run-in with Simpkins.

To Penelope's mind, Jarvis's straightforward evidence supported what Franklin had told them of his movements regarding the emeralds. But as for Simpkins… Penelope glanced around the table. "We're aware Lady Carisbrook and Miss Julia Carisbrook left to attend at least one event later on Monday evening and that Mr. Carisbrook and his lordship also went out. Did Mr. Carisbrook remain in the house for a time before he left?" Penelope widened her eyes. "Did his lordship, for that matter?"

"No, ma'am," Jarvis replied. "Both his lordship and Mr. Franklin left the house shortly after dinner, before her ladyship and Miss Julia. His lordship returned at about twelve o'clock, and Mr. Franklin returned not long after."

"Was that before or after Lady Carisbrook and Miss Julia returned?" Barnaby asked.

"Before, sir. Her ladyship and Miss Julia returned at about half past twelve."

Stokes looked down the table at Wills, Cobb, and Willie. Coachman, groom, and stable boy all nodded. Wills confirmed, "We had the horses rubbed down and the carriage stowed, and we were all in our beds before the clocks struck one. Monday tends to be an early night, and we don't like to waste it."

Stokes nodded and consulted the notebook he'd retrieved from his pocket. After a moment, he looked up and swept his gaze over the table's occupants. "You'll be pleased to know that, in my opinion, the matter of the Carisbrook emeralds going missing has now been resolved, and it's unlikely there will be any charges laid—essentially, the jewels were misplaced and have now been found. Mr. Carisbrook has shared his reasons for removing them from the house with us and his parents, and given your recent answers, I see nothing further to be pursued in that regard."

Penelope took in the relief that flowed over all—every last one—of the faces around the table. The staff truly were devoted to Lord Carisbrook and his children.

Stokes paused and looked around the table again, then still speaking in his official voice, went on, "However, the matter of Simpkins's death is yet to be adequately explained."

Mrs. Jarvis frowned. "I thought she just fell." Her frown deepened. "Was there more to it?"

"That's what we'd like to know," Stokes said.

Seeing confusion flit across several faces, Penelope clarified, "Simpkins did, indeed, die by falling down the stairs. What we want to know is why she fell."

Barnaby glanced at Stokes, who was leafing through his notebook, then said, "We need you all to cast your minds back to Monday night—the night on which Simpkins died."

"Previously," Stokes said, having found his place, "you told us that Simpkins was the last one left in the servants' hall when all the rest of you retired, and that, by that time, all the family were also in their rooms, presumably asleep."

Observing the staff closely, Penelope saw Jarvis and Mrs. Jarvis exchange a glance. More, other staff were also shooting uncertain—questioning?—glances their way.

Standing at the other end of the table, Morgan had noticed as well. His gaze had sharpened, and he was searching the faces, too.

Penelope surreptitiously nudged Stokes.

He looked up just as Jarvis cleared his throat and, folding his hands on the table, said, "As to that, Inspector, Mr. and Mrs. Adair, we"—with a tip of his head, he indicated all of the staff—"have been sharing our thoughts, and in light of developments, there's several observations that might be pertinent."

When Jarvis—and all the other staff—remained silent and still, many looking expectantly at the three investigators, Barnaby obliged and asked, "What observations are these?"

Mrs. Jarvis puffed out a breath. "Well, for a start, as I said earlier, Simpkins was drinking cocoa." The housekeeper met Penelope's eyes.

Thinking back, Penelope frowned. "You said she always...no. You said 'as she often did.'"

"Exactly." Mrs. Jarvis nodded portentously. "That's what I said, because Simpkins didn't normally drink cocoa—she only did when she wanted to stay awake. She said it helped."

"So she wanted to stay awake for a reason?" Stokes looked around the faces.

When all his question elicited was another round of exchanged glances, Penelope asked, "Was she waiting for someone?"

Somewhat reluctantly, Jarvis acknowledged, "That's what we think."

Inwardly cursing her spectacles, Penelope pushed them higher on her nose, then looked straitly at the staff. "Do any of you know for whom she was waiting?"

Mrs. Jarvis started to turn toward her spouse, then thought better of it and looked at Penelope and Stokes. "We've always wondered if it was the gentleman she was waiting for—to let him in and then, later, to let him out again."

Penelope fought not to narrow her eyes. "The same gentleman Willie has seen leaving his horse in the stable?"

Nods came from all around the table. Mrs. Jarvis primmed her lips, then lightly shrugged. "We can't rightly say if it's the same man or not because none of us have ever seen him, and not even Willie knows if he enters the house."

This time, it was Penelope, Stokes, and Barnaby who exchanged glances, wordlessly communicating, then Stokes looked down the table. His expression stern, tending grim, he commanded, "Tell me exactly what you think happens when this gentleman visits."

Jarvis stirred. "Well, we're only guessing, but…" He looked at Wills.

The coachman cleared his throat and said, "Like Willie told you, the gentleman stops in at the mews, comes into the stable, and leaves his horse in one of the empty stalls—me and Cobb, as well as Willie, always know when he's been by."

Cobb nodded. "It's always late, though, and it's only Willie who's in the stables when the man comes and goes."

"And he—the gentleman—was back Monday night," Willie piped up. "Same as usual. He came on Saturday, like I told you, and he came on Monday night, too."

"*If* the gentleman comes inside," Jarvis stated, rather more firmly, "it's always after all of us have gone upstairs to our beds."

"Well, except for me and Peggy." Mrs. Smollet, the cook, dipped her head at the scullery maid. "We share the room down here"—with one large, puffy hand, she waved toward the rear of the house—"but as we've both got early starts, being first up of a morning, we're always first to our beds every night with the door shut tight."

"So," Penelope confirmed, "if anyone came into the kitchen or this hall late at night, neither of you would hear?"

"S'right." Folding her massive arms across her bosom, Mrs. Smollet nodded.

Stokes was busily scribbling, so Barnaby prompted, "What you're telling us is that late on Monday night—or rather, in the early hours of Tuesday morning—Simpkins was the only member of the staff awake, and she was sitting here drinking her cocoa." With his gaze, he swept the faces. "Why do you imagine it was the gentleman she was waiting for?"

Mrs. Jarvis blinked. "Well, because the nights Simpkins sat down here sipping cocoa were always the same nights Willie said the gentleman left his horse in the stable."

Barnaby arched his brows. "I see."

"And"—Penelope directed her words to Jarvis—"you think Simpkins needed to be here, awake, to let the gentleman in."

"I always lock and bolt all the doors before going upstairs, including the rear door." Jarvis paused, then added, "Simpkins never asked me to leave the rear door unlocked, but she was a tight-lipped sort."

"And," Mrs. Jarvis said, "she would've had to stay up anyway to lock and bolt the door after the gentleman left again, or we'd have known something was going on."

Stokes looked up from his notebook. "The rear door was always locked and bolted in the morning—as it was supposed to be?"

"Aye." It was Mrs. Smollet who replied. "Me or Peggy, we're the first to open the rear door of a morning, and it would be locked and bolted proper every day, so 'suming the gentleman did come inside, like we're all thinking, then seems it would have been Simpkins who let him out and locked and bolted the door after him."

Everyone had followed that reasoning, and most were nodding, including Penelope, Stokes, and Barnaby.

Then Mrs. Smollet frowned slightly and added, "Well, except for yesterday morning, of course." She looked at Stokes and Penelope. "The rear door was closed but unlocked and unbolted when I reached it Tuesday morning. First time ever since I've been cook here."

Stokes stared at Mrs. Smollet. "Because Simpkins had opened it, but died before she could relock and rebolt it."

Silence reigned for a heartbeat, then Barnaby said, "That means the gentleman was inside the house when Simpkins died."

"He couldn't lock and bolt the door when he left." Penelope stared down the table, unseeing, while along with everyone else, she examined their deductions and found them to be…incontestable.

She blinked, then refocused on Willie. "Willie, was there anything different about when the gentleman returned to the stable on Monday night? Was he in a rush? Did he seem to be in a panic?"

Willie frowned, clearly thinking back, then replied, "I can't say as he was, ma'am—he seemed much the same as usual to me. And his horse stayed calm and didn't fret, and they usually will if their rider's in a stew." Willie blinked his wide blue eyes and said, "Only thing that was a bit different this Monday night is that I don't think he stayed long. He's usually gone for a few hours, near as I can make out, but on Monday, it didn't seem long at all before he was back. I'd fallen asleep in between, so I can't be sure, but from the way the moonlight was falling when he arrived and then when he came back and left...it wasn't much different."

Stokes looked at Willie and nodded. "That's very helpful." He finished jotting down Willie's observations, even while the implications swirled in his brain.

They were all thinking the same thing—that Lady Carisbrook had a lover who called frequently at the house, a gentleman who insisted on the utmost secrecy, and Simpkins was there whenever he called to let him in and out of the house. But on Monday night, for whatever reason, the gentleman had been involved—either directly or at a distance—with whatever had caused Simpkins to fall down the back stairs and die.

Stokes looked at his notes, then inwardly sighed; he knew better than to leap to conclusions.

He scanned the faces around the table; everyone was now watching him expectantly. "To confirm—other than Willie, none of you here have ever set eyes on our mystery gentleman, and even the glimpses Willie's had are insufficient to identify the man."

Nods came from all around the table.

Stokes continued, "And as none of you have ever seen the man inside, we still have no evidence, beyond Simpkins's behavior and the locked or unlocked doors, that the man ever set foot inside this house."

The staff stared back at him.

Stokes mentally ran through what they could deduce about the mystery man. He rode quality horseflesh and was almost certainly a member of the ton, possibly of the upper echelons—and Lady Carisbrook's social-climbing tendencies made the latter trait even more likely, indeed, virtually obligatory.

Penelope had been studying the staff. Now, she asked, "Is there anything—any observation or inkling or idea you have—that might give us a clue as to this mystery gentleman's identity?"

Most of the staff looked blank, but Mrs. Jarvis and Polly, Julia's maid, shared a quick, uncertain glance.

Penelope caught it. "Mrs. Jarvis?"

The housekeeper reluctantly met Penelope's eyes, then Mrs. Jarvis sighed. "It's just a thought, mind. While none of us have seen the gentleman, and I can't imagine his lordship or Mr. Franklin would have, either—their rooms are on the same floor, but in the other wing—Miss Julia's and Miss Cara's rooms are on the first floor and in the same wing as her ladyship's room, and...well, from the time Miss Cara came to stay, she and Miss Julia were thick as thieves and in and out of each other's rooms all the time." Mrs. Jarvis glanced at Polly and at Abby, the upstairs maid who was sitting next to Polly. "And that included—me, Polly, and Abby suspect—late at night, after they'd come home from the balls and parties and were supposed to be asleep in their beds."

Mrs. Jarvis met Penelope's eyes. "When one or the other was returning to their rooms, slipping through the shadows in that corridor, it's possible they might have seen the man. Of course, it'd be at some distance and in the semi-dark, but those young ladies' eyes are sharp—especially Miss Cara's with her drawing and all."

Penelope blinked, then slowly nodded. "Yes, I see." Her words were distant because her mind had leapt ahead...

Simpkins must have known the mystery man's identity, and now, Simpkins was dead. What if Cara and Julia had seen the man, well enough to identify him...or at least for him to believe they could...

Penelope gripped Stokes's sleeve. When he looked at her, she met his eyes. "We need to speak with Julia and Cara immediately."

Stokes blinked, then his face hardened, and he nodded. "You're right."

He looked at the staff and nodded a brisk dismissal. "Thank you for your time." With a glance, he collected Barnaby and Morgan.

Penelope released Stokes, whirled, and hurried up the steps and into the corridor leading to the front hall.

CHAPTER 10

"Wait!"

Barnaby's call had Penelope pulling up in the lee of the main stairs. All but jigging with impatience, she swung to face him.

With Wilkes, who had spotted them, hurrying to join them, along with Stokes and Morgan, Barnaby halted before her. Before she could ask why they were dallying, he pinned her with his gaze. "Is there any point in appealing directly to Lady Carisbrook?"

Penelope blinked, then frowned and considered, but ultimately, she shook her head. "I can't believe we'll get any joy from interviewing her ladyship." Jarvis and Jeremy moved past their small band, heading into the front hall. She waited until the pair were well past before saying, "After all the shocks visited on Livia Carisbrook yesterday and again this morning, to cap it off by asking for the identity of her until-now secret lover might well push her over the edge into outright hysteria. I, for one, would rather not face that. And"—she met Barnaby's eyes—"I'm greatly concerned that if our mystery man is behind Simpkins's death—if he, for some reason, decided to silence her—then if Julia and Cara saw him and he knows they did, they might be in danger."

"Cara is safe." Barnaby's tone was utterly confident. "Quite aside from Hugo being with her, our people are watching over her."

Penelope nodded. "Which is why I think we should see Julia immediately and make sure she's safe, too."

"Agreed." Stokes started toward the main body of the front hall. "And we need to learn if she knows anything useful."

He asked Jarvis where they might find Julia Carisbrook, and the butler led them to a small parlor at the rear of the house.

There, they found Julia sitting on a window seat and staring, somewhat forlornly, out at the garden.

Jarvis cleared his throat and announced, "Mr. and Mrs. Adair and Inspector Stokes, miss."

Blinking, Julia turned, then she rose, her hands nervously fluttering before she clasped them tightly and regarded Stokes, Barnaby, and Penelope with wide eyes. "Hello."

Penelope smiled and glided forward. "Miss Carisbrook—Julia, if I may?"

Julia blinked warily. "Yes, of course..."

"We have a few questions we'd like to ask you, Miss Carisbrook," Stokes said.

Julia's eyes widened even further. "Oh?" Then as if remembering her manners, she waved to the rattan chairs and sofa nearby. "Please, won't you be seated?"

Barnaby nodded a dismissal to Jarvis, who reluctantly withdrew, shutting the door softly behind him. They'd left Wilkes and Morgan in the front hall. Penelope sat on the sofa, adroitly drawing Julia to sit beside her, where the light from the wide window fell on her face.

Penelope waited until Barnaby and Stokes had subsided into the armchairs facing the sofa, then said, "We now know that, on certain nights, late at night or, more correctly, in the early hours of the morning, a gentleman visits this house." Penelope trapped the startled gaze Julia turned on her; it was obvious from Julia's reaction that she knew of whom Penelope spoke. "Do you know anything at all about this gentleman?"

For several seconds, Julia simply stared, then, slowly, she shook her head. "I know nothing about any such gentleman."

She glanced at Stokes and Barnaby, then looked back at Penelope, as if hoping they would believe her—indeed, almost willing them to do so.

Penelope accepted that this round of questioning was up to her; neither Stokes nor Barnaby was likely to be able to gain Julia's trust, especially not in a matter like this. From what Penelope could read in Julia's expression, the daughter of the house was unsure as to where, exactly, her loyalties should lie—with her mother, with her father, or with the law in pursuit of justice.

"Julia, a woman of this household lies dead, and we don't know why." Penelope held the younger woman's gaze. "Even if you suspect the gentleman we're speaking of is a close friend of your mother's, you need to consider that until we prove otherwise, entirely unwittingly, your mother might be consorting with a murderer."

Julia's eyes grew wide, then wider. Slowly, her lips formed a silent "Oh."

Penelope could almost see the wheels turning in Julia's mind, but they didn't have time for her to vacillate. Still holding Julia's gaze, Penelope sat up. "We're about to return to Albemarle Street to speak with Cara about this same matter." She arched her brows at Julia. "Would you like to come with us? Then you and Cara can speak and, together, decide what to do."

Julia's eyes lit. "Oh—yes. Yes, please." Her tightly clasped hands relaxing, she shifted eagerly on the sofa. "That would be…most helpful."

To us all. Penelope had much more faith in her ability to sway Cara to quickly and without undue fuss tell them all she knew. If Julia could then confirm what her cousin said, well and good.

With a swift glance at Barnaby and Stokes, both of whom nodded in agreement, Penelope rose, bringing Julia almost bouncing to her feet.

"I'll just fetch my bonnet." Julia led them from the parlor toward the front hall. "Mama's taken to her bed—she won't miss me. I won't be a moment."

Stokes dispatched Wilkes and Morgan back to Scotland Yard, then he went out and waited by Penelope's carriage.

With Barnaby, Penelope waited with Jarvis by the front door. But Julia was true to her word and, within a few minutes, came hurrying down, still tying her bonnet ribbons. Informing Jarvis of her destination, she accepted her cloak from him, then at Penelope's wave, joined her in leaving the house, descending the steps, and climbing into the carriage.

Barnaby and Stokes followed, Barnaby having given Phelps the order to return to Albemarle Street.

They covered the short distance in silence—an expectant, impatient silence on Penelope's, Barnaby's, and Stokes's part, while Julia appeared eager and faintly trepidatious in equal measure. As this would be the first time Julia had faced Cara since Cara had been ignominiously marched from the John Street house and Julia felt guilty over not having protested her cousin's treatment, Penelope could understand Julia's trepidation, although she believed it to be unnecessary.

They reached Albemarle Street and were admitted to the house by a smiling Mostyn, who, at Penelope's inquiry, informed them that Miss Cara and Mr. Hugo were in the back parlor with Mrs. Montague.

Penelope led the way into the garden parlor that doubled as her office —and halted.

What Mostyn hadn't told them was that Hugo was posed on a straight-backed chair and Cara was drawing a portrait of him—one that made Penelope and Barnaby blink and kept them all silent as they quietly filed in and waited for Cara to cease the swift, confident strokes of her hand as she laid down more lines.

Despite being executed entirely in pencil, the portrait was far more than just a remarkable likeness. It captured Hugo—the essence of him— in black, grays, and white, and through Cara's magic, revealed a great deal about his inner self. About what made him Hugo. Quite obviously, Cara saw Hugo as he truly was, not as the superficial gentleman-about-town that, until recently, he'd pretended to be.

Penelope had halted at Cara's shoulder. When Cara finally sat back and swiveled on the stool to look up at Penelope, with her eyes still glued to the portrait, Penelope said, "You absolutely must show that to Hugo's mother."

Cara smiled and turned back to the portrait and her subject. "Do you think so? It is just a quick sketch. Would she like to have it, do you think?"

"I think she would be beyond delighted." Penelope moved farther into the room. "Now, if you can pause for a moment, see who we've brought."

Cara turned again to look toward the door and saw Julia. "Oh!" Immediately, Cara set aside her pencil and sketch pad, leapt to her feet, and with pleasure wreathing her face, rushed to Julia.

And then the cousins were in each other's arms, and Julia was babbling about how sorry she was for not standing up for Cara against her ladyship's accusations—and much more in that vein—and Cara was dismissing Julia's apologies and assuring her that Cara forgave her anything that needed forgiving.

Smiling, Penelope walked on to her desk. Violet was seated in the chair behind it, dealing with Penelope's correspondence while keeping a chaperoning eye on Cara and Hugo.

Violet nodded in the pair's direction. "I've been entirely superfluous. They really are an excellent match. Cara is so sweet and kind, and Hugo is head over ears in love and treats her like a goddess."

Penelope chuckled and glanced around the floor. "No Martin?" As the baby still spent much of his time sleeping, Violet often had him nestled in a basket beside her.

"I sent him and Hilda upstairs to the nursery in case I needed to go out with our young couple." Violet eyed the two girls. "You've come from John Street, I take it. What did you learn?"

Penelope watched Hugo, who had risen and gone to stand beside Cara. When Cara appealed to him over Julia's self-recriminations, Hugo smiled and added his reassurances to Cara's.

"Almost there." Penelope met Violet's eyes. "We're hoping Julia and Cara might have caught a glimpse of our mystery man." In a few words, she explained what they'd learned and that identifying the mystery man was now their most urgent priority. "With the matter of the missing emeralds resolved, we need to get to the bottom of Simpkins's death."

Determination glinting in her eyes, Penelope swung back to the trio now chatting animatedly in the middle of the room, with Barnaby and Stokes laconically looking on, clearly waiting for Penelope to take charge. She did so by clapping her hands. When Hugo and the girls turned to look at her, she stated, "If you will, we need Cara and Julia to dredge their memories and help us sort out what happened to Simpkins."

Penelope waved the girls to two armchairs, while she sat on the sofa facing the pair. Hugo perched on the arm of the chair Cara had claimed. Barnaby ambled over to sit beside Penelope, and Stokes moved to stand on Penelope's other side, from where he could observe Cara's and Julia's faces. Violet remained behind the desk, avidly watching.

"Now," Penelope said, "we've learned from the staff of the visits of a mysterious gentleman to the Carisbrook house. We know he arrives very late at night—more usually in the early hours of the morning—stays for a time, then leaves. Simpkins always stayed up to let him in and, later, to let him out again, locking and bolting the door behind him."

Barnaby kept his eyes trained on Julia and Cara. Penelope's mention of the mysterious man had come as no surprise, but judging from the looks the girls exchanged, Simpkins's involvement wasn't something they'd known about before.

Penelope had paused to let her words—and their implications—sink in. Now she went on, "We would prefer not to be forced to subject Lady Carisbrook to further interrogation at this point. She's already been severely overset by the revelations of the past days—her emeralds going missing, then turning up again but confirmed as being fake, and Franklin's involvement, let alone his determination to marry Miss Ives. All these things have preyed on her composure." Penelope paused; Barnaby had to admire the tack she'd taken. Then she continued, her tone even but weighty, "Consequently, if either of you girls know anything at all about this mystery gentleman—if you even glimpsed him through the shadows —we hope you will share what you know."

"We will, of course," Barnaby said, "keep anything you tell us, and anything we might deduce from that, in the strictest confidence." He glanced at Stokes.

The girls followed Barnaby's look. Stokes met their wondering glances and stated, "We at Scotland Yard are not in the business of feeding the news sheets information they don't need to know. If there is some private connection between her ladyship and this gentleman, then beyond us determining the truth of the circumstances surrounding Simpkins's death, we will have no further interest in the matter."

Cara and Julia sat back, then exchanged another long look.

Penelope sighed and rolled out her heavy guns. Her tone formal, she declared, "If either of you have seen or know anything at all about this mystery man, then it is incumbent on you to tell the police"—she waved at Stokes—"everything you know." She caught both girls' now-widening eyes. "We need to identify that gentleman now."

Cara studied Penelope, glanced at Barnaby, then looked at Hugo. After several seconds, finally, she transferred her gaze to Stokes's face. "If you are talking of the man who sometimes appeared in the first-floor corridor outside my aunt's room, then yes, I have seen him three times." She transferred her gaze to Penelope and Barnaby. "But always, it was very late, and I only saw him at some distance, with both of us cloaked in shadows."

Julia's voice wavered as she whispered, "I saw him, too—not at the same time but at other times." She glanced at Stokes. "Four other times." Returning her gaze to Barnaby and Penelope, her voice strengthening, she went on, "After we were supposed to be in bed and the rest of the house had quieted, Cara or I would slip into the other's room, and we'd talk"—Julia gestured—"about everything we'd seen or that had happened at whatever events we'd attended that evening."

Cara nodded. "It was as I was creeping back to my room that I would see him."

"And me," Julia confirmed. "It was always when we were going back that we would spot him—not every time, just sometimes." She swallowed, then said, "It was as Cara said—he was always at the far end of that stretch of corridor, outside or just approaching Mama's door." She raised her gaze to Penelope's face. "I've never seen him anywhere else."

Penelope nodded encouragingly. "Now, I'm going to ask you both to close your eyes and think back to the time you saw the man most clearly." She paused, waiting while the cousins complied. "Keep that scene in your mind's eye—stay focused on it and keep your eyes closed. I'm going to ask you several questions, and I want you to look at that picture in your mind and tell me what you see. All right?"

Both girls nodded. Barnaby remembered that Griselda had used the same trick in a previous case, proving that people very often saw much more than they realized.

Urgently, Stokes waved at Penelope and mouthed, "Simpkins."

Penelope nodded. "First question. Did you ever see Simpkins with the gentleman?"

"No" came immediately from both girls.

"Very well. Now, did the man carry a candle or a lamp to light his path, or did he know to find his way in the dark?"

Both girls frowned, then Cara said, "Every time I saw him, there was a lamp sitting on the small table at the top of the back stairs. A small lamp, like those the maids or footmen carry at night, and it was always turned low."

Julia nodded. "Yes, that's right. I remember thinking that if it wasn't for that lamp, I might never have noticed him."

"The lamplight, though faint, made him into a silhouette and left his face in shadow." Cara paused, then the line between her brows deepened. "Once, I saw him as he came up the stairs and set the lamp down on the table—I saw his face lit by the lamp, just for an instant."

"On a few nights," Julia added, "there was moonlight shafting through the skylight above the main staircase. Those were the only times I saw anything of his face, but the view was never clear."

Penelope glanced at Barnaby, then turned back to the girls. "Describe him as best you can."

Their eyes still closed, both girls stirred, but then they settled, and Cara said, "His hair...wasn't black. And I don't think it was dark brown, either."

"More like light brown," Julia said. "And he was clean shaven."

"Yes," Cara said. "His face was longish—elongated planes—with a wide forehead, and his brows were more like lines than arches."

"He had a strong nose," Julia said. "Like Papa."

Cara frowned. She turned as if to glance at Julia, but with her eyes still closed, instead, she reached out and touched her cousin's hand. "I'm not sure, but I think he might have had a small cleft in his chin."

Penelope met Stokes's eyes and grimaced, then she asked the girls, "How tall was he?"

"Medium?" Julia said.

"A bit taller, I think." Cara offered, "His build, I would call lean, rather than heavy."

Close to despairing, Penelope looked at Barnaby. He pulled a commiserating face; thus far, the girls' description would fit hundreds if not thousands.

Then Hugo, who had been sitting quietly perched by Cara's side, looked from her to Penelope and Barnaby. Then Hugo looked at Stokes and raised his brows. "Perhaps Cara can draw him?"

Cara's eyes popped open, and she smiled and turned her beaming gaze on Hugo. "Yes, of course. That will be much easier."

"Oh." Julia opened her eyes, too, and relief flooded her face. "Yes—and then I can say if it's the man I saw."

Penelope doubted there were two men visiting Lady Carisbrook's room by night, but the confirmation wouldn't go amiss.

Hugo had already risen and fetched Cara's pencils and sketch pad from where she'd set them on a side table. Cara carefully tore the portrait of Hugo from the pad and handed it to Penelope, who carried it to Violet to set aside for safekeeping.

By the time Penelope returned to her chair, Cara was already sketching.

Julia leaned close and watched over Cara's shoulder. The girls murmured, deciding on things like the size of the man's ears and the relative squareness of his chin.

Finally, Cara raised her pencil from the page. She studied her sketch, then looked at Julia.

Julia examined the likeness, then nodded decisively. "Yes, that's him."

Cara considered her effort for two seconds more, then tore off the sheet and handed it to Penelope. "It's at least a reasonable likeness."

Given the evidence she'd seen of Cara's ability, Penelope suspected the sketch was rather more accurate than that. She studied the face depicted, but although she sensed she should recognize the man—he was clearly a member of the upper class with that brow, nose, and chin—she couldn't place him. "I don't know him well enough to name."

Stokes had drawn closer. She handed the sketch up to him. He took it, scrutinized it, then shook his head. "No. He's not someone I've met."

Barnaby held out his hand, and Stokes gave him the sheet. Violet left the desk and came to stand beside Barnaby and study the sketch, too.

Frowning, Violet shook her head. "He has the sort of face one expects to know, but…no. I can't place him, either."

Hugo, Penelope noticed, was staring at Barnaby, a frown spreading from his eyes to his face. Penelope followed Hugo's gaze to her husband's face—to find it utterly and implacably blank.

She blinked and straightened. Then she reached out and laid a hand on Barnaby's arm. "You've recognized him." She didn't make it a question; it was patently obvious that he had.

Barnaby stared at Cara's sketch for a heartbeat more, then he raised his gaze—shuttered and giving nothing away—and met Penelope's and then Stokes's eyes, and quietly admitted, "Indeed, I have."

Before he'd shared the gentleman's name with Penelope, Stokes, and Violet, Barnaby had insisted that Hugo take Cara and Julia into the garden. Refusing to bend in the face of their frustrated looks, pleading eyes, and disgruntled grumbling, he'd been adamant that the man's identity was something the three of them did not need to know.

Only once Cara, Julia, and Hugo were ambling on the lawn beyond the windows, safely out of hearing, had Barnaby sunk his hands into his pockets and told the others the gentleman's name.

They'd been as shocked as he had been—as he still was.

And, sadly, knowing the man's identity hadn't made their way forward any easier. Far from it.

Violet had had to gather Martin and Hilda and go home, leaving Barnaby, Stokes, and Penelope still debating their next move.

Eventually, Barnaby had sent a note to his father, requesting his insight, while Stokes had bitten the bullet and dispatched a carefully worded missive to the Houses of Parliament, seeking an urgent interview with the gentleman in question.

In a final bid to gather every last bit of information possible before any interview, Barnaby had sent a personal note to Neville Roscoe. Given who Roscoe was—and, even more, who he'd once been, a secret Barnaby had stumbled on a good few years ago—Roscoe's opinion could well give them more to go on than even the earl's.

That had been over an hour ago. Subsequently, they'd consumed a quick luncheon, then sent Julia home in Penelope's carriage. Hugo and Cara, after one look at their distracted faces, had taken themselves back out into the garden; they were presently sitting on a wrought-iron bench, chatting companionably in full view of the back-parlor windows.

Penelope stood watching them, although her furrowed brow said her mind was far away.

Stokes flanked her on one side, his hands in his pockets, his face set in harsh lines, his expression even more saturnine than usual.

Barnaby stood on Penelope's other side, his gaze, like hers, on Cara and Hugo. He was conscious of a craven wish that he could forget this case and be as carefree as the couple before him…then he glanced at Penelope and—inwardly—sardonically grinned. She and he…this was what they did. Along with Stokes, they pursued justice for those who no longer could speak for themselves, and his and Penelope's role was to guide Stokes through the shoals of the ton.

In this case, however, exactly where true justice might lie—exactly what it would encompass—was yet to be determined.

It certainly wasn't clear to him, to Penelope, or to Stokes.

After a moment, his mind still circling the principal issue, Barnaby sighed; they needed to face it head-on. Steepling his hands before his face, his fingertips resting on his nose, he said, "I'm having a hard enough time seeing Lord Frederick St. John-Carter as Lady Carisbrook's lover. My mind balks entirely at the notion of him flinging Simpkins down those stairs."

Stokes grunted. After a moment, he said, "I know of St. John-Carter only by repute, but if his reputation is even half true…" He paused, then went on, "One part of my cynical policeman's brain insists that even a saint can commit murder, only I can't think of one who has."

Penelope snorted. "Quite. But Lord Frederick's reputation as an advocate for the downtrodden in all their many guises is, quite simply, unassailable. I've only crossed his path a few times, but I would have said he was…one of those souls who are not so much kind as born defenders. Not of any specific type of person but of people who need defending, whoever they might be."

Barnaby shifted. His gaze on the garden, he said, "That's why we're tying ourselves in knots over this—over the possibility that he's a villain. He's a shining light for justice, and pulling him down… If he's guilty, it's going to be a shocking travesty that will send ripples throughout society far beyond the ton."

After a moment, Penelope said, "You're right, of course, but we shouldn't lose sight of the fact that, somehow, there might be an explanation that accounts for everything that's occurred without our shining light for justice having tarnished his sword with murder."

"That," Stokes said, with a dip of his head, "is why we're waiting for information from the earl and Roscoe before going to call, nice and politely, on Lord Frederick."

Barnaby couldn't help a self-deprecatory laugh. "And we've only been thinking of his good works—we haven't yet given much thought to his position within the government, let alone his standing in the ton."

"I'm hoping—indeed, praying—that Lord Frederick can explain it all." Penelope turned as a tap on the doorframe heralded Mostyn.

Their majordomo advanced to proffer his salver, on which a neat note lay, to Barnaby. "From Roscoe, sir. It came via the back door."

Stokes grunted. "Naturally."

Mostyn's lips twitched. Once Barnaby had picked up the note, the majordomo bowed and left them.

Barnaby unfolded the note, scanned the lines within, then handed the missive to Penelope. Stokes moved to read it over her shoulder.

"Well," Penelope said. She waited until Stokes straightened, then handed the note back to Barnaby. "Even Roscoe sings the man's praises."

Barnaby refolded the note and tucked it away. "And no man in London is more likely to see through a façade of good works to a dark heart better than Roscoe."

Stokes grimaced. "I can't disagree." He met Penelope's eyes. "Like you, I'm praying Lord Frederick will have some explanation I—and the commissioner—can accept."

"It's not, thank God, beyond the realms of possibility," Barnaby said. "We've no evidence he pushed Simpkins, only that he—or at least, something—caused her to fall."

"While he was there." Stokes pulled another face. "And there's the matter of him walking out of the house and riding away, calm as you please, afterward."

Penelope waved as if erasing their comments. "Let's just accept that we'll have to wait to hear his explanation before we can pass judgment either way."

"At least we now know the reason for the secrecy surrounding our mysterious gentleman's visits." Barnaby raised his head as, in the distance, they heard the front doorbell peal. A minute later, Mostyn returned, another note on his salver.

Barnaby took it and broke the seal. "My father." He spread the sheet and read, then as before, handed it to Penelope to hold while she and Stokes read the earl's message as well.

Stokes humphed and straightened. "No surprise there. Proceed with the utmost caution, remembering that Lord F is highly regarded—"

"And valued," Penelope put in. "Don't forget the valued—it's underscored three times."

"Indeed." Stokes inclined his head. "And we shouldn't forget the bit about him being a quiet lynchpin of the government, either."

Barnaby eyed Stokes's harassed expression. His friend would much rather face a violent, dyed-in-the-wool villain than have to negotiate the intricacies of a situation like this—where the only potential villain they had was presented in the garb of a universally lauded saint.

Penelope had refolded the earl's note; she tapped the edge on her palm, then said, "It occurs to me that far too many sensible, experienced, and usually insightful men view Lord Frederick as a sound and trustworthy—indeed, admirable—pillar of society, one who would never stoop to crossing any line, for them all to be wrong."

She looked at Barnaby, then transferred her gaze to Stokes. "We'll need to bear that in mind when Lord Frederick tells us what happened. The odds are good that he'll tell the truth without any great pressure—his character will compel him to it."

Stokes eyed her with faint hope. "From your lips to the Almighty's ear."

The doorbell pealed again, this time more insistently.

The sound cut off, and they heard the door open, then Mostyn was back, this time shepherding Davies, Stokes's favorite police runner.

Stokes straightened. "Yes?"

Davies saluted, grinned, and handed over a note.

Stokes took it, unfolded it, and read, then he dismissed Davies, sending him back to the Yard, and glanced briefly at Penelope before looking at Barnaby. "We've been granted an audience at two o'clock sharp in his lordship's office in Westminster." Stokes glanced at the clock on the mantelpiece; it showed fifteen minutes before the hour. "We'll have to hurry."

Penelope's eyes narrowed, and she folded her arms. "Westminster. Damn!"

Barnaby bent to drop a kiss on her forehead. "You can't come."

Lips and chin setting, she glanced through the window at Hugo and Cara, still seated on the bench in the sun. "I know. I keep telling myself that I have other fish to fry…" She turned back and skewered Stokes with her gaze. "But the thought of you two managing such a sensitive interview without me…it doesn't bear thinking about."

Barnaby smiled. "We'll miss your perceptive insights, but I'm sure we'll manage to stumble our way through it."

She humphed. "I just hope Lord Frederick is as understanding as they say."

Stokes grinned, unrepentant, and saluted her. "We need to go."

"On one condition." Penelope halted them both with an upraised finger. "In return for my forbearance in not seeking to force my way into this meeting, you must both promise to return here immediately afterward and tell me what transpires." She narrowed her eyes at them. "It's the least you can do."

Stokes glanced at Barnaby, then shrugged.

Barnaby caught Penelope's hand, pressed a kiss to the back of her knuckles, then released her with the words, "We do so solemnly swear."

Penelope smothered a chuckle and watched them head for the door, then she remembered and called out, "And don't forget—we have dinner at Violet and Montague's tonight."

Without looking back, Barnaby waved. He glanced at Stokes as they strode for the front hall. "If luck is on our side, we'll have found our way to a conclusion to this confounding case by then."

Stokes sent him a reproving look. "Don't jinx us." With that, he led the way through the door Mostyn was holding wide.

CHAPTER 11

Barnaby followed Stokes into the chambers of Lord Frederick St. John-Carter just as the clocks throughout the corridors of Westminster chimed and struck and *bonged* twice.

A sober individual of indeterminate years, severely garbed and bespectacled, rose from his chair behind a desk to one side of the antechamber and came hurrying to intercept them. His gaze flicked over them both, then he inquired, "Inspector Stokes?"

Stokes halted and nodded. He waved at Barnaby. "Mr. Adair is officially assisting me in this matter."

Adopting a reassuring smile, Barnaby said, "We appreciate Lord Frederick agreeing to meet with us."

The secretary would have liked to frown and put them off, his preference communicated by his reluctant and agitated mien, but then he drew breath and turned to an inner door. "Lord Frederick is expecting you. If you will come this way?"

The secretary opened the door and announced them, then stood back to allow them to enter.

Although Barnaby followed Stokes through the door, Stokes immediately stepped to the side, wordlessly urging Barnaby to take the lead.

He did, going forward with an easy smile to greet Lord Frederick, who, with his gaze rapidly surveying them, rose from behind a large and patently much-used desk.

Lord Frederick St. John-Carter was, Barnaby judged, a few years—

perhaps as many as five years—younger than Lord Carisbrook. Lord Frederick exuded the controlled vigor of a man in his prime; when younger, he must have cut a dashing figure, with his light-brown hair, straight and falling negligently over his forehead, his sharp and plainly shrewd hazel eyes, and his lean, aristocratic face. Despite the difficulties, Cara's sketch had captured something of the distant yet strangely vulnerable quality that hung about the man; Barnaby had no difficulty believing this was a gentleman others would be drawn to, to serve and protect. Just like the secretary.

With well-concealed wariness, his lordship nodded to Barnaby. "Mr. Adair. I'm acquainted with your father and sit on several charity boards with the countess."

"Indeed?" Maintaining his air of relaxed bonhomie, Barnaby shook the hand his lordship offered, then gestured to Stokes. "If you know my father, you might have heard that I occasionally assist Inspector Stokes in navigating the waters of the ton."

Lord Frederick inclined his head to Stokes. "I had heard." He held out his hand to Stokes. "Your successes have been noted, Inspector."

Stokes hid his surprise and shook hands with his lordship; not many men of Lord Frederick's age and stature would so readily have shaken hands with a mere Scotland Yard inspector.

Lord Frederick waved them to the pair of chairs angled before the desk. As they sat, he resumed his seat. "Now, how can I help you, gentlemen?"

Barnaby caught his lordship's gaze and, without turning his head, with his eyes indicated the secretary, who had remained and taken up station to one side of the door.

Smoothly, Lord Frederick looked at the man. "That will be all, Moreland." His lordship glanced at Stokes, then added, "Please ensure we're not disturbed unless the matter is urgent."

"Yes, my lord." The secretary's tone suggested he didn't want to leave, but leave he did.

Once the door shut behind him, Lord Frederick looked from Stokes to Barnaby, then back again. He raised his brows, the action faintly weary. "Well, Inspector?"

Succinctly, Stokes ran through the sequence of events they'd uncovered in the course of their investigation into the recent happenings in Lord Carisbrook's residence. He referred to the until-recently unknown gentleman as a "mysterious man" throughout.

His gaze trained on Lord Frederick, Barnaby concluded that his lordship would be a diabolical poker player—or a brilliant negotiator, which, apparently, he was; his face, even his hands and body, gave away absolutely nothing of his thoughts.

Finally, Stokes reached the point of their push to identify their mystery man. He withdrew Cara's sketch from his pocket, unfolded it, studied it for a silent second, then leaned forward, flattened the page on the desk, and turned it so that Lord Frederick could see it.

His expression impassive, Lord Frederick stared at the sketch for several heartbeats, then he reached out and picked it up. Outwardly unperturbed, he studied it at length, then his lips lifted just a touch. "She's a talented artist. It's a very good likeness."

"A very recognizable likeness, my lord." Stokes waited. When his lordship set the sketch back down, Stokes retrieved it, refolded it, and stowed it away again. Then, after a glance at Barnaby, who had continued to watch his lordship, Stokes followed his friend's lead and settled to wait on Lord Frederick's conscience.

Eventually, Lord Frederick, who had fallen into a reverie, stirred. He cast a sharp glance at Barnaby, then looked at Stokes. "In answer to your unvoiced questions, gentlemen, I never laid so much as a finger on Simpkins, nor did I touch that blasted necklace."

When Lord Frederick sat back, steepled his fingers before his face, and faintly frowned, volunteering nothing more, Stokes glanced questioningly at Barnaby.

Barnaby noted his look, returned his gaze to Lord Frederick, and after a moment, his tone quiet and even, said, "Inspector Stokes and I have been given the task of determining how Simpkins died. I can assure you that nothing you say to us will be relayed to anyone who doesn't need to know." He paused, then added, "We would rather not report our findings to date without hearing what you can tell us about the incident which led to Simpkins falling and breaking her neck."

Stokes approved of that speech and was pleased when Barnaby shut his lips and said no more.

After another taut silence, Lord Frederick's gaze, which had been focused on some distant prospect, returned briefly to Stokes's face, then his lordship looked at Barnaby—assessingly, measuringly—then Lord Frederick faintly, somewhat cynically, smiled. "You are a credit to your lineage, Adair." A second passed, and Lord Frederick more quietly added, "As I hope I am to mine."

Stokes told himself to be patient; working with Barnaby had taught him that, when interviewing nobs, silence was often more effective than specific questions in eliciting information. Nevertheless, it was difficult to sit still while sensing such powerful undercurrents swirling around them.

At last, Lord Frederick sat up, lowered his hands to the desk, looked from Barnaby to Stokes, and said, "Very well. I accept that you do, indeed, need to know, and that I must place my trust in your discretion. That said, I wish to underscore that what I am about to reveal impacts the lives of three others as well as mine—namely, that of my wife, Anne, that of Humphrey, Lord Carisbrook, and of course, that of Livia, Lady Carisbrook." Lord Frederick paused as if gathering his thoughts, then said, "In order to put the events of Monday night into proper context, you will need some understanding of the history that binds us."

Stokes managed not to arch his brows in surprise; he'd thought it a simple matter of an affair, the usual sort of liaison the aristocracy—certainly those of his lordship's vintage—fell into and out of much like a new suit. He glanced at Barnaby and saw him leaning back in the chair, his blue gaze, acute and sober, trained on his lordship's face. Again taking his cue from his friend, Stokes settled back and, with greater curiosity than he'd previously felt, waited to hear what his lordship thought they needed to know.

Lord Frederick clasped his hands on the desk and, with his gaze fixed on his fingers, said, "I should commence by telling you that Livia and I have known each other since our early teens. Her parents' country property abutted an estate my father acquired, and I often spent summers there. Although we didn't grow up together, through the time I spent there, we grew to care for each other." He drew breath, his fingers tightening, and went on, "In short, we developed an understanding—an expectation that, once she reached a suitable age, we would marry. However, I was a younger son with no prospects, and when Carisbrook made his offer, I couldn't compete. He didn't love Livia, but in those days, among our class, love didn't weigh in the scales. Not at all. Livia and I had no option but to accept her parents' decree and put aside our childhood dreams. She married Carisbrook, and subsequently, she and I met as distant acquaintances, nothing more."

Lord Frederick paused. His gaze was locked on his clasped hands, but his mind seemed to be looking far down the years. "After a time, I married Anne, and much the same as with Livia and Carisbrook's union, ours was one of convenience. But while love was never a part of our mix,

Anne and I grew to be, and still are, firm friends—our shared liking of helping others brought us together in the first place, and our ongoing activities in that sphere continue to bind us." His lordship's lips briefly lifted. "A shared passion of a different sort, if you will."

After a second, he went on, "That situation remained in place for many years, until, well-nigh twenty years ago, some years after the birth of her youngest daughter, Livia and I met again…and I learned that she and Carisbrook had agreed to go their separate ways, at least in private. Anne and I had led separate lives for years at that point." He paused; when he continued, his voice held a softness, a subtle glow of wonder and joy, he hadn't allowed to manifest before. "Livia and I discovered that our youthful love had never died—it had simply lain dormant, suppressed by circumstance but very much alive and able to bloom again. We became lovers then, and over the years, I have continued to visit her several times a week."

Lord Frederick glanced up, wry self-deprecation flitting over his face as his gaze briefly touched Barnaby and Stokes. "Somewhat to my surprise, not long after our affair began, Carisbrook sought me out and, without actually speaking of it, gave me to understand that he had no objection whatever to me being Livia's lover—that anything that made her happy was acceptable in his eyes—just as long as she and I maintained the strictest discretion and, as he knew of my own need for that, he had complete faith that we would. Since that time, he and I have met, if not as friends, then certainly as easy acquaintances." His lordship softly snorted. "Everyone was happy—Anne was delighted for me, too. And so it went…until now."

His face hardening, his lordship exhaled, then said, "Simpkins. She was Livia's dresser from long before I became Livia's lover. I would have said—indeed, I still believe—that Simpkins was to-the-bone loyal to Livia. My only error was in believing that that loyalty extended to me." Lord Frederick paused; his guard was down, and his expressions were growing easier to read—he appeared to be examining something in his mind. Then he continued, "I don't know what got into her—whether she'd realized she was growing old and perhaps didn't have enough put by, or if some sudden need had surfaced for which she required immediate funds…" He lightly shrugged. "I simply don't know."

He glanced at Barnaby and Stokes, and his features firmed. "But to come to those events you've been investigating, when I visited Livia on Saturday—more correctly in the early hours of Sunday—everything went as it usually did. There was no indication of anything being amiss—of course, at that time, Livia hadn't realized the emeralds were missing. I came and went as I usually did, let into the house via the rear door by Simpkins. When I left, also via the rear door, I told Simpkins, as I'd previously told Livia, that I would next visit on Monday night."

When his lordship's subsequent pause lengthened, Stokes glanced at Barnaby. Seeing his look, Barnaby infinitesimally shook his head, and Stokes resigned himself to more waiting.

His gaze again on his clasped hands, Lord Frederick's frown slowly deepened. Eventually, he said, "Anne attends Sunday service at St. George's in Hanover Square. She heard Livia loudly proclaiming the theft of the emeralds and blaming Carisbrook's niece, Miss Di Abaccio. I'd briefly met Miss Di Abaccio at some social event, and I suspected Livia's temper had, as it sometimes does, got the better of her. Once I heard the full story—how Livia had summoned the police and essentially thrown Miss Di Abaccio from the house—I resolved to speak to Livia when I saw her on Monday. I seriously doubted Miss Di Abaccio was to blame and felt that Livia had seized on the situation to get the girl out of the house and away from Julia, who Miss Di Abaccio completely outshone. Livia tends to get into states, especially over things she cannot control." His lordship's expression grew resigned. "Loving Livia has never blinded me to her faults. However, usually she will listen to me, and I didn't need the note Carisbrook sent me to know I needed to rein her in over this."

Lord Frederick straightened, glanced at Barnaby, then looked directly at Stokes. "I'm telling you all this, Inspector, so you will understand that when I rapped on the rear door of the Carisbrook residence in the small hours of Tuesday morning, in my mind, I was rehearsing what I intended to say to Livia about her public denunciation of Miss Di Abaccio. I needed to approach the matter in the right way—Livia has a formidable temper, and I didn't want her waking the whole house. As usual, Simpkins unbolted and unlocked the door, then locked and bolted it once I was inside. She followed me into the servants' hall and handed me the small lamp she always had waiting. I took the lamp, walked on into the foyer at the foot of the back stairs, and started climbing."

Stokes couldn't help himself; he opened his lips to ask about Simpkins, but Lord Frederick stayed him with a raised finger and went on, "Usually, Simpkins remained downstairs in the servants' hall, but this time, she followed me. I was vaguely surprised, but I assumed she intended to fetch something from her room, which I supposed was in the attics. But she hurried up the stairs close behind me—I registered her nearness, but thought it must be because I was the one holding the lamp and the beam didn't reach far. Without the lamp, the stairwell was pitch dark. She was right on my heels when I reached the landing and turned to go up the second flight."

"I was still thinking about what to say to Livia as I started up." Lord Frederick closed his eyes; his features suggested he was reliving the events of that night as he drew in a tight breath and went on, "Without warning, from close behind me, Simpkins said…no, she *hissed*, 'I know you took the emeralds. I know you're hard-pressed, but you'll get a pretty penny when you sell those stones—I want ten percent to keep my mouth shut or I'll tell the whole world what I know.'"

Neither Stokes nor Barnaby succeeded in keeping their expressions impassive. Lord Frederick opened his eyes, saw their reactions, and grimly nodded. "If you're taken aback, you can imagine my shock. For close to twenty years, Simpkins has been seeing me into and out of that house, and never did I dream that I—we—stood in any danger of blackmail from her."

Barnaby recovered first and asked the obvious question, "Are you hard-pressed? And if so, how did Simpkins learn of it?"

"I—my wife and I—are perennially hard-pressed, but that's essentially by choice. My income was never remarkable, but it has always been sufficient to easily cover our needs, and long ago, Anne and I agreed we didn't need even that much to live comfortably—by our standards, that is. To Livia, I am always one step away from penury." His lordship's features softened with fond resignation. "Wealth was always more important to her than it was to me. Anne's and my stance of sharing our wealth with as many needy souls as possible is literally beyond Livia's comprehension." Lord Frederick shrugged. "I expect Simpkins got the idea that I was financially desperate from what Livia no doubt constantly let fall, and when the necklace disappeared after my previous visit, Simpkins decided I was the thief."

Stokes had been going over his lordship's revelations, creating a picture in his mind. He stirred and fixed his gaze on Lord Frederick's face. "We need you to tell us exactly what happened after Simpkins spoke." Stokes hesitated, then offered, "You stated you didn't lay a finger on her, and we've discovered no evidence to suggest you did. But we need to learn how and why she came to fall—why she fell as she did."

Lord Frederick acknowledged that with a dip of his head. His gaze again grew distant; this time, as he looked on the recent past, his face paled and a fine tremor passed through him. "That was the most shocking thing of all." He drew in a determined breath and went on, "That stairway is very narrow, and Simpkins was following close on my heels. Her words registered—as you can imagine, I felt stunned. I reached the top of the stairs, stepped onto the floor of the corridor, and swung around to confront her."

His voice grew fainter. "She was too close. I didn't touch her—I don't think even the skirts of my greatcoat touched her. But she reacted. She sucked in a breath and instinctively stepped back…into nothingness. She fell. It happened too quickly for me even to attempt to catch her—even for her to reach for the bannister and try to break her fall." He swallowed. "That's how it happened. I turned. She stepped back and fell…and the next thing I heard was the sickening crack as her head and shoulders hit the wall, followed by the thump as her body landed."

"What happened next?" Barnaby's voice was pitched to lead Lord Frederick without jarring him back to the present.

"I stood and stared down at Simpkins. It was obvious she was dead. I was…beyond horrified. I was frozen—I couldn't think. I tried, but my mind…simply wouldn't work. So I waited. I thought surely someone would have heard and would come…but no one did." He paused, then said, "I don't know how long I stood there, at the top of the stairs, staring down at Simpkins's lifeless body and waiting…but eventually, I realized no one was coming, and it was up to me to decide what to do."

Lord Frederick paused, then, with a shuddering sigh, he blinked and refocused on Stokes. "All I could think of was that if I reported the death, quite aside from the difficulties such an act would cause for me, it would also expose Livia to the opprobrium of the ton, and Carisbrook and Anne would be drawn in, too. Against that, if I simply left the house, no one would know I had been there, and some member of the staff would find Simpkins's body in the morning."

Lord Frederick sat back and drew in a huge breath. "The more I thought of it, the more it seemed to me that Simpkins had brought about her own death—if she hadn't followed me so closely and attempted to blackmail me, I wouldn't have turned as I did, nor would she have been so close to have instinctively reacted and fallen. If she hadn't tried to blackmail me, she would have remained in the servants' hall, perfectly safe, and she would still be alive." He met Barnaby's eyes. "I don't know whether that reasoning is sound or merely self-serving. However, at the time, I acted on it. I slowly walked down the stairs, carefully stepping over and around Simpkins's body. I went into the servants' hall, turned out the lamp and set it back on the shelf, and walked out of the house. I went to the stable, took my horse, and rode home."

He leaned back, some of the tension easing from his frame. "I thought of sending a note to Livia and another to Carisbrook, but decided I shouldn't involve them. I could explain later, once the matter blew over." With faint self-deprecation in his gaze, he eyed Barnaby and Stokes. "I confess that I didn't expect you to come knocking."

Barnaby studied his lordship, then quietly said, "You'll continue your liaison with Lady Carisbrook." It wasn't a question, and he wasn't surprised when Lord Frederick inclined his head.

"Once Livia finds someone she trusts to man the door." Lord Frederick returned Barnaby's regard, then, his lips easing, asked, "Do you love your wife, Adair?"

"Yes." Barnaby saw no reason not to admit that; quite aside from the fact being widely known, he was curious as to where Lord Frederick was leading the conversation.

Lord Frederick nodded. "Livia isn't my wife, but...we are what Fate makes of us. I see Livia quite clearly, flaws and all, yet as I discovered long ago, love isn't blind—it simply has other priorities."

Barnaby considered the statement and, after a moment, inclined his head, not just in acceptance but in recognition, too. He glanced at Stokes and saw he'd read the statement in the same way Barnaby had—as a declaration that Lord Frederick was irrevocably in love with Lady Carisbrook, and in whatever followed, that would influence his responses.

Stokes cleared his throat, drawing Lord Frederick's and Barnaby's attention. Stokes had retrieved his notebook and now held it open on his knee, a pencil in his hand. "If you will indulge me, my lord, I would like to take you through your actions on Monday night—this time, step by step."

Resigned, his lordship inclined his head.

Barnaby listened as Stokes reduced the tale to the bare facts—a process at which Stokes excelled. Lord Frederick gradually relaxed again, finding the recitation of actions stripped of their emotional weight easier than he'd anticipated. Sitting back and listening, not just to Lord Frederick's words but also to his tone, Barnaby felt certain that his lordship had been, and still was, telling the unvarnished truth.

Barnaby didn't doubt that, experienced politician that he was, his lordship could and might prevaricate with the best of them, yet he doubted the man could convincingly tell an outright lie, and Stokes's questions couldn't be avoided other than by lying.

Finally, Stokes reached the end of his interrogation. He studied what he'd written, then shut his notebook, looked up, and met Lord Frederick's gaze. "Thank you, my lord. For your information, my assessment of the incident that resulted in Simpkins's death is that no crime was perpetrated. Instead, it appears that, in setting out to commit blackmail, entirely of her own volition, Simpkins set in train a sequence of events that culminated in an accident that resulted in her own death."

Relief showed in Lord Frederick's face. Formally, he inclined his head to Stokes. "Thank you for telling me of your conclusions, Inspector." He paused, then asked, "Am I likely to hear anything more of this matter?"

Stokes straightened and glanced at Barnaby. "I'll need to make a formal report to the commissioner of my findings regarding the mix-up with the Carisbrook emeralds and Simpkins's death, but that report can and will be made in absolute confidence, for the commissioner's and the directors' ears only." Looking at Lord Frederick, he added, "Any further action will be at their discretion."

Lord Frederick nodded. "When will I hear of their decision?"

Stokes rose and looked at Barnaby as he, too, came to his feet.

Recognizing Stokes's dilemma—he couldn't speak for the commissioner—Barnaby smiled faintly, caught Lord Frederick's gaze, and replied, "In all honesty, my lord, we doubt you'll hear anything at all. As no crime was committed by anyone alive, there's nothing to be done—no action to be taken."

Lord Frederick stood and, across his desk, held out his hand, first to Stokes and then to Barnaby. "Thank you, gentlemen. When I learned I would need to entertain you and your inquiries, I didn't foresee the relief your visit would bring me." He met their gazes and formally bowed. "I wish you luck in your future endeavors. The people of London are lucky to have men like you working to preserve our peace."

When they returned as promised to Albemarle Street and Barnaby led Stokes into the back parlor, it was to see Penelope with her head down, brows drawn, scribbling madly at some translation—apparently having forgotten her chaperoning duties; her back was to the windows beyond which Hugo and Cara were still strolling on the lawn.

Although she hadn't even glanced up, as if reading Barnaby's thoughts, Penelope stated, "They're not doing anything reprehensible. According to his mother, who sent me a note this morning, Hugo has taken Cara's being Italian to mean that she adheres to an even stricter code of courtship than we do, and he's determined to live up to every single expectation and not put a foot wrong in any way." Finally looking up, Penelope met Barnaby's laughing eyes. "His mother has informed me that she wants to hear wedding bells and expects me to nudge matters along."

Swiveling on her chair and leaning sideways, Penelope peered out of the window, then humphed and turned back. "I decided that propinquity without distraction was the only prod likely to work, but thus far, Hugo's held rigidly to his imagined code, and Cara is too unsure to take matters into her own hands."

Setting down her pen, Penelope fixed wide eyes on Barnaby and Stokes. "Well? You both look quietly pleased, but not all that excited."

Barnaby rubbed his temple with one finger and glanced at Stokes. "Your insight, as ever, isn't far from the mark."

Between them, they gave her an edited but accurate recounting of their interview with Lord Frederick. When they related his explanation of how Simpkins had come to fall down the stairs and break her neck, Penelope sat back and blinked several times before saying, "Oh—yes, I can see how that could have happened…" After a moment of gazing into space, she refocused on Stokes. "You know, of all the possible scenarios, that—exactly what his lordship said happened—fits the evidence best."

Barnaby nodded. "We're as certain as we can be that he's telling the truth."

Consulting his notebook, Stokes continued describing the interview to its end, then he shut the book and glanced at Barnaby. "Now, we need to return to the Yard and report to the commissioner."

"Hmm." Penelope's gaze had once again grown distant. She tapped a finger to her lips. "The existence of a thwarted but enduring love between Lady Carisbrook and Lord Frederick explains quite a few things."

Stokes frowned. "Such as?"

Penelope refocused and straightened. "Well, for a start, Lady Carisbrook's insistence on managing her children's marriages. She was managed herself in that way—forced to set aside love—so now it's her turn to be the manager, and she expects her children to fall into line, just as she did."

Still standing, as was Stokes, Barnaby shifted. "I would have thought her experience would make her more sympathetic toward her children in their quest for a love-match."

Penelope looked wise and shook her head. "That would be so were her ladyship a different—a more confident—character. But I suspect she truly loved Lord Frederick and, having bowed to her parents' wishes and turned her back on love as she did, the only way she can reconcile herself to that—to living with the outcome, if you like—is to insist, even now, that adhering to parents' dictates in marriage is the correct and, indeed, only way to go. It's"—she waved—"something that's critical to, a part of the bedrock of, the way Livia Carisbrook sees herself. And when you realize her three older children fell into line, probably because they shared her thoughts on who they should marry rather than anything else, then until now, with Franklin and Julia, her ladyship's way—her emotional need to enforce her matrimonial dictates—hasn't been challenged."

After a moment of digesting his wife's argument, Barnaby met her eyes. "Perhaps I—or you—might have a quiet word with Lord Frederick. In light of what he said of his ability to sway Lady Carisbrook and given his reputation for championing the welfare of those in need, he might be willing to speak on Franklin's and Julia's behalves."

Penelope grinned at him. "An excellent idea." She paused, then tipped her head. "I rather think I should mention my notion of his wife's possible motives to Lord Carisbrook, as well. It might assist him in helping all three—her ladyship, Franklin, and Julia."

Stokes nodded, clearly impatient, yet… He caught Penelope's gaze. "We really need to go but…what other things does knowing of Lady Carisbrook's thwarted love make clear?"

Penelope's expression turned just a touch patronizing. "It explains Lord Carisbrook's apparently overly understanding attitude toward his wife. He's known all along that she loved and still loves another, yet by all the usual yardsticks, she's been an exemplary wife. She's given him five healthy children, seen them grown, and established three with their own families, and she's successfully managed his household for all these years. She may be a difficult person to live with, but she's kept her part of the marriage bargain they made, and he has to honor her for that. And to his credit, he has. He's done all he can to accommodate her, although I suspect that now he's realized that Franklin and Julia need his support in a way his older children did not, he'll be more attentive and find some way to help them all get on."

Penelope met Barnaby's eyes, then looked at Stokes and smiled. "This seems strange. I can't recall us reaching this point in an investigation and feeling happy with all those involved, more well-disposed toward them than at the start, to the point of wishing them all well..." She broke off, then shrugged. "All except Simpkins, of course, but she brought her fate on herself."

Stokes humphed and looked at Barnaby. "I have to make that report."

Barnaby nodded and straightened. "I'll come with you." When relief fleetingly showed on Stokes's hard face, Barnaby grinned and clapped him on the shoulder. "You didn't think I'd leave you to explain all about Lord Frederick on your own, did you?"

Stokes blew out a breath. "I was hoping not." He nodded to Penelope, who grinned and waved them off.

Barnaby turned with Stokes toward the door as Penelope pushed back her chair and rose.

Barnaby had taken only one step when Penelope exclaimed, "At *last*!"

Both he and Stokes halted and looked back—to see Penelope standing, all but vibrating with excitement as she looked through the long windows.

"Yes, yes—go *on*!" She made urging motions with her hands.

Barnaby strolled back to stand behind her. Stokes joined them.

All three looked out onto the rear lawn—to where Hugo now knelt on one knee, both of Cara's hands in his, his gaze locked on Cara's face as he spoke...

The pair were oblivious to their audience. Their faces—Cara's as she looked down into Hugo's and his as he gazed adoringly at her—told a story as old as time, one the three observers had themselves experienced and that, today, still anchored their lives.

All three felt the moment—relived the bright, scintillating emotion of their own moment in the past—as Hugo ceased speaking and waited, breath bated...then Cara smiled radiantly and said one simple word the observers could read even at a distance. Then with her smile brighter than the sun, Cara tugged on Hugo's hands and, as he rose, she slipped her fingers from his, threw her arms about his neck, and flung herself into his arms.

Hugo caught her to him, wrapped her in his arms in a wordless vow that he would never let her go, then he bent his head, and they kissed.

"Yes!" Penelope crowed, triumph resonating in the single syllable.

A second later, by unvoiced agreement giving Hugo and Cara the privacy they deserved, the three onlookers turned away, the lingering glow inside them infusing their smiles.

With a soft sigh, Penelope halted by her desk. "Obviously, my work today is done."

"So it appears." Still smiling, Stokes caught Barnaby's eye. "But now that's settled, we need to go."

Barnaby nodded, leaned down, and brushed a kiss across Penelope's lush lips, then he straightened, tipped her an insouciant salute, and turned to follow Stokes.

As he and Stokes went out of the parlor door, from behind, they heard Penelope call, "And *don't* forget our dinner at Violet and Montague's! I'll see you both there."

Barnaby grinned and followed Stokes out of the front door and down the steps. His darling wife had been right. They'd reached the end of a case, and for once, they were smiling.

At just after four o'clock, Barnaby trailed Stokes into the office of the Commissioner of the Metropolitan Police and discovered his father, along with another director, Lord Hubert Radcliffe, waiting to hear their report.

The commissioner rose to greet them.

When, after shaking hands with the commissioner and Lord Hubert, Barnaby turned to his father, the earl said, "Thought it might be useful for Hubert and me to be here given the standing of those involved in this case."

"Indeed." The commissioner, a stickler for correctness, waved them all to the chairs arrayed around his desk, then resumed his seat behind the polished expanse. "I'm keen to hear just where the investigation stands."

Stokes commenced his report, much as he'd related their findings to the earlier meetings of his co-investigators at Albemarle and Greenbury Streets and, more recently, to Penelope in her office. Barnaby weighed in to add those details that made the unfolding case more comprehensible to the others, especially to his father and Lord Hubert.

Over the years, Barnaby and Stokes had learned how to edit reports such as this to render them simple yet complete. By the time they'd finished describing their interview with Lord Frederick St. John-Carter, and Stokes advanced his conclusion that, based on all the information they'd gathered, no crime had occurred, and therefore, in this instance, they had no victim and no villain to pursue, the commissioner and his supporting directors were relieved, impressed, and very willing to discuss how best to smooth over the situation—namely, the public expectation raised by Lady Carisbrook's trumpeting of her charge against Cara and the consequent widespread belief that the Carisbrook emeralds had been stolen.

"It seems to me," Lord Hubert rumbled, "that her ladyship's accusation of theft against Miss Di Abaccio has been proven to be false, and furthermore, as Stokes has stated, no crime was committed." He looked at the others. "As far as I can see, the emeralds merely went missing without her ladyship's knowledge. They remained in the hands of members of the immediate family at all times." Lord Hubert waggled his brows at Stokes. "Is that correct, Inspector?"

"Indeed, my lord."

"Well, then"—Lord Hubert turned his eyebrows on the commissioner—"I can't see that this case necessitates any further bother, Phillip."

The commissioner, Sir Phillip, grimaced. "It's the press, Hubert—the newshounds are the bother. But you're right." The commissioner looked to the earl for agreement. "If I put out a dull-as-dishwater announcement, with any luck, the newshounds will be so disappointed, they'll go nosing about somewhere else."

"You might say," Barnaby put in, "that the emeralds were found to be not stolen at all but merely misplaced." He shot a questioning look at his father. "That will make Lady Carisbrook appear foolish, and she'll certainly feel so, but with no substance to feed further scandalmongering, attention will swing to something else within days if not hours. That will effectively shield the family from further…er, hounding."

"Exactly so." The earl nodded his approval.

"If I might suggest," Stokes said, "we could use any announcement regarding the emeralds to put paid to all questions about Simpkins's death as well. You could add a coda to the announcement, stating that the death of a servant in the Carisbrook house that occurred at much the same time as the emeralds being misplaced has been found to be entirely unrelated. The maid had grown careless, missed her footing, and regrettably broke her neck in the resulting fall."

Lord Hubert huffed. "Very good—and it's all nothing more than the truth."

The commissioner had seized a pen and scribbled down Barnaby's and Stokes's suggested phrases. Now, Sir Phillip sat back, studied what he'd written, and nodded. "Yes—excellent. That will do." He looked up and met the earl's eyes. "The last thing we need is scandal-laden rumors of a high-class jewel thief, much less a murdering one, wandering the streets of Mayfair."

They all agreed, and the meeting broke up with handshakes and pleased smiles all around.

The earl elected to leave with Barnaby and Stokes. As the three walked along the corridor to the building's entrance, the earl asked, "How is young Cara getting on? Met her the other night at your aunt's. A sweet young thing—your mother tells me she'll suit Hugo very well, if only he'll get himself up to the mark."

Barnaby grinned. "I'm sure Mama, as always, is correct, and it certainly seems that the Adair ladies, one and all, have taken Cara under their wing."

"You're telling me!" the earl grumbled. "Cara this and Cara that—sweet girl, mind, but I've hardly been able to think for having her virtues extolled."

Barnaby exchanged a laughing glance with Stokes. Barnaby waited until the three of them had passed through the foyer and walked out of the door. They paused on the pavement, and when his father halted beside him, still smiling, Barnaby said, "Just before Stokes and I came to the meeting, Hugo proposed, and Cara accepted. And yes, we all agree—Hugo should consider himself a lucky man."

"Huh!" For a moment, the earl stared into his son's face, then his smile widened into a delighted grin, and his eyes started twinkling. "Excellent news, my boy!" The earl thumped Barnaby on the shoulder, then turned to beam at Stokes. "It seems that for once, I have news to share with the countess that she won't already have heard!"

Chortling in anticipation, the earl saluted Stokes, then his son, and whistling a jaunty tune, strode off down the pavement.

Barnaby and Stokes watched him go, then turned to regard each other.

"Another case closed," Barnaby said.

"Indeed." Stokes looked past Barnaby toward the end of the street, then met Barnaby's eyes. "And as it's barely five o'clock and we won't be looked for in Chapel Court before six-thirty, by my reckoning, we have time to share a well-earned pint with Wilkes, Morgan, Philpott, and the rest."

Barnaby grinned and turned toward the public house at the end of the street that was the favored watering hole for the denizens of Scotland Yard. "The fruits of our honest labors, as it were."

Stokes laughed and nodded. "Precisely."

Side by side, shoulder to shoulder, they headed down the street.

CHAPTER 12

Violet was delighted to welcome Griselda and Penelope, now her closest friends, into her and Montague's home and even happier to hear from Penelope that their efforts had borne fruit and the investigation was, to all intents and purposes, complete.

"However, I won't steal Stokes's and Barnaby's thunder—I'll leave today's tale for them to tell." Penelope released Oliver's hand and, with a smile, watched him rush after Megan. "Besides, I don't know the final outcome post the commissioner's verdict. I expect Barnaby and Stokes will come straight here once their meeting breaks up, then we can all hear the result at once."

Together with Montague, who had quit his office on the floor below to follow Griselda, Penelope, and their entourages up the stairs, the three ladies dispensed with dignity, spread their skirts on the drawing room rug, and indulged in one of the joys of motherhood—playing with their children.

As always, Oliver's and Megan's antics, along with Martin's increasing interest and attempts to join in, distracted and absorbed the four doting adults; they didn't notice the minutes ticking by.

Consequently, when Stokes and Barnaby arrived, Violet was surprised to discover that it was almost seven o'clock. In no way behind the others in the doting stakes, Barnaby and Stokes joined their families on the rug. But their children had barely had time to crawl all over them and chatter to them about their day before Trewick appeared to announce that Mrs. Trewick had dinner ready to serve.

Violet looked at Barnaby's and Stokes's faintly guilty faces and asked Trewick to beg Mrs. Trewick for ten minutes' grace.

Barnaby glanced at the others. "As we all know everything has turned out well, perhaps we can wait until after the meal to share the details?"

That suggestion was acclaimed by all; they'd already relaxed, basking in the knowledge that the investigation had come to a successful conclusion—the details could wait.

Finally, the nursemaids were summoned and took the children off to the nursery.

The three men helped their wives to their feet, then, arm in arm, the couples ambled into the dining room. Smiles, laughing quips, and an air of pleasant satisfaction enfolded them as they settled about the board.

Mrs. Trewick's roast lamb was another sort of triumph. The company set to with excellent appetite, and in keeping with their now-established custom, the talk was all of other things—all the absorbing issues of their busy lives.

At the end of the meal, Violet led the company back to the drawing room.

Montague had been given a particularly fine—not to say exquisite—bottle of French cognac by a grateful client, and they all accepted glasses of the golden liquor; even the three ladies were curious enough to attempt a small taste.

Violet sipped, surprised at the smoothness followed by the sharp burn that faded into a taste reminiscent of honey. Griselda had settled on the sofa beside her, while Montague had claimed his usual armchair on the other side of the hearth. To Montague's right, Penelope and Barnaby had settled on Violet's recently acquired love seat—of which she was secretly and inordinately proud—leaving the last armchair for Stokes, but at present, their inspector had taken up station before the hearth.

Violet caught his eye and, a smile on her lips, graciously inclined her head. "The floor is yours, sir."

Stokes flashed her a grin that lit his harsh-featured face. "Where should I start?"

"Why not at the beginning?" Griselda asked. "Just the facts, of course, but Violet, Montague, and I haven't been rushing about as you three have—give us enough to put more recent events in context, then you can explain those more recent events in detail."

All approved of that tack, and Stokes commenced, skipping lightly over the earlier events they'd previously shared, before settling into a blow-by-blow, statement-by-statement, clue-by-clue recitation of the events of the day. Barnaby assisted, and Penelope weighed in with her usual unique observations.

Between them, the three drew the strands together and outlined their conclusions and the case Stokes and Barnaby had subsequently laid before the commissioner and directors.

"All agreed," Stokes reported, "that in this instance, no further action was warranted." He finally walked to the armchair facing the hearth and sat.

"Of course," Barnaby said, "given Lady Carisbrook made the disappearance of her emeralds such a public affair, the commissioner will be releasing a statement by way of dampening expectations."

"Meaning expectations of a scandal," Penelope clarified.

Stokes grunted. "More like pouring cold water over the newshounds." He raised his glass. "Here's to the commissioner's success."

All murmured agreement and sipped; no one wanted to see any whiff of scandal unnecessarily damage the lives of those involved.

"And to cap it all off," Penelope reported, "Hugo finally girded his loins, took the plunge, and proposed to Cara, and the dear girl accepted." Penelope positively glowed. "I am now in very good standing with Barnaby's aunt and her family."

Smiling, Barnaby raised his glass and called for a toast to Hugo and Cara, and everyone hurrahed and drank.

A comfortable silence descended as they sat, sipped, and digested all they'd learned and, in their minds, made sense of the case.

Eventually, Montague said, "When you consider it, this case has been odd." He looked around at the others' faces. "For once, no large sums of money were involved."

Violet nodded. "And there was no question of inheritance, either. We often stumble on that within the ton."

"What strikes me most," Stokes offered, "was that this was that rare case when there was no true victim and no true villain."

"Agreed," Barnaby said. "And yet it seems to me that, on all fronts, justice has been served. It was just a different sort of justice to what we normally see."

"Indeed. Cara was the first almost-victim," Griselda pointed out, "but that prompted Hugo to leap into action and rescue her, and now Cara has gained her heart's desire courtesy of her aunt's false accusations. If that's not justice, I don't know what is."

Penelope chuckled. "*And* Hugo was prodded into action. If Cara hadn't been threatened, who knows how long it would have been before he drummed up the courage to act?"

"Speaking of having the courage to act," Violet said, "Franklin did—acted, I mean—and made himself an almost-victim, too, but now that Lord Carisbrook has had his eyes opened, Franklin and his Miss Ives also seem sure to find happiness."

Barnaby inclined his head. "Another appropriate outcome."

"Lord Carisbrook himself seems destined to find a happier relationship with his younger children," Stokes mused.

"Even Lady Carisbrook," Penelope said, "who is a victim of long ago, so to speak, and more recently of her own making, will not be seriously harmed, and the happiness she derives through her affair with Lord Frederick will continue."

Montague added, "Lord Frederick, his wife, Lord Carisbrook, and his, once the uncertainties settle, all will go on much as before. It sounds like a comfortable arrangement all around, one from which everyone gains."

Stokes nodded. "The only one who lost anything was Simpkins," he said, "and she most definitely brought that on herself."

Companionable silence settled again, their shared thoughts and observations leading their minds down this track and that.

Eventually, Barnaby stirred and looked around the circle of faces. Feeling his gaze, the others looked at him inquiringly. He smiled. "Montague's correct—this has been a strange case. How often is it that, at this point, we're feeling so thoroughly pleased and content with the outcome?"

"I was just thinking," Penelope said, "that when you delve to the heart of it, this case has been driven and shaped by what men will do for love."

The others all looked at her, inviting her to expound. She spread her hands. "Franklin started the case by taking the emeralds, believing that selling them was his only route to securing Miss Ives's hand. And Lord Frederick with his longstanding affair with the love of his life—a gentleman like him willing to slip through the shadows night after night, all for love. That put him into position to be wrongly accused by Simpkins and, subsequently, being there when she fell and died. And last but by no means least, we have Hugo rushing to his Cara's defense—his reaction revealed his love, not just to him but to his family and, most importantly, to Cara."

"Hmm." Barnaby set down his empty glass on the small table beside the love seat. "As is often the case, family was the other element involved—the Carisbrooks and the relationships between Lady Carisbrook, Lord Carisbrook, and their children." Smiling, Barnaby caught Penelope's eye. "But to turn to one of the new families taking shape out of this case, what's the status with Hugo and Cara?"

Penelope was delighted to report, "At this point, they are unofficially betrothed. Hugo will need to speak with Lord Carisbrook and gain his approval before the betrothal can be formally announced, but no one is expecting any obstacles to rear their head. And after that"—she grinned—"his mother is hoping for a wedding within a few months."

Barnaby added, "From what I gather via the family grapevine, fatted calves will be slain in abundance."

Penelope smiled. "The only person likely to feel aggrieved by that result is Lady Carisbrook, but I expect wiser counsel— from both Lord Carisbrook and Lord Frederick—will prevail, and her ladyship will accept the outcome with, if not joy, then passable grace."

"It seems," Violet said, "that even the Carisbrooks have gained from this incident, and as a family, their situation has improved."

Their glasses had been drained, and with the story fully told and, more, fully explored, their comments turned to other things, to their lives, their work, their families.

Not long after, Stokes rose and drew Griselda to her feet. "We must go—some of us have a desk to turn up to in the morning."

Penelope groaned and rose, too. "Don't remind me." She glanced at Violet. "Yes, I know—I really need to get on with that Greek text."

Coming to her feet, Violet mock-frowned and wagged a finger at her friend and part-time employer. "The museum will shortly be hounding you." With that and a grin, Violet bustled off to summon the nursemaids and help with the sleeping children.

All of whom proved to be wide awake.

Giggling and laughing, Oliver and Megan came toddling out, chased by Hattie and Gloria, both apparently having been caught off guard.

The children's shrieks had woken Martin, but he, good boy, lay in Hilda's arms, smiling and sleepily batting at whatever came close enough to touch.

Barnaby stood beside Penelope and watched Oliver evade a lunge from Hattie and, laughing with joy, his face alight, come toddling at speed toward them. Oliver barreled straight into Penelope's legs. He gripped her skirts in his chubby fists, spared a grinning glance for his papa, then demanded, "Mummy! Up!"

Penelope laughed, scooped him up, and settled him on her hip, then, with Barnaby, she looked at the others—at Stokes, who'd grabbed Megan, swung her through the air, then settled her in his arms so Griselda could put the little girl's coat on. And at Violet and Montague, who had their heads together, cooing at their son.

Barnaby met Penelope's eyes. "Family and friends—the most critical elements in any life."

"Indeed." Penelope regarded Oliver, her Madonna smile glowing. Then she looked up and met Barnaby's gaze. "Family is what you make it"—her eyes grew brighter—"and we're going to make ours strong."

The Season was at its height, and in a bow to the expectations of her social mentors, Penelope, along with Barnaby, attended Lady Rutledge's ball.

It had been over a week since the matter of the Carisbrook emeralds had been laid to rest, and as frequently happened, especially during the Season, with no evolving scandal to hold their interest, the ton had moved on to other things; the incident had already been consigned to history.

For Penelope, that wasn't quite the case. She'd finished her translation for the museum and had other projects on her plate, yet the confounding case of the Carisbrook emeralds had piqued the innermost private part of her busy brain; with her and Barnaby's renewed focus on family, she'd found herself wondering about the Carisbrooks and how they were faring. Consequently, when, through the crowd in the ballroom, she spotted Lord Carisbrook, she didn't even attempt to talk herself out of making her way to his side.

With his hands folded over the head of his cane, his lordship was standing by the wall. He saw her approaching and smiled in welcome. As she reached him, he half bowed. "Mrs. Adair—you look ravishing as always, my dear."

Penelope dipped in a graceful curtsy. "Thank you, my lord. I have to confess I'm somewhat surprised to find you here."

"Truth to tell, I'm somewhat surprised myself. But"—with his head, he indicated the couples occupying the dance floor—"I felt that perhaps my presence might be helpful, at least for the next little while."

Penelope surveyed the dancers; the set his lordship had been watching contained Cara and Hugo, and also Julia Carisbrook and Mr. Leyton, one of the quieter, although entirely eligible, younger gentlemen of the ton. In the next set along, Franklin Carisbrook was gazing besottedly at Miss Ives, who smiled radiantly as she twirled under his raised arm.

The morning after the matter of the emeralds had been resolved, Franklin had called at Albemarle Street and, with Hugo looking on, had apologized profusely to Cara and flung himself on her mercy; he had taken the jewels on impulse, never imagining Cara might be accused of the theft, and once she had been, he'd panicked.

Secure in Hugo's love, Cara had readily forgiven Franklin, pointing out to an unconvinced Hugo that if it hadn't been for Franklin's action and its unexpected result, she and Hugo might never have grown close, certainly not as quickly.

Hugo had had sense enough to accept Cara's decree and had extended his hand to Franklin, so the three cousins were now at peace.

Subsequently, by way of advancing Hugo and Cara's cause, Penelope had hosted a dinner at Albemarle Street for the Carisbrooks and the Adairs. Although the conversation was initially stilted on the Carisbrooks' part, the Adairs had blithely carried all before them, and Lord Carisbrook —who had already given his agreement to the match—relaxed enough to address the question of where Cara should live until the wedding.

Consequently, by general agreement, Cara had returned to live under her uncle's roof until she and Hugo tied the knot in early June.

Now, taking in the soft smile on Julia Carisbrook's face as she and Mr. Leyton conversed, Penelope murmured, "I take it there have been changes in John Street."

Lord Carisbrook, his gaze also on his daughter, softly humphed. "To some extent. But that change has been primarily on my part—I find I am no longer content to hide in my study and allow Livia free rein." He paused, then added, "Not with Franklin and Julia, at any rate. The older ones could and did hold their own, but courtesy of our recent contretemps, I've realized the younger ones are of a different caliber. Their strengths are not the same as their older siblings, and they deserve their moment to explore what might be—I've accepted that my attention and presence are the shield that will allow them that." He harrumphed and lowered his voice. "To my regret, neither Franklin nor Julia knew to appeal to me for support—they saw me as uncaring and ineffectual when, from my point of view, I was merely keeping my distance as per long-standing habit." His lordship straightened and nodded toward where his younger children danced. "That, I'm pleased to say, has now changed."

Penelope couldn't hold back a satisfied "Excellent."

His lordship glanced at her sidelong, amused. "Indeed." After a moment, he went on, "As you, in particular, have been a critical agent in bringing about our necessary change, I will admit that once my eyes were opened courtesy of the inspector's and your and your husband's investigation, I had a long-overdue talk with Livia. You might not credit it, but it came as a shock to her that she was, in effect, attempting to visit the same wrongs on her younger children as had been visited on her—that in her deepest heart, she knew had been visited on her and that she still, to this day, deeply resents." Lord Carisbrook coughed and, in an undertone, added, "I believe Lord Frederick told her much the same thing."

Lord Carisbrook raised his head and went on, "To be perfectly frank, my dear, I suggested to Livia that she strive to become the lady Freddie loves."

Penelope was momentarily surprised, yet the revelation explained what she'd heard from her wider ton sources regarding Lady Carisbrook's recent and unexpected reformation. Patience Cynster had overheard several of her ladyship's cronies exclaiming over Livia Carisbrook's "new leaf"—her attempts to be kinder and much less belligerently arrogant, and apparently, she had been overheard apologizing several times.

Yet curiosity was Penelope's strength as well as her weakness. She couldn't resist murmuring, "Lord Frederick mentioned you and he were acquainted."

As she'd hoped, Lord Carisbrook was in the right mood to nod and respond, "Indeed, we have been from the start. I knew when I offered for Livia's hand that Freddie—he's somewhat younger than I—was in love with her, but in those days, love had no place in the calculations pertaining to marriage. And, truth to tell, I believe neither Livia nor I can claim we didn't receive the benefits our arrangement promised. She gave me five healthy children, and in return, I gave her title, social standing, and as far as was possible, the wherewithal to make the splash in society that she craved. For all that he loved her and she him, Freddie couldn't have given her those last two things—not then and not even now. Achieving social prominence has never been one of Freddie's interests. But after Julia's birth, Livia and I reached an accommodation." Lord

Carisbrook paused, then said, "I have never been a man to stand in the way of others finding what happiness they might. I knew and expected and, in fact, accepted that Freddie and Livia would begin an affair, for theirs was a love that had never died."

He fell silent, then in a softer tone said, "It was time—their time—to claim it, and the arrangement suited and served us all, Anne, Freddie's wife, included."

A second passed, and Lord Carisbrook turned to regard Penelope in, she judged, a benevolently patronizing way. His lips were certainly curved when, glancing at the dance floor, he observed, "I expect it's old-fashioned to point this out, but even without love, we can have understanding and affection, fondness and caring—elements that can underpin an effective relationship within our sphere. A life without love may not be perfect, but it doesn't have to be a disaster, either."

Penelope felt forced to acknowledge that; she inclined her head. "I accept that's true."

The dance ended, and they watched the couples halt and, happy and relaxed, converse. Through the shifting throng, Penelope glimpsed Lady Carisbrook standing with several other ladies on the opposite side of the room. "I notice your wife is no longer wearing the emeralds."

Lord Carisbrook sighed. "No. Can't say I blame her, and in fact, after the initial shock wore off, she accepted the necessity and has said no more about it." His lordship glanced at Penelope. "Actually, my dear, I would value your opinion. I'm thinking of asking Bridge to remove the crystals, melt down the gold, and fashion some piece more appropriate for Livia to wear now."

Penelope arched her brows. "That would be a nice touch—especially if you asked Bridge to fashion something unique."

Lord Carisbrook nodded. "Indeed, indeed! An excellent idea."

Penelope hesitated; there remained one issue that, in her mind, she still hadn't resolved. Not to her own satisfaction. After weighing her words, she ventured, "My esoteric interests have led me to become something of a student of human nature, so I hope you will excuse my asking whether Lady Carisbrook had some deeper reason for her apparently irrational yet clearly powerful antipathy toward Cara?"

His lordship's brows rose. "How perceptive of you, my dear." His gaze sought out Cara; he found her beside Hugo, her hand on his arm as he and she chatted animatedly with several younger couples. His lordship smiled faintly. "But yes, I should have been more sensitive over inviting

Cara into our household—not that I could have done anything else, but I should have foreseen the ensuing difficulty and taken steps to avoid or at least lessen it. Livia, of course, knew of the scandal my sister, Meg, caused in throwing aside all social conventions in pursuit of love—a love she embraced and enjoyed for more than twenty years. From what little we heard, Meg lived life to the hilt and was deliriously happy with her Italian painter. She, therefore, was the living antithesis of Livia. Meg had counted the world well lost for love, while Livia had taken the opposing stance. Meg reaped her just reward, while Livia…reaped hers. To then have Cara—a living, speaking, sparkling reminder of what, I suspect, Livia had come to see as her own lack of courage in failing to own and embrace her love for Freddie—foisted upon her… Well, I can't be surprised it grated on Livia's soul and found expression in her temper.

"Even though she and Freddie are now together, they cannot be openly so. Livia knows she made a bargain in which she deliberately turned away from their love—that she didn't have the inner strength Meg had—and every time Livia sees Cara, she's reminded of that."

Penelope studied Lady Carisbrook with new—and much clearer—understanding. "Luckily, Cara will soon leave to live with Hugo."

"Indeed. And I cannot be other than glad that Cara and Hugo have found each other." His lordship's smile bloomed anew, his gaze again resting on his niece and Hugo. "Meg and Giovanni would have been delighted with the match."

After a moment, Lord Carisbrook turned to regard Penelope. "Before I forget, I must thank you and yours for introducing Cara to Mr. Debbington, the painter. She tells me he's invited her to show some of her works alongside his, and she's utterly in alt at the prospect. Hugo gave me to understand that having gained Gerrard Debbington's imprimatur, Cara is well on the way to becoming a recognized portrait artist in her own right." His lordship arched his brows in question. "Of course, given Hugo's bias, I'm uncertain how much value to place on his words."

Penelope laughed. "I can assure you Hugo was speaking nothing more than the truth. Indeed, after Gerrard saw the sketches Cara had done of his children, he was knocking on our door within the hour. Gerrard is adamant that Cara is extremely talented, and as Hugo's wife, she'll have the entrée to the circles within society that will most appreciate and value her skills." Penelope met Lord Carisbrook's gaze. "Gerrard gave me to understand that he feels honored to be able to act as Cara's mentor."

The quiet joy that infused Lord Carisbrook's expression warmed

Penelope through. "My dear," his lordship said, "Meg and Giovanni would be beyond thrilled to hear that, and to know of the happy and fulfilling life that now stretches before their daughter. It is everything and more they would have wanted for her."

Penelope felt her own smile deepen. She looked out at Cara and Hugo—at the joy and happiness that lit both their faces—and deemed her job well done. "They face a life full to bursting with love."

Lord Carisbrook nodded. "Indeed. I might not have experienced that joy myself, but I recognize its value." He turned his head, caught Penelope's eye, and arched a brow. "As I know you do, my dear."

Penelope allowed her own inner happiness to invest her smile and show in her eyes. She inclined her head. "Indeed, I do, my lord. A life filled with love is indescribably precious."

And makes life worth living.

For her, at least. Still smiling, with all of her lingering questions answered, she took her leave of Lord Carisbrook and glided into the crowd—looking for her own love, for he who gave her so many reasons for living.

She found Barnaby farther down the ballroom, chatting to Melissa, Hugo's sister.

The entire Adair clan seemed unable to do anything other than smile.

After eagerly exchanging several wedding-related comments, Melissa moved on.

Her arm linked with Barnaby's, Penelope turned him toward the long windows that stood open to the terrace. "Come and walk with me."

He regarded her, concern lurking behind the cerulean blue of his eyes. As they passed out of the ballroom and into the cool of the night, he bent his head and murmured, "Are you all right?"

She glanced up and met his eyes, smiled, and patted his arm reassuringly. "I'm perfectly well." She'd started exhibiting the first signs of pregnancy—namely being nauseated in the morning—only that morning. "Ton stuffiness, whether atmospheric or behavioral, doesn't sicken me—it merely drives me crazy."

He laughed, still a trifle uncertain. "You'd think I'd be an old hand at this, but I find I'm as nervous as the first time."

She patted his arm again. "We'll see it through, just as we did with Oliver." She slanted him a smiling glance. "I have confidence in us."

He tipped his head. "I suppose I do, too."

They'd fallen into step pacing along the moonlit terrace. There were other couples taking the air, but the flagstones weren't crowded; there was plenty of space to walk and talk in private.

After several more steps, Barnaby murmured, "So why are we out here?" Through the shadows, his gaze touched her face. "Or should I ask what subject your busy brain is dwelling on?"

Her smile deepened; he knew her so well. "Lord Carisbrook deigned to explain several things. But what caught my attention was how central to his revelations was one undeniable, inviolable truth."

"Which is?"

"That, ultimately, love is what you make of it." After a second of gathering her thoughts, she elaborated, "For some—like us, like Cara's parents—love finds us, and we recognize it, seize it, and hold on come what may. But for others, like Lady Carisbrook and Lord Frederick, love wasn't—indeed, still isn't—within their ability to seize. First, they let it slip through their fingers, and even now, they can only allow it life in secret. Regardless, love that strikes of its own accord never dies. It's a living force that, no matter the hurdles people place in its path, will do its damnedest to find a way to connect the two people it wants to link. For however long those two people might live, love will strive to find a way. *However*"—she tipped her head, frowning as she searched for how best to communicate her meaning—"that is only half the tale. That type of love—what we call true love—is only one part of love's story."

She paused, then went on, "We all accept that true love begets another sort of love—familial love. And if you don't have true love, then familial love might be all that much harder to secure, *but*"—she emphasized the point with an upraised finger—"as Lord Carisbrook has just reminded me, it's not impossible. Familial love *can* be founded, as he put it, on understanding and affection, fondness and caring—in other words, a relationship underpinned by a conglomerate of emotions other than true love."

After replaying her words, she looked at Barnaby and met his eyes. "I think, being as we are, with our friends in a similar boat, we—I, at least—have tended to forget that. Have, perhaps, tended to look down on that and not accorded due credit to the effort of building familial love on such a base."

Barnaby held her gaze, considered her words, then nodded in understanding. "It's...if not easy, then certainly easier for us to fall into the ways of familial love, being already conditioned to the demands made by the love that binds us."

"Exactly." Penelope pushed her spectacles higher on her nose. "Nevertheless, while familial love might not be exclusively dependent on true love giving it birth, considering all the couples and the families we know, the chances of forming a strong and supportive family seem that much greater if true love stands at the core."

"If true love is the family's foundation." Barnaby halted, drew her to face him, trapped one of her hands, and raised her fingers to his lips. Holding her gaze, he pressed a kiss to her fingertips, then, at the questioning look she threw him, smiled. "As ever, I bow to your insights and have no argument whatever with them. And in light of that, and of the fact that we are one of those families with true love at its core, might I suggest that we leave all others to their own endeavors and direct ours toward caring for our expanding family—with all the love in our souls?"

Even wreathed in shadows, her smile was radiant. "Yes. Let's."

She gripped his fingers and laughed, and together they turned, slipped back into the ballroom, found and farewelled their hostess, then made their way to where their carriage waited. Minutes later, they were on their way home.

To their son.

To their marriage bed.

To their future founded on, defined, and underwritten by a love they knew to their souls would never die.

Later, Penelope lay staring at the progression of the moon's light across the ceiling of their bedroom. Her hand lay over her still-flat belly, and her lips were gently curved.

In life, fulfillment came in many forms, with many and varied flavors—the shared triumphs of their investigations, the comfortable bustle of their household, the pleasure found in the company of their friends and the wider family they both embraced, the unalloyed wonder of Oliver, and the joyful promise of the child to come—yet at the center of all stood one thing.

One combined force.

Her love for Barnaby and his for her lay at the heart of it all.

THE END

Dear Reader,

The Confounding Case of the Carisbrook Emeralds featured several different types of romances—an innocent budding romance, one innocent but secret, an illicit but accepted relationship of longstanding, plus a conventional marriage of convenience and one much less conventional—all contrasting with Barnaby and Penelope's, Stokes and Griselda's, and Montague and Violet's happy, contented, and rock-solid marriages. I hope you enjoyed reading about how the various characters coped with the emotional challenges they faced.

THE CASEBOOK OF BARNABY ADAIR series is one I continue to add to. This volume is the sixth, and the next installment, *The Murder at Mandeville Hall*, will be with you soon (August 16, 2018). More information about earlier volumes—*Where the Heart Leads*, *The Peculiar Case of Lord Finsbury's Diamonds*, *The Masterful Mr. Montague*, *The Curious Case of Lady Latimer's Shoes*, and *Loving Rose: The Redemption of Malcolm Sinclair*—can be found following, along with details of my other upcoming releases.

Barnaby, Penelope, Stokes, Griselda, and their friends continue to thrive. I hope they and their adventures solving mysteries and exposing villains entertain you as much as they do me.

Enjoy!

Stephanie.

For alerts as new books are released, plus information on upcoming books, exclusive sweepstakes and sneak peeks into upcoming novels, sign up for Stephanie's Private Email Newsletter
http://www.stephanielaurens.com/newsletter-signup/

The ultimate source for detailed information on all Stephanie's published books, including covers, descriptions, and excerpts, is Stephanie's Website www.stephanielaurens.com

You can also follow Stephanie via her Amazon Author Page at
http://tinyurl.com/zc3e9mp

Goodreads members can follow Stephanie via her author page
https://www.goodreads.com/author/show/9241.Stephanie_Laurens

You can email Stephanie at stephanie@stephanielaurens.com

Or find her on Facebook
https://www.facebook.com/AuthorStephanieLaurens/

COMING SOON IN THE CASEBOOK OF BARNABY ADAIR NOVELS:

The seventh volume in
The Casebook of Barnaby Adair mystery-romances
THE MURDER AT MANDEVILLE HALL
To be released on August 16, 2018

#1 New York Times *bestselling author Stephanie Laurens brings you a tale of unexpected romance that blossoms against the backdrop of dastardly murder.*

On discovering the lifeless body of an innocent ingénue, a peer attending a country house party joins forces with the lady-amazon sent to fetch the victim safely home in a race to expose the murderer before Stokes, assisted by Barnaby and Penelope, is forced to allow the guests, murderer included, to decamp.

Well-born rakehell and head of an ancient family, Alaric, Lord Carradale, has finally acknowledged reality and is preparing to find a bride. But loyalty to his childhood friend, Percy Mandeville, necessitates attending Percy's annual house party, held at neighboring Mandeville Hall. Yet despite deploying his legendary languid charm, by the second evening of the week-long event, Alaric is bored and restless.

Escaping from the soirée and the Hall, Alaric decides that as soon as he's free, he'll hie to London and find the mild-mannered, biddable lady he believes will ensure a peaceful life. But the following morning, on walking through the Mandeville Hall shrubbery on his way to join the other guests, he comes upon the corpse of a young lady-guest.

Constance Whittaker accepts that no gentleman will ever offer for her—she's too old, too tall, too buxom, too headstrong…too much in myriad ways. Now acting as her grandfather's agent, she arrives at Mandeville

Hall to extricate her young cousin, Glynis, who unwisely accepted an invitation to the reputedly licentious house party.

But Glynis cannot be found.

A search is instituted. Venturing into the shrubbery, Constance discovers an outrageously handsome aristocrat crouched beside Glynis's lifeless form. Unsurprisingly, Constance leaps to the obvious conclusion.

Luckily, once the gentleman explains that he'd only just arrived, commonsense reasserts itself. More, as matters unfold and she and Carradale have to battle to get Glynis's death properly investigated, Constance discovers Alaric to be a worthy ally.

Yet even after Inspector Stokes of Scotland Yard arrives and takes charge of the case, along with his consultants, the Honorable Barnaby Adair and his wife, Penelope, the murderer's identity remains shrouded in mystery, and learning why Glynis was killed—all in the few days before the house party's guests will insist on leaving—tests the resolve of all concerned. Flung into each other's company, fiercely independent though Constance is, unsusceptible though Alaric is, neither can deny the connection that grows between them.

Then Constance vanishes.

Can Alaric unearth the one fact that will point to the murderer before the villain rips from the world the lady Alaric now craves for his own?

A historical novel of 75,000 words interweaving romance, mystery, and murder.

RECENTLY RELEASED:

The first volume in THE CAVANAUGHS
THE DESIGNS OF LORD RANDOLPH CAVANAUGH

#1 New York Times *bestselling author Stephanie Laurens returns with a new series that captures the simmering desires and intrigues of early Victorians as only she can. Ryder Cavanaugh's step-siblings are determined to make their own marks in London society. Seeking fortune and passion, THE CAVANAUGHS will delight readers with their bold exploits.*

An independent nobleman

Lord Randolph Cavanaugh is loyal and devoted—but only to family. To the rest of the world he's aloof and untouchable, a respected and driven entrepreneur. But Rand yearns for more in life, and when he travels to Buckinghamshire to review a recent investment, he discovers a passionate woman who will challenge his rigid self-control…

A determined lady

Felicia Throgmorton intends to keep her family afloat. For decades, her father was consumed by his inventions and now, months after his death, with their finances in ruins, her brother insists on continuing their father's tinkering. Felicia is desperate to hold together what's left of the estate. Then she discovers she must help persuade their latest investor that her father's follies are a risk worth taking…

Together—the perfect team

Rand arrives at Throgmorton Hall to discover the invention on which he's staked his reputation has exploded, the inventor is not who he expected, and a fiercely intelligent woman now holds the key to his future success. But unflinching courage in the face of dismaying hurdles is a trait they share, and Rand and Felicia are forced to act together against ruthless foes to protect everything they hold dear.

ALSO RECENTLY RELEASED:

The first volume in Lady Osbaldestone's Christmas Chronicles
LADY OSBALDESTONE'S CHRISTMAS GOOSE

#1 New York Times *bestselling author Stephanie Laurens brings you a lighthearted tale of Christmas long ago with a grandmother and three of her grandchildren, one lost soul, a lady driven to distraction, a recalcitrant donkey, and a flock of determined geese.*

Three years after being widowed, Therese, Lady Osbaldestone finally settles into her dower property of Hartington Manor in the village of Little Moseley in Hampshire. She is in two minds as to whether life in the small village will generate sufficient interest to keep her amused over the months when she is not in London or visiting friends around the country. But she will see.

It's December, 1810, and Therese is looking forward to her usual Christmas with her family at Winslow Abbey, her youngest daughter, Celia's home. But then a carriage rolls up and disgorges Celia's three oldest children. Their father has contracted mumps, and their mother has sent the three—Jamie, George, and Lottie—to spend this Christmas with their grandmama in Little Moseley.

Therese has never had to manage small children, not even her own. She assumes the children will keep themselves amused, but quickly learns that what amuses three inquisitive, curious, and confident youngsters isn't compatible with village peace. Just when it seems she will have to set her mind to inventing something, she and the children learn that with only twelve days to go before Christmas, the village flock of geese has vanished.

Every household in the village is now missing the centerpiece of their Christmas feast. But how could an entire flock go missing without the slightest trace? The children are as mystified and as curious as Therese—and she seizes on the mystery as the perfect distraction for the three children as well as herself.

But while searching for the geese, she and her three helpers stumble on two locals who, it is clear, are in dire need of assistance in sorting out their lives. Never one to shy from a little matchmaking, Therese undertakes to guide Miss Eugenia Fitzgibbon into the arms of the determinedly reclusive Lord Longfellow. To her considerable surprise, she discovers that her grandchildren have inherited skills and talents from both her late husband as well as herself. And with all the customary village events held in the lead up to Christmas, she and her three helpers have opportunities galore in which to subtly nudge and steer.

Yet while their matchmaking appears to be succeeding, neither they nor anyone else have found so much as a feather from the village's geese. Larceny is ruled out; a flock of that size could not have been taken from the area without someone noticing. So where could the birds be? And with the days passing and Christmas inexorably approaching, will they find the blasted birds in time?

First in series. A novel of 60,000 words. A Christmas tale of romance and geese.

AND FOR HOW IT ALL BEGAN...

Read about Penelope's and Barnaby's romance, plus that of Stokes and Griselda, in

The first volume in
The Casebook of Barnaby Adair mystery-romances
WHERE THE HEART LEADS

Penelope Ashford, Portia Cynster's younger sister, has grown up with every advantage - wealth, position, and beauty. Yet Penelope is anything but a typical ton miss - forceful, willful and blunt to a fault, she has for years devoted her considerable energy and intelligence to directing an institution caring for the forgotten orphans of London's streets.

But now her charges are mysteriously disappearing. Desperate, Penelope turns to the one man she knows who might help her - Barnaby Adair.

Handsome scion of a noble house, Adair has made a name for himself in political and judicial circles. His powers of deduction and observation combined with his pedigree has seen him solve several serious crimes within the ton. Although he makes her irritatingly uncomfortable, Penelope throws caution to the wind and appears on his bachelor doorstep late one night, determined to recruit him to her cause.

Barnaby is intrigued—by her story, and her. Her bold beauty and undeniable brains make a striking contrast to the usual insipid ton misses. And as he's in dire need of an excuse to avoid said insipid misses, he accepts her challenge, never dreaming she and it will consume his every waking hour.

Enlisting the aid of Inspector Basil Stokes of the fledgling Scotland Yard, they infiltrate the streets of London's notorious East End. But as they unravel the mystery of the missing boys, they cross the trail of a criminal embedded in the very organization recently created to protect all Londoners. And that criminal knows of them and their efforts, and is only too ready to threaten all they hold dear, including their new-found knowledge of the intrigues of the human heart.

FURTHER CASES AND THE EVOLUTION OF RELATIONSHIPS CONTINUE IN:

The second volume in
The Casebook of Barnaby Adair mystery-romances

THE PECULIAR CASE OF LORD FINSBURY'S DIAMONDS

#1 New York Times *bestselling author Stephanie Laurens brings you a tale of murder, mystery, passion, and intrigue – and diamonds!*

Penelope Adair, wife and partner of amateur sleuth Barnaby Adair, is so hugely pregnant she cannot even waddle. When Barnaby is summoned to assist Inspector Stokes of Scotland Yard in investigating the violent murder of a gentleman at a house party, Penelope, frustrated that she cannot participate, insists that she and Griselda, Stokes's wife, be duly informed of their husbands' discoveries.

Yet what Barnaby and Stokes uncover only leads to more questions. The murdered gentleman had been thrown out of the house party days before, so why had he come back? And how and why did he come to have the fabulous Finsbury diamond necklace in his pocket, much to Lord Finsbury's consternation. Most peculiar of all, why had the murderer left the necklace, worth a stupendous fortune, on the body?

The conundrums compound as our intrepid investigators attempt to make sense of this baffling case. Meanwhile, the threat of scandal grows ever more tangible for all those attending the house party – and the stakes are highest for Lord Finsbury's daughter and the gentleman who has spent the last decade resurrecting his family fortune so he can aspire to her hand. Working parallel to Barnaby and Stokes, the would-be lovers hunt for a path through the maze of contradictory facts to expose the murderer, disperse the pall of scandal, and claim the love and the shared life they crave.

A pre-Victorian mystery with strong elements of romance. A short novel of 39,000 words.

The third volume in
The Casebook of Barnaby Adair mystery-romances
THE MASTERFUL MR. MONTAGUE

Montague has devoted his life to managing the wealth of London's elite, but at a huge cost: a family of his own. Then the enticing Miss Violet Matcham seeks his help, and in the puzzle she presents him, he finds an intriguing new challenge professionally…and personally.

Violet, devoted lady-companion to the aging Lady Halstead, turns to Montague to reassure her ladyship that her affairs are in order. But the famous Montague is not at all what she'd expected—this man is compelling, decisive, supportive, and strong—everything Violet needs in a champion, a position to which Montague rapidly lays claim.

But then Lady Halstead is murdered and Violet and Montague, aided by Barnaby Adair, Inspector Stokes, Penelope, and Griselda, race to expose a cunning and cold-blooded killer...who stalks closer and closer. Will Montague and Violet learn the shocking truth too late to seize their chance at enduring love?

A pre-Victorian tale of romance and mystery in the classic historical romance style. A novel of 120,000 words.

The fourth volume in
The Casebook of Barnaby Adair mystery-romances
THE CURIOUS CASE OF LADY LATIMER'S SHOES

#1 New York Times *bestselling author Stephanie Laurens brings you a tale of mysterious death, feuding families, star-crossed lovers—and shoes to die for.*

With her husband, amateur-sleuth the Honorable Barnaby Adair, decidedly eccentric fashionable matron Penelope Adair is attending the premier event opening the haut ton's Season when a body is discovered in the gardens. A lady has been struck down with a finial from the terrace balustrade. Her family is present, as are the cream of the haut ton—the shocked hosts turn to Barnaby and Penelope for help.

Barnaby calls in Inspector Basil Stokes and they begin their investigation. Penelope assists by learning all she can about the victim's family, and uncovers a feud between them and the Latimers over the fabulous shoes known as Lady Latimer's shoes, currently exclusive to the Latimers.

The deeper Penelope delves, the more convinced she becomes that the murder is somehow connected to the shoes. She conscripts Griselda, Stokes's wife, and Violet Montague, now Penelope's secretary, and the trio set out to learn all they can about the people involved and most importantly the shoes, a direction vindicated when unexpected witnesses report seeing a lady fleeing the scene—wearing Lady Latimer's shoes.

But nothing is as it seems, and the more Penelope and her friends learn about the shoes, conundrums abound, compounded by a Romeo-and-Juliet romance and escalating social pressure…until at last the pieces fall into place, and finally understanding what has occurred, the six intrepid investigators race to prevent an even worse tragedy.

A pre-Victorian mystery with strong elements of romance. A novel of 76,000 words.

The fifth volume in
The Casebook of Barnaby Adair mystery-romances
LOVING ROSE: THE REDEMPTION OF MALCOLM SINCLAIR

#1 New York Times *bestselling author Stephanie Laurens returns with another thrilling story from the Casebook of Barnaby Adair...*

Miraculously spared from death, Malcolm Sinclair erases the notorious man he once was. Reinventing himself as Thomas Glendower, he strives to make amends for his past, yet he never imagines penance might come via a secretive lady he discovers living in his secluded manor.

Rose has a plausible explanation for why she and her children are residing in Thomas's house, but she quickly realizes he's far too intelligent to fool. Revealing the truth is impossibly dangerous, yet day by day, he wins her trust, and then her heart.

But then her enemy closes in, and Rose turns to Thomas as the only man who can protect her and the children. And when she asks for his help, Thomas finally understands his true purpose, and with unwavering commitment, he seeks his redemption in the only way he can—through living the reality of loving Rose.

A pre-Victorian tale of romance and mystery in the classic historical romance style. A novel of 105,000 words.

ABOUT THE AUTHOR

#1 *New York Times* bestselling author Stephanie Laurens began writing romances as an escape from the dry world of professional science. Her hobby quickly became a career when her first novel was accepted for publication, and with entirely becoming alacrity, she gave up writing about facts in favor of writing fiction.

All Laurens's works to date are historical romances, ranging from medieval times to the mid-1800s, and her settings range from Scotland to India. The majority of her works are set in the period of the British Regency. Laurens has published more than 70 works of historical romance, including 39 *New York Times* bestsellers. Laurens has sold more than 20 million print, audio, and e-books globally. All her works are continuously available in print and e-book formats in English worldwide, and have been translated into many other languages. An international bestseller, among other accolades, Laurens has received the Romance Writers of America® prestigious RITA® Award for Best Romance Novella 2008 for *The Fall of Rogue Gerrard.*

Laurens's continuing novels featuring the Cynster family are widely regarded as classics of the historical romance genre. Other series include the *Bastion Club Novels*, the *Black Cobra Quartet*, and the *Casebook of Barnaby Adair Novels*. All her previous works remain available in print and all e-book formats.

For information on all published novels and on upcoming releases and updates on novels yet to come, visit Stephanie's website: www.stephanielaurens.com

To sign up for Stephanie's Email Newsletter (a private list) for heads-up alerts as new books are released, exclusive sneak peeks into upcoming books, and exclusive sweepstakes contests, follow the prompts at Stephanie's Email Newsletter Sign-up Page

Stephanie lives with her husband and a goofy black labradoodle in the hills outside Melbourne, Australia. When she isn't writing, she's reading, and if she isn't reading, she'll be tending her garden.

www.stephanielaurens.com
stephanie@stephanielaurens.com

CPSIA information can be obtained
at www.ICGtesting.com
Printed in the USA
LVHW04s1703160618
580974LV00013B/792/P